17

The Norfolk Library

THE RABBIT SKIN CAP

Also in The Norfolk Library

NORFOLK FOWLER by Alan Savory
WITHIN LIVING MEMORY edited by Zita James
NO HALT AT SUNSET by Elizabeth Harland
I WALKED BY NIGHT edited by Lilias Rider Haggard

THE RABBIT SKIN CAP

A TALE OF A NORFOLK COUNTRYMAN'S YOUTH

Written in his old age by

GEORGE BALDRY

Edited by

LILIAS RIDER HAGGARD

Illustrated by

EDWARD SEAGO

BOYDELL PRESS

WAVENEY PUBLICATIONS

Published by The Boydell Press Ltd
PO Box 24, Ipswich IP1 1JJ
in association with Waveney Publications
Ditchingham Lodge, Bungay, Suffolk

First published 1939
Reprinted in The Norfolk Library 1974, 1975 and 1976

ISBN 0 85115 045 4

Printed in Great Britain by
REDWOOD BURN LIMITED
Trowbridge & Esher

You who read this fickle page
Illustrated by the sun,
Scribbled by the shower's rage,
Altering as the minutes run;
Think how alteration must
All endeavour bring to dust—
All that's mortal, man and house
And of mercy pray for us.

Scratched on the glass of a window
at Oxford by Laurence Whistler.

PREFACE

MANY PEOPLE may say "Why is this book called *The Rabbit Skin Cap?*"

Because if you wish to read it as it is meant to be read you must put the Rabbit Skin Cap on your own head, just as the hero did before he went adventuring down the long meadow by the river on that summer day more than seventy years ago.

You must read the story with the eyes of the boy who wore it —who looked forth on a rural England which is not as our England is. You must suffer his apprehensions and despairs, his terrors and excitements, go hungry with him, laugh at country jokes which are not your jokes, have patience with tales of those who lived a life far different to anything you have imagined. You must feel the cut of the leather strap as he crouched naked against the wall in the little bedroom with the window looking on to the river, the sting of the cane on his palm because he would write in school with his left hand.

So it will become an enchanted cap. It will show you that which always escapes us—try as we will to remember—the mind of a child. Here you will find it, set forth with meticulous detail and simple approach. It will show you—incident by incident—an England which has gone and will never come again, a picture of boyhood and youth lived within a mile radius yet not lacking in incident and adventure.

What is written here has nothing to do with cities or those who live in them. Nothing to do with books or the written word, for most of the men and women who people its pages could neither read nor write, and these things touched their lives but lightly.

In one particular its author differed from them for he was born with a mechanical brain. Denied its proper outlet one sees, again and again, how it strove for expression. His endless curiosity as to how things were made. His unchildlike patience in conquering the problems of braiding and netting and eel-trap making, his passion for tools and woodwork, his absorption in methods, his desire to always try something new.

In the mind of this child who had never even seen a mechanical toy or a box of bricks, there was so much tow waiting for a match. One day the tow was lit, by a tale told in a Pub kitchen about the man who tried to solve the secret of perpetual motion, who broke his heart because he thought he had succeeded and then destroyed his secret with his own hand. The little boy sitting unnoticed by the fire listened and in that moment the ambition of a lifetime was born For ever after "it seem to draw me," that mystery of a machine that has the principal of motion within itself. It was a lode star, the unattainable towards which he always travelled hopefully, the private and particular mistress of his soul, in pursuit of whom he grew not discontented, crabbed, and thwarted, but the skilful, industrious, happy-hearted man he is with an alert brain always reaching forth after new knowledge.

As to the truth of this story if those who read it care to come they will find the scene as he has set it down. The old Mill House by the river, the very inns by the roadside and the fields—Turkey Pightle, Brickle Hill and Bakers, all the same as when he was a boy. They will find the author and his boats and his workshops filled with the unimaginable collection of wood and iron work which has given him his nickname of 'Old Iron.' The place where three generations of children from my family have gone with the familiar plea, "Please, George, could you mend this for me ?"—unthinkingly demanding the ungrudging service and meticulous attention which they have always known. For what he has to give cannot be bought with money, which, anyhow, means little to him.

As life went on and we ceased to play with cap pistols, toy boats and clockwork trains, our demands have, I fear, grown no less. If rooves leak which no one can mend, if staircases are taken out of cottages and mysteriously refuse to go in again, if boats want painting, locks have to be picked or mended, keys made, wood turned, odd bits of metal cast or filed, an awkward repair needed to stable, boat-house or summer-house, someone says brightly, "We had better go and see George." And from that moment the problem is solved.

Of the Seven Famous Snobs[1] only one, the youngest, is still alive. The other day he was telling me that "come Michaelmas" he must go away from this village where he had lived all his life "because he couldn't manage no more." Neither he nor I could bring ourselves to mention the place to which he was going—where he himself said he would be well looked after—it remained nameless. Because of a painful pause in the conversation I remarked hastily that he was getting on a bit these days. He nodded an old head, nose and chin nearly touching and said that was true enough, over eighty years he was, he could not rightly say how much over eighty as he could not read his club card.

"It's like this, yew see. I had that there card when I wur just gone two and twenty, and Postmaster he say to me—'Yew have had that there card sixty-five year and more, but how much more I be danged if I knows, not bein' able to read yew see.'" He bid me good day, caught the bridle of the old mare and ambled away down the road to "du a little job fur Keeper up in the rearin' fields." I stood and watched until the spare bent little form in high hat and skirted coat vanished round the corner to take his way through the park and down by the lake, where Nosey had hidden behind the oak and the Keeper had let fly and copped the Burnt Ass on the waxy seat of his trousers.

I feel in a way it is the Snob's book. One of their sons wrote it and it has been my care to put it together so that a piece of English countryside history shall not be lost for ever, nor the memory of the Seven Famous Snobs who in their youth ran, and poached, and worked, and fought, in this corner of a simpler and a younger England.

[1] Old term for shoemaker.

My warmest thanks are due to Mr. A. S. Harvey for permission to include "The Cambric Shirt," "The Old Grey Mare," "Old Thyme" and one or two smaller rhymes from his *Ballads, Songs, and Rhymes of East Anglia.* To Mr. Peter Upcher for "The False Old Mawkin," "The Cruel Wife," "Gossip Joan" and "The Lincolnshire Poacher" from his collection. "The Farmer's Boy," "The Ploughman's Song" and "The Farmer and the Maid" were written down for me by the author of *I Walked by Night.*

Also I should like to acknowledge my deep gratitude to Mr. Fred Cannell, who gave me the great advantage of his advice on various points. He also took the greatest trouble to help me arrange the dialect so that it should not be too unconvincing to the eye—nor too wearisome to the reader—no easy task. He is one of the few people who can write broad Norfolk as it is (or used to be spoken). He had, for the comfort of the general reader, to leave much that he would like to have changed, so as to reproduce his native tongue more accurately. As regards discrepancies in the spelling, readers are asked to remember there is no accepted way of spelling dialect. It is a matter of inflection of the voice, and therefore the author's version has often been left as he wrote it.

The same applies to the sometimes marked changes in style. They are not, as the eagle-eyed critic will no doubt suspect, the Editor having a little flutter on her own—but typical of the man as he is.

LILIAS RIDER HAGGARD.

Ditchingham, Norfolk.
May, 1939.

CONTENTS

BALLADS AND SONGS

ILLUSTRATIONS

Sir Roger[1]

Sir Roger is dead and laid in his grave
Laid in his grave
Laid in his grave
Sir Roger is dead and laid in his grave
EE—AY——
Laid in his grave.

A child goes out of the ring and holds her pinafore over the form of Sir Roger to represent apple tree.

They planted an apple tree over his head
Over his head
Over his head
They planted an apple tree over his head
EE—AY——
Over his head.

The ring still dancing pretend to catch the apples thrown by the child in the centre.

The apples got ripe, they all fell off
All fell off
All fell off
The apples got ripe, they all fell off
EE—AY——
All fell off.

The child in the centre gathers the apples the ring doing the same.

There came an old woman a' picken 'em up
Picken 'em up
Picken 'em up
There came an old woman a' picken 'em up
EE—AY——
Picken 'em up.

Dead Sir Roger jumps up and thumps the Old Woman.

[1] Traditional Singing Game from Mrs. Page, Trimingham-on-Sea.

Sir Roger jumped up and gi' her a thump
    Give her a thump
    Give her a thump
Sir Roger jumped up and gi' her a thump
    EE—AY——
    Give her a thump.

The Old Woman limps sadly off.

Which made that old woman go hibbeldy hop
    Hibbeldy hop
    Hibbeldy hop
Which made that old woman go hibbeldy hop
    EE—AY——
    Hibbeldy hop.

CHAPTER I

Old Rags, Old Bags, Old Bonnets or Stays,
Pull 'em out Ladies and takes your Pays,
Pull 'em on Ladies and take their praise,
Whether they be old Woollen or Cotton,
Any old thing be it ever so rotten
Haul 'em all out
I shan't be shamed to lug 'em about.

THE RAG AND BONE MAN OF BUNGAY.[1]

I WAS BORN in the Loke, six-fifty-seven on a Sunday evening so I've heard my parents say, coming into the world the time the bells of St. Mary's Church, Bungay, were tolling in for service. I've lived within sound of them bells all my days, for all that I live in Ditchingham in the county of Norfolk, and Bungay is over the border in Suffolk, this village being half in one and half in t'other as one might say, the river Waveney running between.

Bungay bells tolled me into this world and I don't doubt they'll toll me out when my time come, as they have done many a worse and many a better man than me and will many another yet, when there's never one that remembers me. There's a rhyme used to be on a stone that lay in the churchyard which the old folk said had been took out of the Church when the heating were put in which I always thought spoke the truth about most of us—ran this way.

Without a name forever senseless, dumb
Dust only now contains this silent tomb,
Where t'was I lived or died it matter not,
To whom related, or by whom begot.
I was but am not, ask no more of me,
T'is all I am, and all that you must be.

[1] The Town Crier, James Revell, known as "Cock Robin."

There's a clump of apple trees down the Loke,[1] not many can tell you a house stood there when I was a nipper—back of Garroulds, the shop—where you could buy most things you had a mind to, if you had the brass. Striped bull's eyes, and sugar sticks, brown liquorice, marbles and whipping tops, bacon and twine, linsey wool cloth and corduroy. A little old house built of clay lump with walls two feet thick.

They don't build housen that way these days, too old-fashioned may be, but for all that clay lump'll keep you warm winter and cool summer better than any brick ever shaped. Thatched it was with them old winders of bottle glass it would puzzle you to see through. When I was a little 'un I used to think it were all the world like looking into the bottom of the river, fishing for tiddlers[2] on a summer day, looking into them winders. That house ha' been gone this sixty year and more, but them old apple trees have a way of hanging on where there's been housen, not that they gits a chance to carry an apple till it's ripe, them there varmints of boys sees to that. Still I'd miss 'em if they was gone. Come spring-time they're a sight for sore eyes bein' so loaded wi' blossom. Old trees will bear a deal more blossom than young ones any day, and when you gits old seems you think as much of that as you did of the apples when you was a nipper.

I remember well enough collecting a rare lot of bricks but could not say of what make—might be of my Grandfather's making, he being in the brick trade—and building a house with them. I was mighty pleased with that house, as Father and Mother when they come to look had a good laugh at it and made me think I had made a good job of it. I must have been about three and a half year old, but it seem only yesterday. It was the first thing I ever remembers making and was the start of a lot else, as I've set to and made most things with my hands I've had a mind to ever since, never being one to be carried.

[1]Loke, an enclosed alley or lane with no road out of it except the entrance. From the Icelandic "loka" to shut.

[2]Minnows.

Shortly after we left the old house in the Loke and went to live in another cottage close on to the Ditchingham Four Cross Ways and were there for about six months. During that time what must I do but go and fall downstairs and give my head a proper wallop, striking it on a nail that stuck out of the woodwork of the stairs, making me ill for a month. When I got over that we left there to go to the Mill House down by the River, where I am living at the present day.

The Mill House stood on the banks of the river Waveney, and had been burnt down in 1778.[1] It seems the house was rebuilt after that and the oak-timbered plates which supported the mill wheel still remain in the bank of the river.

An old Miller called Lock was carrying on business at the time of the fire as a grist miller, that is to say, grinding corn into what is called "whole meal" for the farmers round. It seem he did not do a very flourishing trade, and his poor old pony was more fit for the knacker than the poke-cart.[2] When it was laden with a couple of combe of corn it had a hard job to git along, so when they come to a hill, Lock, who was a very strong man, used to sling a combe out of the cart on to his shoulder, and holding it with one hand push with the other—easy as if it was a sack of straw.

[1]Extract from *The Ipswich Journal*, July 13th, 1778: "Situation for a Water Mill.—To be sold.—A piece of Meadow-ground containing about two acres and a half where-on a water-mill stood which was lately burnt down, lying at Ditchingham in Norfolk within a quarter of a mile of Bungay. There is a good stream and it is a very desirable situation to erect another mill upon as the river is navigable from thence to Yarmouth.—For particulars apply to: Messrs. Negus & Bonhote at Bungay."

Note.—From State records of fishery rights, etc., it appears there was a mill on this site known as "the Mill of Cliff" in 1240. The "cliff" is explained by a high sandy bank rising behind the meadow grounds.

[2]Poke-cart. Miller's cart, so called from "poke," bag or sack.

My grandfather on the mother's side knew him well as a very old man, infirm, and only able to git about on two sticks.

He used to tell me he reckoned Lock was the honest'st miller ever born, never taking more'n a peck for every combe of corn he ground, considerin' that his toll. There was others separated the rooks from the jackdaws, that is took out all the fine flour they could with a hand sieve, stealing out of a bushel as much as five peck.

After he grew a man my grandfather took over the Mill House as tenant, but the mill was no longer working. Grandfather was born in 1800 and went to work as a boy of eight year old on a farm. What with short vittals and hard work he grew that shambly the men called him "Hoggity-hoy, he's not a man nor yet a boy!" but he never took no notice and was soon as big as any on 'em.

Being allus in the open he never had a day's illness in his life. He walked two miles to his work every day and had a family of eight children to keep, of which my mother was one. To help bring in a living he had a couple of cows and a few pigs and fowls, and my grandmother looked to them and made sheep-skin gloves and buskins[1] by candlelight at night.

She used to have to walk twelve miles to get her supply of leather and trudge home with it herself. That way they managed well enough till the family was growed up and out in the world. One autumn afternoon when she was gettin' on in years she picks up the 'slings' or bucket yoke and away to milk the cows out grazin' on the Common. The bounders had strayed—she was a long time a'gettin' them up, and by the time they was milked it was day-end, and a fog with it thick as a feather bed. She missed her way among the dykes and wandered all night, not knowing which way to turn, still a-carrying the milk pails, and when dawn come found herself right over by Bungay. She got home six o'clock time, exhausted—and died two hours after.

Through her loss my grandfather lost heart—couldn't abide the place no longer, sold the cows and pigs and went to live with an old

[1]Buskins: sheepskin gaiters.

The Mill House stood on the banks of the River Waveney.

friend of his. My father took over his place as tenant going in Michaelmas, 1869, and that's how we come to go to the Mill House. As to Grandfather he worked to the end of his days, and died at the ripe old age of eighty-seven.

I was then nearly four years of age and can picture it now in my mind, going for the first time down the long drive holding my Mother's hand, and saying, "Where do we go?" not knowing then that there was a turn that led across the medder to the house, and

could not make it out, nor where I was being led to. Had not been there long a'fore I begin to pipe my eye and cry out wanting to be back agin to my old home, little knowing it was going to be my home for life.

It felt right strange to see so many trees and a big river running just a'low my bedroom winder. I went to bed and the wind was blowing hard, making the trees moan and rattle and scaring me so that I blared for my Mother and she soon told me what the racket was and tuck me up close, and I laid as quiet as a mouse till morning.

After a bit of breakfast Mother turned me out with my sister and brother to play on the medder, saying, "Don't you go near that river—du you du I'll thrash you." We did not, never having seen one before, the look was enough, but when we got used to the place playing round the river become a wonder to us, and the ducks and the water hens made us long to get on it ourselves, but this wasn't to Mother's liking. She told us to keep playing on the medder but somehow the pull of the water drew us back to it again.

One day I see something jumping up and falling back and wondered what they were, and said to my sister, "I've got to go and see what that is a-jumping up," but she was a year and six months older than me, and pulled me back and we started scuffling. Then Mother come out and my sister said, "That there boy Gearge will keep going to the water," so Mother says, "Take him up the Bath Hills," and we were soon climbing up and down until I seen something running across the path—a rabbit. My first step was my nearest but when I gets to where I thought it was hiding up it had gone down a hole.

When we gets home and I tells Mother and asks what they does with rabbits, she says, "They skins and eats them, and good they are, but you can't catch 'em you're not old enough for that." I thinks why can't I—it won't be long afore I'll git one if they're good to eat. I tried many a time after that but they always runned off making me think it was my rabbit skin cap what scared them from me, in case any of them would have to give up his skin to make me another, which made my brother and sister laugh, saying, "You run too slow and make too much noise."

We wanders on and when we gets home Mother says, "You've been on the Squire's lawn—after them rabbits—don't you tell me because I see you there. You keep off the Squire's lawn or the Policeman'll come and take you."

That scared me, but all I could think on was them rabbits and catching them. But next time we went along the hills we came to a very steep slope and started climbing up and down, and then running, until my brother lost his foothold and going heels over head on part of a glass bottle, cut his face and hands cruel and ran crying home. Then I started rolling and half-way down the hill come bump up against a tree hurting my ribs and had to be carried home and put to bed (rubbing my bruises with milk) where I had to stay for weeks, putting an end to my pranks for a time. Father come home from work and come up and says, "That 'ull learn you a thing or two, and mind it du or I'll send the three of you to school."

Here was I just five years of age with a second accident and having to lay in bed for weeks—such is life when young and silly—it sees no fear. When I was about agin Father says, "You can have this piece of ground under the winder to make a garden, that 'ull keep you out of mischief."

That pleased us and we were soon digging it up and planting it with what we could find growing in the medder, and soon had a garden full of wild flowers. I being the eldest was foreman gardener. Father says, "They can talk and make plenty of noise—I'll set 'em some work cleaning some tarnips for the cow." We found up an old stump of brush and piece or two of stick and soon rubbed and probed at 'em till they were all clean and thought we was rare men.

After a day or two we tired of that and came a day when I could not stay anyways long at a time and kept thinking of the Common, knowing I had only to go out of the yard gate into the Common Lane and down to the bridge over the river—and so off I go. I got in the middle of the bridge and see the water deep and rushing under me, my foot slipped and in I went. The stream was running so fast I had no time to sink but was carried along into the whirlpool beyond the bridge and washed to the verge of the medder below where I felt my feet touch the ground. I soon scrambled out and looked round for my rabbit-skin cap and saw it floating down the river and a black dog coming up the bank after rats. I called him and sent him arter my cap. He swam and soon got it to my delight and come ashore with it in his mouth, biting and shaking it as though it were a rat; and when I runned to take it he was off across the medder and I never see it again.

Looked to me I was in for a throshing, wet through, and lost my cap which was one my mother had made me from a rabbit skin, cut in four quarters and sewn together having no peak, so didn't matter what way it was put on being like a half-coconut, fitting anyway. My suit was made of my Father's old corduroys and a rare man I thought myself when I had it on.

I ran about to get my clothes dry in the sun, and then drew near the house where my brother was fudging about in the garden but I did not tell him, thinking he might let the cat out.

Kept very quiet at dinner but no one notice my clothes or that my cap was gone and made up my mind to look up the lane afterwards to see if the dog had left it laying—as I did—in the medder. But no cap and I thought he must have eaten it, making me shed tears to think my beloved cap had gone and I should see it no more, and I should have to tell Mother. Then she comes into the yard and says, "Boy, put your cap on," and I say, "I can't as it's lost—a black dog has runned away with it," and she says, "Don't tell me that nonsense, unless you throwed it to him—tell me the truth or I'll give you one of the most tarnishing wallopings you ever had in yer life. Me taking all the trubble to make it for you and all." So I had to tell her what happened and she felt my clothes and they were still wet, and off I had to go to bed while they was dried.

"No more rabbit skin caps," says my Mother, "du I make you, one off your Father's old cord trousers will be plenty good enough."

So I got over that better than I expected but it was a long time afore I went near the bridge again. Though I had better pay more attention to my gardening, which I did, it taking me all my time to keep the old hens from a'scrabbling all my flowers up. I chased 'em into the mill stream and they floated down under the bridge and landed on the medder as I had done, and come marching into the yard looking as if they had lost half their feathers—a proper set of draggle tails.

Mother see them coming and said she'd sell the pair of us boys for a tanner if she could make it, next time the Rag-and-Bone man come round, and not to run the hens any more but build a fence round the garden with sticks.

I knew well enough who she meant, having heard him a week or two before making a terrible noise, and when I asked what it was Father said, "Cock Robin was crying the Sweep's Old Woman." (He being the Town Crier of Bungay, as well as a Rag Merchant.) So I scuttles off to listen and sure enough there he was making the winders shake with his bellowing—

"Early this morning while our worthy town sweep was on duty up a flue his old girl Susan wearing a crinoline, black stockings and poke bonnet become lost, stolen or strayed. She wake up and see her husband lying black with soot by her side and her reason being gone astray did think he was the devil himself sleeping beside her. When he returned home his wife had runned away. All who bring news of her dead or alive will be rewarded."

I remember standing there and listening to the women round wagging their heads and saying, "Poor dear, poor thing, if they finds her she'll be took away for sure. It's in the river she is, I'll be bound."

Coming home across the bridge what should I see but two men in a boat a'pulling at something in the water with boat-hooks—something that rolled over when they touched it and a bit of black skirt which was blowing out with the air under it. I didn't see no face nor nothing, but I takes to my heels and runs home as fast as I could lay feet to the ground with a cold feeling in the pit of my stomach. I said nothing to nobody, but all my days I have remembered that bit of black skirt blowing out of the muddy water, for child as I was, it was then I begun to realise what us poor humans can be druv to, when things go amiss.

And so we got stakes and brush wood and Mother trimmed them and showed us how to set them with the ends in the ground the width of your hand apart. We soon had our garden fenced-in all good and proper, we in and the hens out, as we had forgot to leave a gateway, so we had to pull the sticks up every time we went in and out. That was no matter as we did not value time in them days, having just eternity to play in, as it seem to a child. The old hins couldn't scratch our flowers no more; it didn't worry us they was only wild ones, we were not fortunate enough to have any other kind, and did not as much as know seed could be bought. If we did it would not have mattered as we had no money—not a brass farthing.

Well, we got fed up with gardening and I says, "Let's go on the Common," but my brother kept saying, "Mother has said we must never go across the bridge." I says, "If you wont go I am, so here's off," and was soon over and away, as I had seen boys swimming in the Common side of the river and thought I'd like to have a try. It was not long afore I had my clothes off, picked a nice sloping part of the river bank and was soon in. It was deeper than I expected and I was quickly in trouble. I determined to have a swim and a swim it was, as I went down like a stone with the water roaring in my ears in a black suffocating dark, choking for breath and swallowing mud and water.

Lucky for me I had been missed from home. Mother come running along the bank and see me struggling in the mud and was quick into the water waist deep and had me out by the hair of my head in a crack. She landed me on the shore and lifted me up by the feet to empty the water out of me, and then dropped me down on the grass and rolled me backards and forrards a dozen times to restore me back to life. She was young and strong in them days and I can see her now standing over me in the medder drenched to the skin and covered in mud. I began to come round a bit and squeal and she said, "You'll have something to squeal about when I tell your Father your goin's on, if it hanter been for me you'd a' bin drownded and put in the Church hole, and never seen no more." I started blaring at that so she picks me up as though I was only made of cork, twisted me round, landed me across her shoulders and took me home and to bed, while she went and fetched my suit I had thrown down on the bank.

After a bit Mother says if we're any more trouble we shall go to school and perhaps she, git a bit of peace and we shall get a taste of the stick for a change, as it was sartin shure we'd be up to something else afore long.

We promised we'd be good 'uns so one day she sent us off into the medder and told us not to go near the river no more. No sooner there than my brother see a tree laying along side the river bank and we soon found it had been blown down from the island and lay across the top part of our medder making a bridge. That suited me up to the dick, as I'd never been on the island afore, so off we go among the branches.

It was all easy going till we got through the branches to the trunk, and then we had to hang on like a couple of squirrels and were soon over the other side, had a good look round and then come back again. When we were nearly over my brother slips and into the mud near the shore. So I leans across from the bank and catching hold of the branch of the tree started to pull him out when the branch broke and in we both goes, and a nice job it was getting out, with me collecting bits of wood and putting them so Bill could git something under his feet. Our trousers were covered with mud and we were black up to the waists, looking more like a couple of niggers than ought else, and it took us an hour cleaning of ourselves with bits of grass afore we thought we were good enough for Mother to see, and then we went up the hills and dried our trousers as best we might.

When we made home Mother asks where we been to all that time, and when we says the Bath Hills she says:

"Yes, very likely, but what's the matter with yer trousers, yer didn't git that mud up the hill, yer been in the dykes. I s'pose there's no out-thinkin' you young varmints, allus up to suffin'. Pull 'em off the pair o' you and up to bed before I give you the best troshing you ever had, makin' me all this work a' washin' out yer clothes. Yer

Father 'll give yew the strap when he come back and yew wont git no supper to-night, so hook it."

Off we went thinking ourselves lucky and were soon into bed, and when Mother come up 'tended we were sleeping, but when she were gone we wondered what we'd do, as we were that hungry.

We knew there was some apples stored in a cupboard in their bedroom, with a chain and padlock on the door, and knew they laid on straw spread over the floor of the cupboard. It was still light enough for us to see across the room, so we out and crept to the cupboard, and I lay down on the floor and put my feet agin the wall and got hold of the bottom of the door and pulled it out from the door stud far enough so my brother could git his hands in and reach the apples. We were soon back in bed enjoying them, saying to ourselves—now we dun 'em and had our supper arter all!—and soon had forgot everything.

Next morning down we comes and looked to see if we had left any straw pulled under the cupboard to show what we had been at, but all was straight so out we goes and starts climbing up the tree in the yard and swinging from a branch with our hands and then pulling ourselves up and turning our legs between our hands—turning the pudding out of the poke—as we called it.

Bill did it all right and lit on his feet on the grass, but when I tried—oh, lor! I couldn't git my feet in between my hands, and slipped and lost my hold, and down I go a lump on the ground and bursted the seat out of my trousers—the only pair I had. It gave me such a bump I could not speak or even cry out, but soon got up thinking I must be like the cat that had nine lives.

In we went to breakfast, me careful to sit on the stool with my back to the wall, so Mother could not see I'd bursted my trousers, got my skim milk and piece of bread and packed it away as quick as I could. Then out I go, but Mother twigged me and off them busted trousers come, and up I goes to bed again while she draws them together. Soon she flings 'em up to me, and says:

"Now don't you bust 'em no more or I'll skin yer," and I ups and into 'em and thinks there's suffin' the matter and they are sewn up all round. Going through the kitchen, Mother she yell at me, "Boy, you got 'em on hinder part for." And so I had, but couldn't stop to change, and was off to see what my brother might be doing.

After a bit I found him and he says, "Let's gorn have a look into this 'ere field; at that man and all them there sheep he's got." This field was the fifteen acres and cropped with swedes to be folded and fed off with sheep. This being so the shepherd had his hands full, had to pull up all the swedes, clean 'em, grind 'em, then serve 'em out in the fold. We were soon through a gap in the fence and went across to the shepherd, and as we got near he says, "Well, boys, what do you want?" And when we says "Nothing," "Well," sez he, you wont find none o' that here, so scurry off and hint somewhere else."

We was turning to go back when he calls out for us to put a few swedes in the grinder for him, and we was pleased enough to have the chance to stop along o' him and all them there sheep.

We hadn't been long a' hulling the swedes in the grinder afore he sezs, "Boy, who made yer trowers?" And when I sezs "Mother," he sezs, "When you go along home you ask her if she can't make me a pair like them"—making me right proud to feel he wanted a pair like mine, wrong sides round and all.

He was glad of our help—such as it was—though we was too small to reach the hopper till he'd piled some mould for us to stand on and when he said, "Now, boys, you can't throw in as fast as I can," we sezs, "Can't we, you keep on a' turning that there crank," and we fired away at the job lumping them in one at a time hammer and tongs, and soon had the ole man a' puffing and enough swedes ground to last him for the day, and he with his shirt a' sticking to his back.

Us two nippers had warmed him up all right. He promised us if we'd come and help him on the morrow he'd give us a swede each, and we said, "Right, Master, if you mean that, we'll be coming."

Next morning we were up bright and early, Mother asking where we were off to. We told her and she sezs, "You git your breakfast fust, set down and have that salt sop I got ready, that'll stop yer noise," and we set to it. Salt sop was a few pieces of bread crumbled into a basin with small pieces of butter, lard, or dripping with hot water poured over, the water dipped up out of the river, making our sop like good broth with bubbles of fat floating on top. A few bits of weed and an insect or two didn't matter to us. We didn't know good from bad and the latter being mostly our share we were happy and contented. My brother got fat on it but I was that poor and skinny I was nick-named "Bones." If my parents could have fed us better they would have done, but we had to live on whatever we could get.

Boys and girls of to-day live in paradise compared with us. If we did do anything wrong we were likely to get our heads banged or thrashed within an inch of our lives and no one worry except him as got the throshing. To-day parents are not allowed to punish their children, nor should it be so, it's a question of bending the twig when young, but not too sharp.

We sat there with our salt sop between our knees and our wooden spoons, having a race to see who could finish first. I soon burnt my gills and my brother bolted his spoonfuls, burning his crop, and had to go and get some water from the river to cool himself. At last we was off and what must I do but catch my foot in an old stump, going heels over head and wrung my ankle, but I limped along and we were soon helping the shepherd. I couldn't git along so well because my ankle hurt me, but I kep a' going and thinking of that swede he was going to give us to take home.

About mid-morning along come the Farmer, "Cribby," as they used to call him, to look at the sheep, and say what piece was to be fed off first so they could start and git on with the ploughing. He asked what we were doing there, and the Shepherd sezs how we were Jack Baldry's boys, and Cribby sezs:

"Ah, I knows him, he's a deep 'un he is, I dare say they'll be wantin' a swede or two; well, don't you let 'em take 'em corse they belong to Farmer Wilson who I sold 'em to for feed, so his sheep 'ud muck the land."

We felt bad about that, but Cribby went off and we helped Shepherd draw the hardles in to make another fold, and he sezs presently, "Don't you worry what Cribby sezs, you aren't gonter work for nothing, and I'll pick you out a couple of good boilers." So he did and we went home feeling as big as Johnnie Gant (who he was I

niver did know) and lay awake half the night thinking of the rare good fill of boiled swede we'd earned.

Next day we helped him again, and towards evening, coming along home with our swedes, we sees old Cribby, and he starts calling out at the top of his voice for us to stop, but we, not being mugs enough for that, runs the faster. He comes looping at us, covering a yard and a half at each loop, and when we was near the fence I tripped over a standing swede and down I go flat, and Cribby coming behind at such a thundering rate, he went heels over head, and before he could get on his feet agin I was off a' sticking to my swede like a monkey to a handful of nuts, running for all I was worth, my brother being nearly home.

Mother hears the racket and sees Cribby running us off the field, and come along with her fists up, saying:

"I'll pull yer limb from limb you long lanky lout you, if you don't leave my boys alone. Git off my medder—they ain't yer swedes—you sold 'em and you begrudes the poor boys a swede when they been working like blacks this two days to help Shepherd. You don't care if the pot boil fat or lean, wait till my husband gits at yer, he'll make you wish you'd niver been born, you old hike."

Cribby stops and looks at Mother, then goes off saying he can't waste any more time over her but he'll serve Father the same as he'd have served us if he could have caught us. Away he go to blow at the Shepherd, and Mother hurry us home and say, "Now keep you away from those swedes or old Cribby 'll have the Policeman after you."

The Shepherd was a nice old man and we shed tears to think we could not go and help him any more, but comforted ourselves thinking of the good blow out we would have from the swedes boiling in the pot when Father came home.

He was late that night, having a pair of ladies shoes to finish—so I heard him say. I was hungry, the time seem long and I kept looking at the old clock, not being man enough to tell the time, but was able to count the number of the strokes. It struck eight as Father come home, and I can still hear the same old clock ticking off the time as I sit writing this—sixty-six years since I was a boy.

The Cambric Shirt

I pray you make me one Cambridge shirt,
(Savory, sage, rosemary, and thyme),
Without either needle, nor yet needle work,
And then you shall be a true lovyer of mine.

And wash it all over in a dry well—
(Savory, sage, rosemary, and thyme),
Where niver was water, nor niver rain fell,
And then you shall be a true lovyer of mine.

I pra' you to hang it all on to a thorn,
(Savory, sage, rosemary, and thyme),
Where niver was bud since man was born,
And then you shall be a true lovyer of mine.

I pray you to hire me one acre of land,
(Savory, sage, rosemary, and thyme),
Aquixt the salt water and the sea sand,
And then you shall be a true lovyer of mine.

Plow it all over with one ram's horn
(Savory, sage, rosemary, and thyme),
And crop it all over with one pepper corn,
And then you shall be a true lovyer of mine.

And pick it all up with a cobbler's awl
(Savory, sage, rosemary, and thyme),
And stow it all into the moussen's hall
And then you shall be a true lovyer of mine.

CHAPTER II

If I should die diddle diddle,
As well may hap,
Bury me deep diddle,
Under the tap,
Bury me deep diddle diddle,
You ask me why?
That I may drink diddle diddle
When I am dry!

Traditional

MOTHER heard Father's step and lit up the rushlight (that was the pith of a rush with the outside peeled off for the wick, dipped in fat), and we could begin to see one another through the shadows. It only give enough light so we could see one thing from another in the room, but Mother used to say all the likes of us wanted was to find the way to our mouths.

The rushlight was used by rich and poor and then followed the tallow candle of mutton fat with a cotton wick, but they were not for such as us. Mother did not hold with trying new ways, as my Grandmother had near burnt the house down thinking she'd light it better.

One winter a Turnpike Sailor called at her door, one of them with a business smile and a soft manner of speech. My Grandmother was a hard-working, good dispositioned woman—would do any one a good hand's turn, and thought no evil when he asked her if she would not like to try his Californian Candles. She said she'd never heard such prate and what did he mean, and they looked to her more like sticks of rock than candles with the red and black lines round 'em. But he had her on that they were a new sort of candle, would light up the whole house and last all night, and he had not as much as a latch-lifter[1] in his pocket, and he'd take it kindly if she'd buy some.

My Grandmother thought to herself they would be rarely useful when she was making gloves and such like and save her eyes, and not having much in the teapot (where the money was kept) she give what she have, and a good pair of sheepskin gloves as a makeweight for a bundle of Californian candles. Away go the sailor and tell her to be careful and burn one at a time and they'll last her all winter—she'll be surprised. So she was, poor soul, for them candles was made of pitch and tar with a little red ochre mixed in to make 'em look nice. She lights one and went outside the house to get some wood, and coming back finds black smoke pouring out of doors and windows and all the room flew a'fire. They lit up the house all right, and it was a marvellous mercy (some neighbours being handy) that the blaze did not last all night as the Turnpike Sailor had said.

So we always sat in the firelight, Mother not thinking of lighting a candle, until Father come home to supper, saying, "Well, ole gal, and what's for us to-night?"

She told him she had a fine stew of the swedes we had brought back, making us feel proud that we had begun to work for a living.

When she and my elder sister had it dished out, with Norfolk dumpling steaming hot, we could hardly see ourselves for steam in the little back kitchen, making the rushlight look like a distant star in the heavens. She filled up our pannikins, hot swede, a little bit of dumpling, a spot o' dripping and a pinch of salt to add to the flavour and help them down, the best meal we had had for many a day. Mother told us to eat all we could "Cos you 'ont git no more once this is done."

Father asked, "How's that, then?"

Mother told him how us boys had been across to the shepherd, and he had given us the swedes for helping him, and how old Cribby see us coming home and near blew his teeth out and spauled[2] for us

[1]Enough money to open a pub. door.
[2]Spawle—to spit out with force. Anglo-Saxon "spaw."

to stop. How we runned, how she out and told Cribby off about running us off the field, and said she'd push his ugly mug in, and he said he'd see her Old Man about that, and she said it was the best thing he could do, as her Old Man would surely square him up.

Father thinks a bit and says he won't go out shoemaking to-morrer but spud some of the thistles up on the medder, and then if old Cribby came down to the sheep he'd see him and come across. Mother made him promise he wouldn't never go off his own medder on to the field arter him whatever Cribby say to anger him, and Father say:

"I shan't du that you can be sure, let him come on the medder

after me and I'll show him what I can do, I'll fatten his head up for him as he never had it afore, or I'll eat my old hat," and out he goes to cut Mother's sticks and do her little jobs before they shifted themselves for bed.

Next day eleven o'clock time Father gets his spuddin-stick[1] and tells us to stay in the yard and not come on the medder. He hadn't been working on them thistles more than half an hour when Cribby spies him and come across the swedes, not waiting till he gits to the fence afore he begins to unwind hisself yelling, "What yer mean lettin' yer boys come inter my field and carry swedes home."

[1]A long stick with a spud on the end; a flat metal point for cutting through the top root of thistles. From the Danish "spyd"—a lance.

"They h'aint took only what Shepherd give 'em."

"He don't want any boys' help, I tell yer—they must keep off, and you too."

"It'll take a better man than you to keep me off have I a mind to go on."

"Don't yer let me catch you on my fields or I'll sune put yer off."

"What you—stow it man, I'd go round yow like a wapsy[1] round a cask—I'd soon tighten yer hoops for you, I would."

"I've a good mind to come through the fence arter you now."

"Come over then and I'll give you a dressin' down you 'ont forget."

"What you ——! You ain't man enough for that, you got the duck disease, you short little brat, and I can give yer a licking any day."

"That's as may be, but I can lick you any day I chose, and as I'd as soon chose to-day, as any."

That was enough for Cribby. He was through the fence and on to the medder—made a rush at Father and swung his long arm round, knocking his dog-skin cap off, sending the toe of his boot into it and come round to give him another blow.

My Father ducked in an instant, being a rare quick one on his feet, though small, and landed Cribby a good 'un in the bread basket, bringing him down to about his own height, and quick as thought landed him another bunger on his paste horn, nearly flattening it down on his face. The claret begun to run, making Cribby wild in his hitting. He made another rush at Father, who stepped to one side, and quick as light gets in a blow in the short ribs with all his force behind it, twisting Cribby round like a ninepin, making him think p'raps he'd met his match.

Cribby gets a bit vicious at that, made another rush at Father, pretending to kick him in the stomach, but he caught the back of the heel of his boot and over he went sprawling on to his back. Father was soon on top of him, Cribby got him by the throat, but

[1]Wapsy—wasp. Anglo-Saxon "woeps."

Father got hold of one of Cribby's little fingers and bent it back near to breaking, till he hollered with the pain and let go, then gripped him by the back of the neck, trying to get on his feet again. Over and over they went, striving to see which was the best man of the two, till Cribby begins to get exhausted and cries out he's had enough and Father is a better man than he thought he was. So Father says:

"So you've had enough of it, yew b . . . bully, yew only got what I promised yew. Don't yew come on to my medder upsettin' of me no more—seems to me yow'd better be gettin' along back on to yer own field, or I'll soon be at yer again."

But Cribby had had enough—said he was sorry it had happened, and the end of it was they shakes hands and patches it up, and Cribby sezs come to think of there's no harm in the boys giving old Shepherd a hand and getting a swede or two for payment, and off he go through the fence and across the field to the sheepfold, a wiser man about upsetting of Jack Baldry than he was afore. Father looked around for his thistle spud and picked it up and walked off towards the house with his head dropping down, thinkin', no doubt, of what had happened.

Now me and my brother had to look lively. Father had told us not to leave the yard, but when we hears the argufying we slips into the Common lane running along the medder where they was, and keeping our heads well down below the bank, creeps along till we gets nearby where they were at it hammer and tongs, and peeping through the lower part of the fence could see and hear what was doing, as were less than thirty yard off. Billy getting in a rare stew, saying:

"He'll wholly kill Father, he will," and I, "Not he. Father'll lick him, Father can fight, look at 'em a' rolling over each other, let's be off and go across." But Billy wouldn't, thinking he'd only get a throshing when Father was finished with Cribby.

That was the first fight we had ever seen and thought it was great fun to see two grown men knocking each other about, and I kept wishing I was big and old enough to go in and help, being young and silly in them days. Since then I have had a hand in many a fight and brawl and find they are best left to those that starts them —which cannot be laid to my door—being a man peaceably inclined in all my ways. Otherwise all one gits is a black eye, sore ribs, and a chip or two off the hull, not to say anything about being stiff and sore for days.

Well, we sees Father making for home and dare not go back the way we come as he'd a' caught us, so we slips through the fence the other side of the lane and down the marsh that runs to the back of the yard and away home in a crack, and busy playing pussy when Father come by. He says nothin' to us as he go past but to take care and not break his winders, and went indoors to Mother, not knowing we had seen and heard all that had happened and had one of the greatest days in our young lives—a day I couldn't never forget.

When Father come out again and told us we could go and help Shepherd and we would git a swede or two for our pains, that made us feel as proud as fighting cocks. It was a good thought we should have a chance of another fill up of boiled swede, it being a hard struggle in those days to git enough to eat.

Water was about the only thing there was enough of as the River Waveney run by, washing the wall as it passed the house. All we had to do was to dip a pail in, and some lucky days we would get a few small gudgeon—anything went down the same way with us and all was welcome as we often knew what it was to be hungry. Father only made a few shillings a week at his trade of shoemaking, and I have known him work till twelve o'clock at night to get a job finished and a shilling or two extra, which was badly needed for our clothes.

It was a day or two before we went back to see the Shepherd, and he sent us off to collect all the swedes we could find about the field as there were not many more left. He told us that he was moving on the morrer, a long way off, where we could not come and help him, and we dropped our heads, feeling our combs were cut, and no more swede dinners for us. He promised we could come and give him a hand getting the sheep off the next day, if we were there early. So we off home, had supper of a crust and skim milk, and to bed happy as sandpipers to think of going droving on the morrow, sleeping one eye at a time.

We was up and dressed at six next morning. Father hollered at us to git into bed again, but then let us go down if we didn't go near the river. We slipped out and got two of his droving sticks out of the cow-house and hid 'em in the fence so they'd be handy when we come to drive the sheep, and then come in, and Father calls, "Du yew git some sticks and make a fire," which we soon did and put Betsy on to boil.

Mother come down grumbling what was all the hurry for, and set me to watch the swede she put in the frying-pan while she went to milk the cow. Back she come and said I'd done that job well, and we were begging her to get our breakfast till she says:

"What's the matter with you boys, fair crazin' me about them sheep fare as thow you hadn't another minute to live—just be steady or you shan't go arter them sheep at all."

That made us pull in our horns like a couple of Dodmen,[1] and we set quiet as mice, blowing at our breakfast bowls, and was then sent off to have a good wash in the river, as Mother said we were as black as a couple of Tinkers, and where had we been pugging to that morning. At last she let us git along, telling us not to go on the road with the sheep lest we got lost.

We found the Shepherd and he set us to droving, getting rare and ratty because we didn't know how to block the sheep at first, the silly things allus a' running up driveways and all manner of foolishness. We were so busy at that we never stopped to take any notice of which way we were going so we might know the way back till we gits more than a mile from home, and the Shepherd calling out to one of us to stand on Alma Bridge and block 'em, the other to run down the road and open the gate of the pasture in Pirnough Street. They were soon in, and then Shepherd sezs

[1]Dodmen—snails.

he's off for a drink at the Tuns and we'd better be getting home.

Away he goes and leaves us with never a penny for our pains, to get back as best we can. We got to the three cross-ways and could not think which way to go as everything seemed strange. Then we saw the railway and the man swinging the big gates across the road and the train puffing along and stopping—such a thing as we had

never seen before. It made us stare and wonder and forget we were lost and hungry and not got a penny for driving the sheep.

When it was gone we runned up and down the road and could not find the way—lost heart—and started piping our eyes and snuffling till the village policeman come along and wanted to know what was wrong and what our names. were. We told him George and Billy, then he said, "Hain't you got no other name?" and when we said we didn't think so, he asked Father's, and we said 'Happy Jack' and that he was a shoemaker and worked near Falcon Bridge. He took us home then, hungry as hunters, not having had a bite all day. Mother was in a rare taking wanting to know where we had been all day when she had told us never to go on the road, and we saying we'd never heard her say so.

"No, I don't suppose as you did, might as well talk to a couple of blocks of wood as you two masterpieces. You will do as you like, and what have you been and got by it this time, no dinner—lost yerselves—and then brought back by a perliceman. Bin a good job if he'd took yer both and shut you in, till you'd learnt a bit of sense. Now mind what I say—git your supper and away to bed afore Father come home and give you a drubbin'. Thanks be it won't be long afore you be a' going to school. You'll soon find the way to do as yer bid then. They keep a stick for all bad boys there."

"What du we du there?" we asked.

"Find out the difference between a great A and a bull's foot," said Mother, which set us thinking.

It seem, looking back to when I was a lad, that most of what I remember when I was a little nipper had to do with summat to put in my mouth, perhaps because more often than not it was over ready to be filled and there was not as much as a hen's nose full[1] to put in it. Anyway there was one day make me laugh now to think of.

Father went in for a raffle at the Falcon Inn, they having killed a sheep and thought they would raffle the head. Well he wins the head and no doubt they were all three sheets in the wind and got argufying over whose it was. Anyways when Father come home I remember well enough following him into the house to see what was in the parcel under his arm—like a couple of kittens after an old cat. When he lumped out the sheep's head we thought there weren't much difference between him and it, for he had a cut on his cheek and all the blood had runned down and dried. When Father told Mother he won it from his old pal Blazer High, she said it looked to her as if he'd been blazin' all right, as there was as much blood on his face as there was on the sheep's head, but anyways it 'ud make a fine Sunday dinner.

[1]Hen's nose full—a very tiny quantity.

Blazer High led Father into many a spree, and they was a sight to see—Blazer and Happy Jack—being what you might call the long and the short of it.

Blazer was a wheelwright who had his shop at the foot of Bridge Street. He was a great hero to us boys, being a noted boxer who fought many a Sunday morning match at the Pubs round about, which was agin the law and more often than not the police were after him. I remember well one story Father had of him. How he had a match on with a Norwich grocer called Perowne on St. Andrew's Green up in the Parishes. Blazer went over and lay doggo in Lowestoft, knowing the police had wind of the match. When the time came he walked over to St. Andrews. The police were on his track but he got a lift in a brewer's dray and hid up among the casks. As soon as Perowne had an eye full of him he wanted to shake hands

—Blazer was over six foot and when I knew him weighed near eighteen stone.

The Bungay backers would not hear of this and the fight started, but in the first round Blazer knocked Perowne down and broke his thigh. By this time the police were up to them and collared Blazer, who got ten weeks in Norwich jail.

Sunday come, the pot was put on, and Mother made five Norfolk swimmers[1] and then slipped across to a neighbour telling me to look to the pot and keep it boiling because of the dumplings. I thought that was a great job, tended the fire up and kept it going full gallop.

Presently the lid lifted a bit with the steam and I peeps in and see the sheep's head going round the pot with his mouth open, like old Nick after the sinners, and only one swimmer to be seen. I thinks to myself that there old sheep ha' gone and swallowed the other four and if I don't look slipper he'll have the last at the rate he's chasing it, and what'll Mother say then, and I runs as fast as my legs can carry me, blaring:

"Mother, come quick, the sheep's hid's goin' round the pot like old Wop and swallered four of the swimmers."

She come running and—dang me—if I hadn't been in such a mortal hurry I'd left the top of the pot off and in wallops a great whack of soot. Mother starts trying to fish that out and up come the swimmers from the bottom of the pot, Mother muttering, "This what come of leavin' a silly young lout to watch the dinner."

Then come the 14th of May—Bungay Fair day—which had been held that day for seven hundred years, so my Father always told me. He wouldn't have missed Bungay May Fair—it being the only day out he had in the whole year—and told us if we was good boys he'd bring us some Rock. Didn't the day seem long, we thought night would never come, and we run and ask Mother when Father was coming to give us the rock.

She told us not to worrit but fetch the cow in to milk, and git the sticks and boil the kettle and get off to bed so our sister could mend

[1]A dumpling dropped in the broth, known in the Eastern Counties as a "swimmer."

our clothes. "Allus a job to be done on 'em, you young rascals, tearing yerselves to rags. When yer Father git along with them Donkey Dealers and have a glass or two of beer a lot he'll remember."

Once in bed we lies and listens and hears him quiet-like (for he was a soft-footed man) a' coming down the lane, and we ups and looks out and sees him in the dusk with his head dropped on his breast, as his habit was, and his eyes on the ground where all his life he see more than most people all round him, a' singing to himself his favourite song:

Good bye John, don't stop long,
Come back again to your chicky-biddy
For my heart beat so and the wind doth blow—
And will leave me a weeping widdy.

We hollered for our rock and he'd forgot it, and then we started singing a different tune, hollering and screeching for all we were worth, till Father called up from the staircase door to be quiet, and go to sleep, or he'd come and rock up the devil to us with his big stick. We were scared, knowing he was in no mood to be plagued, and cried ourselves to sleep. We dasn't murmur nor say a word for Father was a tarryfying man at times. Never made no racket—of few words—and soft-voiced to the day he died, but for all that he had a power with him which was ill to cross.

Next morning we were wakened with the cow calling to be milked. It seemed she felt the same as we did without our rock and was standing blaring away under the trees by our window. About six Father calls out to us to go and get the fire going and the kettle on, as he wants a drop of suffin' to drink and curse the beer, as dang him if a man weren't dryer after he'd had a good drink than he was afore.

Mother said she believes they put salt in it and Father saying he knew that's done as he's helped old Long Sam to do it many a time at the Turnstile Inn, and Mother saying she knows more than enough about that and that's where all the money's gone—money he'd best left

He wouldn't have missed Bungay May Fair.

at home to get suffin' for the children, they only having what they stand up in and those no more than rags, and what good has it done him messing about with that drunken click getting full up with the cussed stuff so he don't know A's from B's.

"What du you know about it?" says Father.

"Quite enough to see the more you drinks the more you wants, and then you git arguing 'bout other folk's business and orders another quart and then the trouble begins. How did you git that black eye and the bruise on yer cheek? Not that I want to ask any questions—I know what you are—if there's a row on yer sartain shure to be in it."

"Well, you're right," says Father, unwilling like. "Du you remember that long Dealer bloke what come down here a day or two back wanting the brindle calf? Well, I see him on the Fair ground and he axt me if I'd sold it, and I sezs 'No, I h'aint,' and he sezs, 'Let me buy it off yer and I'll give you a fair price, it ain't one of the best—I'll give yer fifteen bob.'

"'Fifteen bob for a calf like that,' sezs I. 'Do you think I'm soft, I'll see yer neck as long as my arm fore I'll sell you a calf three week old for fifteen bob.'

"Dealer sezs, 'Let's go and have a drink, p'raps we can make a deal.'

"But I sezs, 'No, you don't go and get the best of me that way,' and we goes at it.

"The dealer say, 'If you don't shut yer gob[1] I'll shut it for you,' and that was enough for Happy Jack—for my blood was up—and I goes for him. Standing head and shoulders above me, he was, but I soon brings him down to my height, caught him on where he had just packed a couple o' pints of beer away and got going good and proper with my left hand. I should soon have licked him if it hadna' been for his click, which didn't want to see me git the best of him, gits in my way all they could and one landed me a blow on the top of the eye, and I see I was up against a pretty party of Dealers,

[1]Gob—mouth. From Danish *gab*.

so I watches for my man and lands him one on the bridge of his nose and flattens it—there being no chance of a fair fight—and was off as quick as a mouse-hunter[1] into the crowd."

We listened with our ears stretching out, thinking the Fair must be a rum place and how easy it seem to git a black eye, let alone a broken arm or leg and your pockets emptied for you. Then thinking it mighty odd Father would not miss it—for nothing Mother could do—the only place he went the whole year to enjoy himself. And I remember it all well enough sitting listening to the two of them, but dare not so much as open my mouth to say a word but was just a proud listener.

I remember it weren't long afore we were in mischief again. It was May and the garden we had didn't look to our liking for we had no flowers. We noticed Mrs. Eastaugh had some in hers about 300 yards away—her husband being gardener to Squire—so what do we do but up one morning early and pinch her gillyflowers and stocks and plant 'em out in our garden under Mother's window. When Mrs. Eastaugh come along to git the milk what do she see but her flowers all a' blowing under her nose.

Father was away at Tibman's the shoemaker's shop, where he work at his trade of shoemaking and journeyman, which stood close to the Falcon Inn on Ditchingham Dam. Mrs. Eastaugh was in a fair taking over her flowers and Mother promise that when Father come home he'd square us up, and off she go with the flowers to put 'em in again where they belong. We'd been standing behind the faggot pile and heard poor Mother making the best of it, and thinks we'd best be away up the Bath Hills when Father come to dinner, and so we were and slips home later. Mother—like all of them she couldn't bear to see her boys throshed—give us a bite o' supper and pack us off to bed.

When Father come home we could hear he was mortal angry and muttering to hisself as Mr. Eastaugh and he were like two brothers, what one had the other had to go without, as there was

[1] A small weazel.

not much to share between the two of 'em. He called out to Mother where were we, and Mother said—quiet-like:

"They're gone off to bed."

"You mean you sent 'em to bed outer my way, wait till I gits my coat off and they'll git some strap oil, I'll have no more of this, seems they think they're a' goin' to dew as they likes—the young varmints."

We hears what's said and scared nearly stiff slips out under the bed, our teeth chattering with the fright. Mother come to the staircase door begging him to let us alone, but he push her aside and up he come strap in hand. He soon found out we was under the bed instead of inside, and took hold of the bedstead and turned it on its side as if it was a light door, and see us a-laying in the corner strip star' naked.

Being eighteen months older than my brother I was considered the worst of the two, but I coiled as close as I could against the wall, my brother in front, so he got most of it across his sit-me-down-on. Father couldn't get me according to his liking, so he reached forrard, caught me by the back of the neck and swung me into the middle of the planshard,[1] as though I were a spinning top, and give me a troshing so I remember every detail of that evening to this day. Mother tried her best to save us, but to stop him in one of those rages would be like trying to stop the wind. He'd started and meant to finish. We kicked up such a row Mrs. Eastaugh hear and come a-running begging him to stop, crying she wish she'd never said a word about the flowers, and Father turned on her with:

"Du you think I am goin' to have them up to tricks like that, they'll git me inter a proper muddle if I don't look to it. I'm going to be Master and have my lads do what I want, not what they like. I'll make 'em mind now they're young. An old Man used to be telling me bend the twig while green, Jack, and I find what he says is right. If they do as they choose now—dang me—they'll be kicking

[1]Plancher—boarded floor. From the French.

my legs later and I'll square 'em up now I've got the chance, and if you wimmen hinders me, I'll serve yer all alike."

So there was one lesson learned, and we did not forget that dose of strap oil nor what it were given for, and maybe 'twas the better for us as the lesson was sharp.

The False Old Mawkin

There was a false old mawkin,
In Bungay she did dwell,
She loved her old man dearly,
But another twice as well.
Sing to the fol de ra!

She went to the doctor's shop
As hard as she could go,
To see if there was anything she could find
To turn her old man blind.
Sing to the fol de ra!

She made him a stew of two red toads
And made him eat 'em all,
Says he, "My dear beloved wife
I can't see you at all."
Sing to the fol de ra!

"If I could find my way to go,
I'd go to the river and drown."
Says she, "I'll go along with you,
In case you go astray."
Sing to the fol de ra!

She got up behind him,
All ready for to plunge him in,
He stepped a little to one side
And headlong she went in.
Sing to the fol de ra!

'Coo, how she kicked and wholly shruk
As loud as she could bawl,

Says he, "O my dear beloved wife,
I can't see you at all."
Sing to the fol de ra!

Him being tender-hearted
And thinking she could swim
He got him a great long pole
And shoved the old mawkin in.
Sing to the fol de ra!

CHAPTER III

One is some—two is none—three is a sort—four is a mort.[1]
Old Norfolk Proverb.

ONE Sunday morning soon after this Father went ratting with the ferrets which settled the question of our schooling for us. He had two does with nine and ten young 'uns a' piece.

He slips the does into the hay bag, lets off the dog and away, calling to my brother to go along o' him, and telling me to stay with Mother so she warn't alone—as my sister was with Aunt Bet what lived in the cottage at the foot of Hollow Hill. So I wasn't allowed to go ratting and had to stop at home feeling as if I could kick any one's legs as came near me.

Mother tells me to content myself else she'd soon square me up, and starts to try and teach me to tell the clock, which lightens up my spirits a bit. I kept on looking at one hand and then at the other, but was soon too long for her patience and she tells me I'm a stupid young owl, and can't I see the long and short hand and that it's ten minutes to two. I kept on looking and repeating that over and over till she gits fed up and tells me to shut my row; but after that, though I couldn't tell the clock, I could always tell when it was ten to two.

Presently Father come across the medder and I runs out with the pepper box in my hand (having been helping Mother set dinner), anxious to see the rats. Father laughs and says the ones he'd got didn't want no more peppering. Fifteen he had and one old buck was a whopper—nineteen inches long. Father said he was a great-grandfather and must ha' been living on Billy Garrould's fat bacon for years and he was going to give him to the "cats"[2] In he went and we were fair delighted to see the doe out and tear him limb

[1]Mort—a great number. [2]Cats—local term for ferrets.

from limb for the young 'uns, killing him a second time, biting and sucking and pulling and tugging.

After dinner, when Father took his nap, we outs and thinks we'll give the cats another, and see some more fun—which we did. We made such a row yelling and laughing to see the ferrets after the rats Father wakes up and comes out in a tearing temper and finds all the ferrets' lockers undone, which set him storming at us good and proper, for if the ferrets gits out at night they hides up and will kill chickens by the score for blood lust and the fun of murdering. So he clouts the two of us and we starts blaring fit to bring the house down, we not being short of wind in them days, and made the house tremble with our roaring.

Father says, "Dang me, I can't stand this no longer, them boys fair craze a man, they're as stupid as a couple of Dickeys,[1] and near as headstrong. Let's see, what's ter-morrow—Monday—you and the girl Liza go and see the School Missus, and git 'em off to school and let 'em larn 'em, if they can."

So Mother tidies herself next day and off she goes. Billy and I starts playing with a pop-gun made of a short length of elder wood with the pith bored out. We used to fit a ram rod to it and chew up paper into pellets for bullets and the pop-gun worked fine. We starts shooting at each other and soon I catches him a banger in the eye and he starts to run for home and I arter him. He hulls a stone and hits me on the chin, I throws it back and breaks the keepin'-room window, which was lead glazed, driving all the glass in on to the flower pots standing on Mother's window board. We scurried round and clears up the bits and chucks 'em in the river, and Mother comes along and gits tea and tells Father she fixed we start next Monday, all three of us, and a penny a piece to pay every week for each of us for books and pencils.

Father grumbles at the expense but Mother say she don't care no-how as long as she can git rid of us for a few hours, and she should feel as though she was in heaven. Not long after that they notice the draught from the window, and by the time that trouble

[1]Donkeys.

was squared and brown paper put in to fill the hole, we was feeling p'raps we was best at school.

June 4th, 1871, we sets out to school for the first time, I being six years and seven months old, my sister eighteen months older than me and my brother Billy fifteen months younger.

Mother tells us to be careful crossing the road, but 'twasn't likely we'd meet more than a horse and cart and a wheelbarrow, so we gits there safe and sound and were put on a form in the infants' room. While prayers were said we were gaping at all the boys and girls and feeling very shy.

The Teacher give us each a slate and pencil and tells us to look at the blackboard and the letters she was a-chalking and copy 'em on our slates. We does the best we could, but Teacher with an eye like a hawk soon sees I'm using my left hand, and I get a rap on the knuckles for doing it. We goes out to play and I gits pushed over and starts howling till she comes over and picks me up, and back we goes and does some more scribbling.

We goes home for dinner and Mother says she missed us cruel, couldn't ha' believed she would, and my sister tells how that boy George would keep using his left—and teacher hit him—and if that wasn't silly enough he must git pushed and fall down rushing about at play-time. Then Father says:

"That'll du, I don't want to hear no more," and when Father spoke out we knew what that meant and shoves down our dinners and off back to school.

I soon tumbles to it and gets on all right and could write the alphabet from the blackboard and was put on the top seat of the gallery with the best scholars in the infant room. It was easy there to see if I used my left hand, but one day when I thought she weren't looking I changed the pencil over and soon had my copy done. Teacher sees and calls out:

"Put that pencil in your right hand, young Baldry, if I catch you using your left again I'll give you the cane." And I says:

"My Mother uses her left hand, why shan't I?"

I didn't make much progress using my right hand and my copy was allus being crossed off, so when ever I see a chance I'd slip the pencil into my left hand, keeping one eye on the teacher, and soon she twigged me. She called out for me to come down from the gallery as she had something to show me, so of course I was down in a crack, and only when she pulled out the cane I see what it was I was to see. Twisting up her lip she told me to hold out my hand and down it come but I was quicker and the cane come down on her knee. Then she got the wind up—called one of the assistants to hold me—and she caught my wrist and let me have it—one—two—three—four, and some extra to make up for the one she missed. Then there was a storm of tears and blubbering—the rest of the Class sat as quiet as mice—and the teacher took no more notice, feeling sure I wouldn't use my left again. Nor did I, for it was so sore and tingling for days after it cured me for life of writing with it, though there's many a job to this day I'd sooner use my left hand for.

We used to have lessons on the Bible, and one day teacher tells us about Adam and Eve—the first man and woman God created—and asked us if we had ever heard about 'em. We looks at each other and thinks every one has a Father and a Mother and that's all we knows. My pal Edward Sharp whom we called "Blunt" looked at me and whispered, "Now we be going to learn summat."

Then teacher tells us God made the earth, all animals, birds, fishes, trees and everything that you can see and us as well, and God had been looking over the world ever since at all the things he made, that he could see us and if we done wrong he wouldn't be long punishing us. We sit there like a couple of dummies a-staring at her and listening, for we had never heard nothing about the Creation of the world and it was all a wonder to us. After a few weeks of this religious training we had become a couple of small earth saints—we were that feared to do a thing we should not in case we should be punished by that God—but being very young at the time our religion was only skin deep.

If there was any fruit about me and my pal Blunt would have our fingers on it. One day I say:

"Think the gooseberries'll soon be fit?" and he say:

"Yes, I had some, just what I wants is a good fill up."

So I tells him I knows where we can git plenty out of the Old Lady Garden down the Common Lane—she got a lot under herring netting—and we can git 'em next day which was Saturday, and

she'll be busy with her baking because I know them there old people, they don't bake Sundays they be too religious for that.

Next marning we was there—through a weak place in the fence and under the herring netting—laying on our backs under the bushes eating the lovely ripe gooseberries as fast as we could git 'em down our throats. Soon Blunt say:

"Lay low, I heerd the old Lady coming to scare the birds off her fruit," and out she come and round she go to see if there was any, a-flapping her apron and clapping her hands, but never thinks to look under the bushes or she would have seen three birds what couldn't fly but was fast creepers blowing themselves out on her fruit. Back she go into the house to her baking and we finds we was full and off we went the way we come, pleased as punch we'd filled our little pods to the brim, never thinking we'd left the prints of our hands and knees in the fresh dug soil of the cabbage patch we'd crossed to get in.

When the Old Man sees them tracks and find the fruit gone, he git in a rare taking with his ole Woman and hollers out. She come running, thinking he'd happened on an accident.

"The fruits gone," says he. "Tha's them dratted boys. How is it yew didn't see 'em, thought I towd yer to keep a good look out." Well, she gits proper ratty at that and says:

"Can't dew everything, yer silly old mawkin[1], yew and yer fancies be such it takes me three parts o' my time ter look arter yer grub."

"Yes," says her old man. "And yarning with them old wimmen up the lane and nursing yer apron take the other part. You best stop at home and mind yer business and leave other people's alone."

We hears all this a-going on but as luck went they never thinks it was us took the gooseberries, going past to school every mawnin' with faces like glass saints, and soon the fruit was picked and we hear no more of that.

Harvest time was near and we was looking forward to running rabbits in the big field along side the road home from school. I thought if I could git a piece or two of Father's herring netting and put over some of the holes along the fence, the rabbits'd draw away there as the field was cut.

One morning away come ten harvesters with their scythes on their shoulders—no reaping machines then—and start mowing by the field gate. I slips round to the other end with my netting ready hid up and puts it over the most likely holes I thought they would bolt into, laying it loose over a stick to keep it from being pulled inside. Then I hides in the fence well under cover, armed with a short stick.

The cutters come along up the top end of the field and started

[1]Mawkin—scarecrow.

The cutters come along up the top end of the field.

a-shouting, "Lo—lo—lo"—and bounce come a fat rabbit into my net. Had it in a moment and taps him sharp behind the ears with the side of my palm which soon finished him, that being the only right way to kill a rabbit—done in a second. Wasn't long afore another slips out of the standing corn and into one of my holes and I soon had him. Then I hid 'em both up in different places, as I heard my Mother say, "He who hides can find."

The reapers begun to work round by my end of the field then, so I had to be careful. If they'd caught me it would have been goodbye —a clout on the ear and the toe of the shoemaker's boot for me. Soon there was only a long strip standing and the rabbits started running hard out of the last little bit o' corn. I gits six afore I finished and then thinks the reapers being so close this is the one the cobbler threw at his wife (the last) and packs up and off home with a rabbit stuffed into the front of my trousers.

So I went bakkard and forrard fetched the lot and stowed 'em in an old rabbit locker at home. I then went to see the harvesters finish—which I did—the boys calling out:

"Yew should ha' stopped, Happy, we had some fun running rabbits." But when I asks how many they got they says, "None," which made me laugh and think of my locker full which I warn't going to feed but was going to feed me, hollow-meat[1] being rarely welcome.

Father bring me a doe that night—a tame 'un—and was fair surprised to find the locker full o' rabbits. When I tells him what I done he laughs and says I was darn lucky and did I bring the netting home and not get found out? When he finds that's all right, he says, "How did I git 'em home?" and I sezs:

"In the top o' my trousers—plenty of room—as they's made out of hissen."

He laughs some more, and so do Mother, and she give him a look

[1]Hollow-meat. Poultry, rabbits or game, not butcher's meat. Before modern cropping methods were employed on farms and land lay fallow, rabbits were very abundant, and farm "servants," i.e. "labourers," had an agreement that they should not be given hollow-meat more than so many times a week.

and say, "It's sartin shure he ought to be able to catch a rabbit now he's got his Father's trousers on."

We had a good blow out from them rabbits which fill up Father's old trousers so tight there warn't no more room to put a rabbit down the front.

It happened we got a month's holiday just then from school, and Father tells me to git along and see if the farmer up the hill had a job for me pig keeping when the pigs was turned out on the stubble to shack[1], now harvest was off the fields. I finds the farmer in the yard giving orders and asks him. He looks me up and down, laughs and sezs I ain't big enough for pig keeping, but when I sezs, "Try and you'll soon see," he says, "All right, I'll give you a shilling a week du you du the job," and I runs home that pleased at getting my first work.

Next morning I was away early and the Farmer tells me to see if I can count the pigs—three sows and twenty six young 'uns. I manages that, ticking 'em off on my fingers, and he says:

"That'll be right, take 'em down to Turkey Pightle[2] to shack on the bean stubble and bring 'em home when you sees 'em stop off about noon-time."

Off I goes and found it an easy job while there was plenty of beans to shack up. Had a fill out of blackberries and counted the pigs, found some had filled up and laid down. Come noon-time I started home driving the big 'uns fust but found they 'ont be druv from their pigs, and one runned at me with her mouth open till I took to my heels and fled. Thought a bit and then druv the little 'uns fust and got 'em onto the road.

That worked champion as the sows followed along and soon got into a shag-trot home. I follers puffing and was outter wind by the time I shuts the farm gate on 'em and gits off home myself pleased enough with my first day's pig keeping. Shilling a week, thinks I, that be tuppence I earned to-day, and tomorrer I'm a-going

[1]Shack—Pick up the loose corn.
[2]*Pightle*—A small angular enclosure of land, possibly from Anglo-Saxon "pycan"—pointed.

ter take a good stick to that rare savage old sow what runned at me, and I'll give her beans.

Up with the lark I gits, thinking now I had become a British workman, and off with the pigs afore the farmer were about. He come down to see me later in the day—it had started raining—and he tells me to put my coat on. I sezs:

"I can't do that, Master, I hain't got no coat." So he tells me to put a sack on my shoulders and come to the backus when I gits in with the pigs and he'll find me a coat, which I does.

Back I goes trapsin along proud as a horse with the farmer's coat hanging near on the ground, wondering if there would come a day when I should be wearing his boots and be a proper farmer. When I come marching into the yard all of 'em started laughing fit to split, wondering who the little ole man was a-coming. I tells 'em how the farmer said it would keep me warm all right, and any night I was late home it would do as a bed as well.

Father tries it on and says, "Watcher want this for, it'll du me all right," and I ups and says, "It's mine—farmer give it me to wear pig keeping—and I'm gornter du so—time there's wet days."

So he lets me have it. One of the first times I finds "He who has had best hold."

Well, the shacking got short and the sows terrible hard to keep in, allus making for the weak places in the fence, and kept me a-running. One day the farmer looks over the gate and sees me keep a-heading 'em off, that please him and he sezs:

"Boy, yew done that well—didn't think yew could a' runned sur hard as that," and I tells him:

"Yes, I kin run so be there's anything to run for."

That made him laugh and say I be the sort he want and he'll shift me tomorrer to Baker's field where there is good shacking on the bean stubble. I wonders whatever a baker is doing on a bean stubble, but I sezs nothing.

Next day he helps me take the pigs down on a new field and they starts a-picking up the loose beans as hard as they could go and the farmer he sezs:

"They wont be much trouble to you for a day or tew, take 'em home about the same time—yew can ask someone what o' clock."

I tells him I know what a clock is Father got one at home, and he laughs at that till he shake and sezs:

"Yew don't onderstand me, Bor—ask somebody what time

of the day it be—and if it be fower of the arternoon. If they sezs Yes, boy—drive 'em home."

Off he goes and I thinks I'll have a look round, and see if I could find out where the Baker live—the pigs being busy filling theirselves. I git round to the other side of the field but could see no sign of him anywhere. I looks through the fence and what does I see but a pretty lot o' bards making a funny noise and spreading out their tails as big as my Mother's frying pan. I thinks to myself it would be rare fun to have one o' them, if Father would buy me one. I looks a bit further and finds there is a beet field near by and remembers the Farmer sezs, "See them there pigs don't git into the beet."

Then it starts to rain, a'coming down in torrents and washing my pigs right clean. I buttoned up master's old coat round my neck, pulled my rabbit skin cap well over my head—the water dripping from it as though it were from the eves of a house. I took no harm and after a bit the rain clears away and the sun shined out. I looks round and finds my pigs were a-drawing towards the beet field, the savage old sow was within twenty yards of a gap in the fence.

I got up to her and stood in front and the old sow and another with her and she circles round me a few times and looks with her wicked little eyes peeping out under her flapping ears. Then she raised her head and made up her mind—come at me full trot with open mouth and savage grunt, the other following close behind. Over I goes heels over head, and afore I was up the old sow had a beet in her mouth and the other after her, both getting them down their necks then looking round as if to say:

"Yew little old boy, we done yew after all."

But I gits 'em in the end and see a man with a wagon and horses a-tuttering along the road and ask him if it were four of the clock.

He sezs, "Yes, Bor, half arter," so I hurries and druv my pigs home, and tells farmer about the old sow getting in the beet, and he sezs he'll git the gap mended so she shan't play that trick on me no more.

So I off home and Father ask me about what happen, and I tells him I couldn't find no baker's shop in the field same as I thought, and he sezs, "Yer dunderhead, that's the name of the field, that is called after the old feller as owned it." Then I tells him about them funny bards with tails like frying pans and he sezs, "They call 'em peacocks."

"Well," I sezs (allus getting things wrong way round), "they, doesn't need no calling—they come arter me when I was there making such a funny noise."

Then Father tells me they are werry pretty bards, but werry fierce and'll kill boys if they gits near 'em, which made me shudder to think on, not wanting any birds be they never so pretty, if they be boy eaters, and kept well away from that fence and never looked over there no more. Knew when I was older Father told me that so I shouldn't be getting inter mischief and go on Squire's lawn and be meddling, or upsetting of his peacocks.

The days went on and I gits on all right till one day when they had been moved to the Thwaite field where there was a sandy pit and a hill a few yards from the gate. The pit were full of rabbit holes and the fences too, and I asks the farmer if I can try and git some rabbits with one of Father's nets? He sezs, "Yes, git all yer can," and I were that pleased it seem as if my trousers worn't big enough, although made of my Father's old 'uns.

Well, I were busy with the nets on this morning and then I finds some small black plums in the hedge and starts trying them, thinking here's summat to have a good fill up on, but they stung my mouth and drawed up my throat (I didn't know then they was sloes and give you a belly ache, unless you have 'em in sloe gin, which is rare good in cold weather).

Spat 'em out and looked round and see it had clouded up. Was putting on my coat when off goes one of the sows as if she was mad, shrieking and grunting and bust through the fence and away down the road for all she was worth, me arter her with my ground ash Father give me for pig driving (he having cut it in case we needed correcting) and mortal glad I was I hadn't had that across my back, as yet. But I'd learned to sock 'em over the ribs with it and give 'em a good larding, and they looked to me for master now, did my twenty nine pigs.

She run, did the old bounder, and me after her, had to take my coat off and throw it by the hedge so I could git along faster, in a mortal fright lest I should lose the master's sow, and she running up Brickle Hill and me getting further behind and it raining and me wet to the skin with the rain a-pouring. Down another hill we went through Belsey Bridge Watering, me getting through as best I could, she going full pelt up another hill—nearly out o' my sight—me puffing behind, and when I gets to the top I sees her half a mile ahead. I starts to howl then thinking I'd lost her and what'll Master say to me losing his sow.

Well, in the end she gits tired and turns round, bolts past me and off home. There I finds her when I gits the rest home at the end of the day (tired out and wet) thinking she had gone for good. Worn't I glad when farmer tells me and sezs, "Spect you had some trouble along o' her, Boy?"

When I tells him she runned me near to Thwaite Church and back and I thought she were going and wondered whatever was the matter—she a-carrying on like that—he laughs and sezs:

"I know what's up, boy, she'll be better tomorrer. Yer wet, boy—git off home—I'll shut the pigs up."

So off I goes and tells 'em all about it at home and sezs, "I never did know sows had fits and went off shrieking fit to bust 'emselves, and could trot like horses and lick me a-running and jumping."

Father laugh and tell me old sow will be better on the morrer, and I don't know yet awhile how many beans make five. I go to my work thinking what Father had just said to me—"I didn't know how many beans made five."

Well, I could count the pigs—three big 'uns and twenty six young 'uns—can't see what that's got to du with old sow going mad, if that have I'll ask Master. So getting the pigs out of the yards I asks him and he sezs:

"Blame it, Bor, what du yu want to know that for? Best use the eyes in yer head."

"Corse I'd like to know," sezs I.

"All right," sezs he, "come here, Bor[1]," and he catched me by the back of my neck saying, "Count these," and I thought now I shall find out about these beans, and—bang—his heavy hand comes first on one ear and then on the other, and number five the toe of his boot meet the seat of my trousers and I was not stopping for number six. Off I go in a quicker hurry than I ever was afore, druv my pigs into the field and contented myself for the day. And t'wasn't that way I finds out how many beans make five.

[1] A usual form of address in East Anglia.

The Farmer's Boy

The sun had set behind the hills
Across the dreary moor,
When weary and lame a poor boy came,
Up to a Farmer's door,
"Can you tell me" said he "if any there be
To give me some employ,
To plow and sow and reap and mow,
And be a Farmer's boy.

"If none there be to give to me,
The favour that I ask,
Is there a roof to shelter me,
From this night's wintry blast,
At break of day I'll trudge away
Elsewhere to seek employ
To plow and sow and reap and mow,
And be a Farmer's boy.

"Father is dead, Mother is a-bed
With her five children small,
And what is worse for Mother still,
I am the biggest of all.
Tho' little I be I fear no work,
If you give me employ
I'll plow and sow and reap and mow,
And be a Farmer's boy."

"Try the lad" said the Farmer's wife,
"Let him no further seek,"
"Yes try the lad" the daughter cried,
While the tears ran down her cheek,
"T'is hard to want for any work,
And wander for employ,
Don't turn him away but let him stay
And be a Farmer's boy."

In course of time he grew to a man,
The good old Farmer died,
He left the lad the farm and he
Had the daughter for his bride.
The lad that was the Farmer is,
He often thinks with joy,
On the lucky day he came that way
To be a Farmer's boy.

To plow and sow and reap and mow
And be a Farmer's boy.

CHAPTER IV

Whit-whit-whit-whit-whit-whit-whee-ee
No shoe-maker can make boots for me-ee
Why-why-why-why-why-why-so-o?
Because my heel is as long as my toe-o!

Old rhyme on lark's song.

NEXT day Master say, "We'll have 'em pigs put on Bobby Field." Bobby Field, thinks I, now which might that be, but dare not ask where it was. Asking about the beans make me a bit more careful what I sezs. So he takes me down to Bobby's field and sezs, "There yer are, Bor, look arter 'em well hereabouts, corse if they gits out and du du a power o' damage ter people's gardens I'd likely have ter pay for it."

So I kept a good look out, and trailing round and round that there field was soon that hungry I didn't know what to put inside me, till I sees some small bulbs which I thought was artichokes, and thinking here's a find—I'll have a good fill up now, pulled some up and bit the end off one and started to eat it. I did not get far, it was like biting the end of a hot cinder. I spitted and slavered and wrung and twisted myself about all shapes. My tongue begun to swell up in my mouth and I thought I was going home, there and then, but after about two hours I got better again, not having swallered a lot. I found out afterwards they was Lords and Ladies or wild arums, and deadly poison.

Thought it was time I looked to my pigs, and went down the field to where they was feeding, past some thick bushes. The savage old sow was near by with sixteen small pigs and by some mischance one of them got entangled in some briars.

I went to loose it and it shruck out ten thousand murders. As I got it out of the bushes the old sow rushed to defend it, and I dropped the little one just in time within a foot of her open mouth before she attacked me. If it had not been so, I might have finished pig keeping there and then, as an angry sow is an aw'kard customer.

After that along comes an old farmer jogging to market. He stop to pass the time o' day and has a look over the fence and asks whose pigs they be. I tells him they belongs to my Master, and he sezs they looked a nice lot o' young shotts[1] and he would be seeing Master about 'em—draws his whip across his pony and off he goes. When I gits back I tells Master that a farmer going to market wanted to buy some of the pigs.

"Who's he, Boy—I'd have you remember I'm Master here and Farmer tew, and can look arter myself. Yew look arter them pigs, that's what yew are paid for."

Thinks I to myself it would be a mortal long while before I buys one with what I was paid—a shilling a week—what with getting near poisoned, running half over the country after the old sow, and nearly being killed, all thrown in.

When I gits home Mother say:

"Whatever have yew been a-doing on—you look that white—

[1]A young pig.

don't look to me as if you could eat anything if it was sugared."

I tells her and she make me something up in a mug and tells me to get that down me, and I did. In a moment I runs outside and thought I was going to be turned insides out, spitted and spluttered and brought it all up. Felt like pegging out, but after a bit was better and ask her what she give me.

"Salt and water," said she. "That's how my grandmother used to doctor any one who have been eating such stuff as yew have." And true enough in the morning I was near well again.

Next day we was changed onto the Brickle Field—them pigs and me—which was a paradise for them, plenty of loose corn laying around, large oak trees standing in the fences, a good crop of acorns and a pond with sloping banks that they could go in and out of with ease, which they loves to do, does pigs; rolling and laying in the mud and then drinking of it and come out as black as tinkers, the mud drying on 'em and making a fine over-jacket. Then they would pick a nice spot in the sun and lay down, as is usual with pigs, higgledy piggledy side by side, head to tail in a row (a natural instinct I should think from the time they roams at large in the oak forests of Britain), so they can see both ways and hear the approach of danger.

Another habit with them—I come to notice—was when the sow was near her time. She give birth to the first of the litter and after a few minutes—young and weak as it is—she starts calling in her language and it seems as though the youngster knew and struggle along towards its mother's head, fudges about until it finds a dill, and if suited, sticks to it. Number two come along and it is his turn to find a dill and if he takes that of number one there is a fight between the two, and so it go on until the last one is born.

It happen sometimes the sow has only twelve dills, and give birth to thirteen pigs, which is unfortunate as the thirteenth is often the smallest and weakest—the pippin—and has to hunt about while the others are sucking. When the sow feel her milk gone she gets up and walk off and the pippin's chances are over, so it follows her making a rare hullabaloo, but she wont take no notice of it, as in nature the weak is meant to go to the wall.

Well, I soon had a look round this field; I wanted a frail basket —like the men on the farm take their dinner in—thought I would like to make one and saw plenty of rushes growing alongside the horse pond. There was a deep, dry ditch which overlooked the field so I gits some sticks and laid some rubbish on top and made myself a shelter which was now to become my basket factory, when I had learnt myself how to braid.

I got a good lot of rushes and laid 'em to dry. Standing upright I could see my pigs anywhere on the field, and if it turned wet I had a roof over my head. Next day had a look at my rushes, found they was dry and thought now I'll make a start and try and du a bit of braiding. Picked three rushes, fixed them on a crotched stick and started, but had not done anything of the kind before and was three or four hours afore I gits into the knack of braiding three, but it come to me all at once.

Went on pleased as whoop and getting near the end of my rushes thought I should like to make a long braid, so tied more to the end. Was careful braiding past the knots and in a short time had braided a length two yards long, but thinks to myself, it weren't wide enough —too much work to make a basket of that. So I tried four rushes and found they wouldn't work, then five, and found I got on well with that number and tumbled to it that they must be odd. Then I got fifteen fixed them in between two sticks, put 'em in a line, hung 'em up on two crotched sticks and, seeing the pigs was busy shacking, started to see what I could do with that number.

The wrong way is sure to come first but I stuck to it and after a time found out how—started in the centre taking one from each side—and then went on one after the other and in a short time a braid begun to appear, wide enough to make a frail basket.

The rushes were getting short—I didn't want to knot 'em this time, scratched my head and it come to me all at once, why not braid 'em in clear of the edge then trim them off arterwards. Did so and in two days had enough braiding made for my frail. But now, how was I to put my basket together? When I got home I had a look round to see what I could find and come across a piece of old sack. Plenty in that thinks I, took it and went into Father's cow shed and see laying there some old scissors he used for trimming up the cow. On the winder among the cobwebs I found a needle made of an old umbrella rib that he use for making the babs for eel catching. Now had all I wanted so took all the things and hid 'em up.

When I gets down to the field next morning the Farmer come along and say:

"Hullo, Boy, what have you been rigging up here?" And when I tells him I made that fur shelter if it hap-ter rain, he looks at me with a twinkle in his eye telling me not to go to sleep in it, and let the pigs out, then away he goes.

My fingers were itching to be putting my frail basket together, so seeing my pigs was all right I pulls out my scissors and needle from under my braces—where I had wrapped 'em for safety in a bit of sacking—and started pulling it to bits to get string—threaded my needle—and was off. Took the wide braid—doubled it—thought that's big enough for me, cut it, and found I had plenty to make the bottom.

Sewed the two ends together and put the bottom in, careful to get the side-joint that formed one of the handles. That done, finished sewing in the bottom, stitched together the sides, used my three rush braid for the handles, sewed 'em on and my basket was finished. Found a nob stick trimmed it up and it was just the thing for the basket so now was set up, had a frail and stick of my own I could carry on my shoulder like the men on the farm.

When I got home that night (I knew the time to start from Bobby's field because if the sun was out at half arter four the sun shined through the middle of a crotch in a big tree), Father ask me where I'd been and got that frail basket from? When I tells him I made it, he took it and turned and twisted it about muttering:

"Wont'er thought it—yew done that well. Yew'd better let me have that—just what I want."

But I sezs, "No, I ain't a-going to let any one have it, I wants it myself," and he laughs and looks at me and sezs:

"That's it, boy, you be a-feeling the ground under yer feet—if yew can't have a thing, go out and find a way to git it—and when yew got it—stick to it."

When I said to him I'd make him one time I'd done pig keeping, he goes on eating his supper and never lifts his eyes nor sezs "Yes" nor "No," but presently he looks up at the clock and sezs, "Boy, time for bed," and I took the hint and off I goes, and leaves something I wanted to ask till the morrer.

Next morning I tells him the field where the pigs is is full of burrows and if he'll let me have the dog and a net or two I'm sure as I could git a rabbit—Farmer sezs I might—so he say:

"Right, boy, yew can have the dog and some nets, don't lose em," and I go off on top of the world with the nets in the frail and my dinner and a piece for Rover.

Pigs were out—hungry—and busy shacking. I put some nets over the holes, went down the fence and let Rover loose. He was soon hunting like shot in and out of the fence. It was early, the rabbits was still laying out, soon away go one across the field, his white scut a-bobbing as he ran and I said goodbye to him.

Rover was running another I ha'nt seen at the bottom of the hill towards my nets and in he popped. In a jiffy I had him out, Rover pulling too, and soon he was in my basket and hung on a tree. Rover started another, but that went down a hole with no net, so he scrabbles and whines and I takes a long bramble with plenty of thorns and put it down and twisted it round two or three times, drew it out with rabbit's dome[1] sticking on so reckoned it was in about two yards.

The young shoots of the blackberry will grow to the length of six to ten feet in a season and are the thickness of a man's finger

[1]Dome—Fur.

through. The thorns run the whole length and are very sharp and bent like a parrot's beak. With one of these brumbles as the country folk call 'em put down a hole and twisted round, the thorns' hooks soon get entangled in poor bunny's felt, and struggle as he may out he must come.[1] So it was this time, Rover getting him by the leg, and me pulling till I got a good hold and finish him the warrener

way. Rover, hot and panting, look up at me as if to say, "We got him pal," licked my face and poked his nose under my chin. The two of us had a rare happy day, and little did I think as how it was to be my last at pig keeping.

Next morning I had to go without Rover, as Father had lent him to a man with the nets. I felt lonely without him but busied myself gathering elderberries for Mother to make wine, which I could do well and not lose sight of my pigs, as the hedges was loaded with them hanging down in great black bunches. I knew it was

[1]In Kent these brambles are called "Lawyers." When my informant asked an old woodman the reason, he received the following reply: "When you gets into the clutches of a lawyer he'll take the skin off you—same as this briar will off the backside of a rabbit!"

now or never for the birds have such a fancy for them they will strip the tree bare three days after they have ripened.

Mother set rare store by elderberries. If any of us was ill she could not afford to call in a doctor, but that did not mean she was asleep to nature's remedies that grew in her garden and round about. She made an elderberry wine[1] from grandmother's recipe that was a grand tonic and livener on a cold winter day—many a quiet man fancied he was master of all when he was full up with that drink.

My basket now full of elderberries I set it in the shade and wandered into the next field, round a clay pit, and see, growing on the edge, a great bore thistle with its main root uncovered three parts of its length through fallen clay. Thinking I'd take it home and plant it in my garden, fudged out the rest of the root and found its end in the sand below. Took it and wound it round me, as it was the only way to carry it.

The old sow was restless all day, running and grunting and charging the fence to get out. Presently she charged it in a weak place, went through it snorting—over the road—jumped another fence—through a deep holl[2]—and onto a medder where there was a plain smooth wire fence. The wires were about nine inches apart and a bit slack, she was going full gallop and tried to get between the wires. She put her front feet over the lower one—it slipped up and caught her front dills—she was trapped and shruck out, poor thing, as though she were being killed, and me thirty yards behind, running my hardest.

I stood on the bottom wire beneath and with both hands pulled up the wire that was pressing her back down, set her free and off she went and was quickly out of my sight. Was mortal glad when

[1]Grandmother's recipe for Elderberry wine: Take 2 quarts of plump elderberries and 4 quarts of water and boil for half an hour. When cool, bruise the berry with a wooden spoon and pass the pulp through a muslin strainer, and to each quart of juice add three-quarters of a pound of sugar. Stir well, boil again for 20 minutes, add a few cloves and a little ginger essence, and when cool strain again into a wooden tub. Ferment with a little brewer's yeast, spread on a slice of toast, and when the liquid has ceased to work lift it out and skim the surface. Add one-quarter of a pint of brandy to each gallon of wine, bottle and cork very lightly, and when all fermentation has ceased, cork firmly and store for at least six months before using, or ten years if liked.

[2]A ditch. From Anglo-Saxon "holh"—a ditch.

I got back with the rest to find she was in the yard all buried up in the straw. Father asked me what I wanted with a great thistle wound all round me, as if we hadn't enough rubbish at home and took hold of one end, saying:

"Keep on a-turning, boy," and soon had it off. He took his rule and measured the root and found it was 13 feet 6 inches.

"Glad you brought it home, boy, dang me, if I don't have a bet on that," and he did and won ten bob, so he told me. (Rare fond of a bet was Happy Jack.)

Next day it was a lovely still September morning with the dew on the grass and the gossamers a-hanging all over the bushes and the sun shining; the larks a-singing as if it were spring, making the young with no troubles feel light and gay. I went along whistling "The monkey cocked his tail up" till I gets to the farm, and there I see Master standing near the pig yard, his hat on the back of his head, hair hanging over his eyes, and another man whom I knew was the butcher standing nigh him, both looking black as thunder. Master says to me, savage as a cow with no calf:

"I'll give you summat, you young varmint, coming whistling onto my place 'Monkey cocked his tail up,' I'll cock yer tail afore I ha' done with you. You've been and kilt one of my best sows."

"I h'aint kilt none on 'em!"

"Oh, h'aint yer, burst yer, look you what's this 'ere, the old sow's dead as mutton, yer must ha' done it. The butcher says she been hit with a stick or stone on her dills and thats what's now kilt her."

I had a look and see my poor old savage sow lying dead in the straw, but I looks 'em both in the face and sezs again:

"I h'aint kilt her."

But my master catcht me a clout on the ears with his heavy hand, and the toe of his farm boot in my trouser seat, and I went flying out of his reach, him saying, "P'raps that 'ud larn me to speak the truth." I gets up in a tearing temper, for all I was only a little 'un, and sezs:

"That's just what I have done yew two disbelieving ole men, and when I gits a man I'll give yer both a clout on yer lugs and git my own back, if you git in my way then and give me any trouble."

I blew off at them until they was forced to smile, and my Master ask, "If yew didn't hit her, who did?"

I tells him what happened and how the old bounder gits hung up on the wire fence and shruck blue murder, and how I gits her out and she run off home and I sees her in the straw when I got back, and how I never told no lies about my poor old sow. Master looked at the butcher and ask what he thinks, and they come to it that was the way of it and talk a bit.

Then Master looking at me sharply, say, "Well, maybe—but it's like this, boy—I shan't turn these 'ere pigs out shacking no more. Yew can go along home. I h'aint got ought yew can du now, and tell your Father I'll pay him yer money when I see him."

Off I go, like a dog with his tail burnt. The sun a-shining still but it seemed the day had gone all dark and cold to me. Reckoned I had killed a sow that 'ud lost me my job, done a month's pig keeping for nothing, lost my month's holiday, sent home with no money, and perhaps git another clouting when I tells Father why it was.

As it happen he was just going back to work after his dinner, and when I tells him I finished pig keeping he only ask if I has the money. When I sezs "No," he sezs:

"All right, I'll git that," and off he goes and I keeps quiet about the dead sow, but tells my brother when we gits to bed.

Thinking it over we comes to the conclusion I ain't done so bad. Learnt to braid and made a frail basket, got two rabbits (and six in the harvest fields), found a thistle 13 feet long and Father gave me a penny for it that I'll spend on four farthing sticks of rock at Garrould's shop, and p'raps if Master think better of it I'll git the four shillings he owe me. My brother say anyways we got to go to school Monday, and back we goes, feeling a bit strange after four weeks on our own.

Looking back I see it was then I first begins to learn what you loses on the swings you gains on the roundabouts, and also a man's life is all learning, even to the way a leaf swing on a twig, set so it may best catch the sun.

The Cruel Wife

There was an old couple and they were poor,
Tweedle, tweedle dee.
There was an old couple and they were poor
They lived in a house that had but one door,
Oh, what a poor couple were they!

The old man went out one day from home,
Tweedle, tweedle dee.
The old woman she couldn't stay moping alone
Oh, what a weak woman was she!

The old man he came home at last,
Tweedle, tweedle dee.
He found the door and the windows fast,
"Oh, what is the matter?" said he.

"Oh, I have been sick since you've been gone,
Tweedle, tweedle dee,
If you'd been in the garden, you'd heard me groan."
"I'm sorry for that," said he.

"Oh, I've a petition to make of thee,
Tweedle, tweedle dee,
Go pick me an apple from yonder tree."
"Oh, that will I do," said he.

The old man he got up in the tree,
Tweedle, tweedle dee.
She plucked down the ladder, and down fell he.
"This is cleverly done," said she.

Come all pretty maidens, wherever you be,
Tweedle, tweedle dee.
And do to your husbands as done by she,
That's the end of matrimonie.

Hedenham Brickyard as it is to-day.

CHAPTER V

The childhood shows the man
As morning shows the day.
Milton.

WE settled down again at school and I was moved up into the Big Room, as it was called. It was getting on into the autumn when I got another job. The Sister at the Hospital wanted a Yard Boy to carry coal for the wards and asked the School Mistress to find a suitable one. I was picked on, and went meat for manners.[1] I crept about very carefully not to drop coal or make a noise in the wards, pleasing the Sister-in-Charge, and was nearly too good to live, having become very religious.

My school teacher had told us of heaven up above, the starry heights far above the blue sky, where all good girls and boys went to live for ever with God and his angels. That heaven was beyond space, and the stars were windows which God looked through to see what bad boys and girls were doing down below. If they quarrelled or took that which didn't belong to them they would be thrown into a great pit, where there was fire and brimstone burning for ever.

I thought, small as I was, I wont last long—should soon be burnt up in a fire like that—having burnt myself a time or two with Mother's fire. Give me a terror of such a place and asked where it was. Teacher told us it was the home of the devil, and he use a long fork to stir the fire now and again and poke back the ones who try to git out. The boy sitting next to me say, "Why don't he burn too?" But I told him, "Hold yer row—or both of us'll git the cane."

Teacher told us the Devil like to see boys and girls do wrong

[1]Work for keep.

so he can throw them into the Pit. I thought wherever could this awful hot place be, had never seen it nor its owner, and didn't want to. Thought I would repent of my sins quickly—did so—and wished I could die and go to Heaven straight away, before I did any more, but it was not to be—I was to know a deal more of this old world first, and its ups and downs.

I went home one night after one of these lessons. It was a night with clear sky and hundreds of stars winking at me, and for all I was so feared it was a bit of comfort thinking heaven was p'raps big enough to hold every one on the earth. I went to bed and dreamt of the great Horse Chesnut tree that stand to this day a few yards from the door of this house, and that a ladder was set up it to heaven—the top was lost in indefinite space, lit up with a dazzling brightness—and angels a-going up and down, and I stood at the bottom but felt I must not try and climb. Then I looked up and see the stars like great windows, just as teacher said, and the saints looking through them down on to the earth, all glorious in intense light. Such a vision as could not be imagined. After that I was never so frit of the things teacher told us. Not that I'm finding fault, they did their duty to the best of their ability and belief, they hadn't only the ideas they'd been reared with.

In most country places the working man and woman stayed in the village they was born in, and was reared according to the family tradition. Many a genius must have come into the world his Father following at the plough's tail and followed in his footsteps, on the same farm. Seeing the sun casting its shadow as it rose in the east going to work, toiling on till it set in the west. Growing from boyhood, blooming into manhood with his breast full of that spirit and creative instinct with which nature endowed him, but no learning and no chance to go out into the world to better hisself, rooted deep down in the soil, till at last he go feet first the way of all men, only known to have lived by his family and the farmer he worked for.

Meanwhile I wasn't getting on so bad at school and was always for picking up what I could. One play time I was standing looking at the girls knitting cuffs to keep their wrists warm in the coming winter, and one look up with a smile and say:

"George, would yew like tew learn tew knit?"

"That I should," I say, and they soon set me to work showing me how to set my fingers till I gits the knack of twisting the wool round the needle, until the bell rang and it was time to go in, when I kisses 'em for the trouble they had learning me. I soon got the way of it they showing me how at odd times, and knitted myself a scarf for winter, getting the wool from an old crossover which was worn by women at that time.

One night Father asks, "How I be a-getting on at school, and what have they learnt me, and can I count this way?"

A ha-penny wet and a ha-penny dry
Fourpence ha-penny and a ha-penny by
A ha-penny behind and a ha-penny before
Four pence ha-penny and a ha-penny more.

"There yew are, boy—count that up then I shall know if you be a-larnin' ought at school."

I went outside, as I knew where some gravel lay, picked up two small stones, called 'em four farthings, then four big 'uns—called 'em one penny each, that made five pennies, four more small ones that made one penny, counted 'em up they made six altogether. Thought if there be six in one half the other must be the same, twice six is twelve, that's a bob. In I go pleased as punch and Father asks if I has a-counted 'em yet.

"Yes, that I have," says I.

"Lay yer a penny yew h'aint."

"I know I hev—that's a bob, that is—give me yer penny."

"No! No! Boy, you niver laid yer penny down."

"I won, Father, you knows I have—give us it."

"I'll be blowed boy, yew've cost me pennies enough and I can see yew ha' been to school long enough for the likes of us. I'll find yew a job afore yew git too much learnin' and start a-runnin' round yer betters all ways, shan't know what to du with yer. I'll have yer at work come spring time else my name's not Happy Jack."

It was then November and not for me to choose. Wanted to learn all I could while at school, so made the best of the few months I was to be there. Paid all the attention I could to try and learn to read and write, not like most boys paying much more attention

to the girls. Till one afternoon when with the other boys I were a-running up the school yard fit to bust ourselves, to see who could git to the end first, I see a girl going past the school gate, hand-in-hand with a young sister of hers. I was so struck I fell in love there and then, the first time I had ever known what it meant.

Such a change had come over me, young as I was, that she was always in my mind's eye, and very often if I knew she was out for a walk or on an errand I would go round another way so that I might meet her and git her to smile. Many and many a time have

I done that. I was very shy at the time with girls, and it was many a day before I plucked up the heart to speak to her. The amusing part of it was, as I have thought since, I was courting her in my boyish way hoping she would some day be my wife, as come to pass in the end after many a long year, when we was neither of us young no longer. She not knowing anything about it gave me no encouragement which but strengthened my love, and I only a kid—just out of the cradle—dare not tell any one. I kept it quiet for years and waited my time.

Unfortunately for me the spring time was near at hand. I had to cry—the tears running down my cheeks—to think that after a year's schooling I had to leave and git a job. Heard that a boy was wanted to barrer off newly made bricks at Hedenham Brickyard about three miles from my home, so went after the job. The Brickmaker sezs to me:

"Boy, du yew think as how yer big enough to barrer off brick?"

"Yes, Sir," sezs I. "Nearly tall as yew are, Sir."

It happening that he was a short man a few inches taller than me, making me feel older than I was.

"Well, let's see if yew can run a barrer—take this up to the brick hale[1] and back."

I soon showed him what I could do, tho' it was a spring barrer and I had never seen one afore. He looks at me and sezs:

"Yew'll do, boy, come on Monday marnin' six o'clock, not half after mind, and I'll give yer five bob a week."

Got home and Father asks, "Got yer job, boy?"

"Yes, start on Monday," sezs I.

Monday marnin' come and I was up afore five o'clock. Mother packed my grub in the frail basket I had made and I was off to my job getting there before six. Master tell me to put the grub in the shed and shut the door, handed me a shovel and tells me to fill up the table with brick earth first and then he'll start making. It was

[1]Hale—a pile—term generally used for clamps of beet or potatoes.

not so easy a job as I thought, the earth was more like dough and would not leave the shovel until Master sezs:

"What du yer think I stood that there pail of water there for, Boy—dip yer shovel in." I did so and found the earth slipped off the shovel easy then and the table was soon loaded up. Then he tells me to sand the brick boards, get the spring barrer and stand it by—I did so. "Now," sezs he, "I'll start making."

He handled the earth like dough, cutting lumps off and made me think of my Mother making loaves of bread. He began lumping the earth like fury into the mould, filling up the corners careful, and then struck it off level on the top with what he called a striker. Then he placed the board on top, the one that I had sanded, quickly turned the mould over, so the sanded board was at the bottom, lifted up the mould, and there was the first bricks I had ever seen made, standing on the board ready for me to barrer away.

"Now then, Boy, be yew careful when yew sits them on the barrer, look yew here yew seems a bit stupid, I'll load the first barrer up. Watch how I does it, yew'll sune be used to it, and then I'll show yew how to set 'em in the hale."

I took the barrer and drove it up the sixty yards to the hale with sixteen new made bricks, while he took the spare board. He placed it on top of one brick saying:

"See here, Boy, how I takes hold of both boards with fingers and thumb, holding them tight agin the brick, standin' it on edge, then draw both the boards away, and that'll leave half an inch space in a'tween each brick."

He done half the barrer load to give me a start and then leave me to see how I git on. I bin watching and started—going very careful—and got 'em all set safely down on the hale, and he tells me if I go on like that he'll soon make a brick maker of me, and to bring all the boards back, leaving one to start the next load.

Back I goes, and boy-like stood looking at him making, till he tells me he don't pay me to stand looking at him and to put some earth on the table, and be sharp and load the barrer again. Off I goes, he telling me to be quick and so I was. Set my foot on a rolling stone and over I go—barrer and all—spoiling my load of bricks which were bruck all to bits. Master hear the splutter and come running up the hale, cursing and swearing.

"You stoopid young b——, spoiling all the bricks, yer Father should ha' wrung yer neck when yew was born and reared a pig up on the milk—he wudder done suffin with that."

I tells him it was his fault telling me to hurry with a heavy barrer, but he say he don't want no back-chat, and sends me flying into the spoilt bricks. Nearby was plenty o' small stones and my wool was up, him calling me what he did, and I pelted him with 'em quick as I could and tell him:

"I'll have yer know I can move as quick as yew can, I shoont ha' turned the barrer over hanter bin fur yew a-sayin' I worn't quick enough, that's yar fault the bricks is spoilt—not mine—so there yew are." And he sezs:

"Well, Boy, yer a plucked 'un anyhow, come on and clear up this mess, and don't let it happen agin."

Thinks to myself he ain't much bigger than I was anyways, why should I be frit of him, looks more like a beer barrel on a couple of stumps, let me git a bit bigger and I'll soon go round him like a cooper round a cask, du he call names any more. But I soon forgets about that and was careful not to spoil any more bricks.

Worked from six in the morning till six at night, barrering and setting on the hale, careful to keep the line straight, handling each brick made three times. On a fine day he would make two thousand bricks, being very active with his hands and arms, more so than with his feet as they was covered with corns.

I walked many miles during the day with my barrer, not counting the four mile or more to my job and back home at night, and all for ten pence a day. If it turned out wet I was cut off—no work no pay—so some weeks I earned not more than 2s. *6d.* Fortunately my father was a shoemaker or I should have cost as much as I earned in boots, but I was happy enough and contented with my work.

After a bit we had thirty thousand bricks made, dry, and ready to be burnt in the kiln. Was anxious to see how a kiln was loaded up, and one day it was started. The bricks were sun dried and hard and we used ordinary barrers to cart 'em to the kiln. Kept my eyes open to see how they were put—and found they were placed at about the same distance as on the hale so the fire could git in between. They were set one over the other forming a tunnel about two feet wide in which the fire was lit looking altogether like a large honey comb with passages in between to allow the smoke and hot air to escape. Then the fire was lit, the smoke pouring forth like a volcano, and after about a fortnight of burning the kiln was ready to be unloaded.

We took down the bricks that were laid temporary to block the archway through which the kiln was loaded—not so bad a job though they was still hot, as long as we could still git at them standing on the ground. Then we began on top, Master throwing 'em down and I thinks I'll catch 'em—one at a time—but he soon tells me off, "Be a month of Sundays doing that," sezs he. "Catch 'em in pairs—look out here comes the first pair!"

I was feared to catch 'em and down they come plump on the top of my feet, and I wrung and twisted about hollering out I was gornter be killed if I had to catch hot bricks, but Master tells me to stand closer and not be feared of 'em coming and draw my hands under 'em and then I'll catch 'em right enough. Down come two—one on top of t'other—and I catched 'em and nearly goes over forrard on my nose and Master yell:

"Stick to 'em, Boy, I'll soon larn yer to load hot bricks," and so I did, not letting any more on my feet, learning like an old uncle of mine learnt a monkey he had to dance.

He put that monkey on a hot malt-kiln floor and played the hornpipe with his fiddle while it was dancing about. The monkey got so used to it whenever he see that fiddle he'd start dancing. Uncle, like all our family, had an eye to business and made his living with his dancing monkey.

Round Pubs he went with his Dickey and cart keeping the monkey covered up so as he didn't see the fiddle. When he found some good company in he'd go and play a dance tune or two, and then say, "Would you like to see Mike dance?" and they a-wondering who Mike was sezs "Yes."

Out goes Uncle and walks Mike in, puts him in the middle of the floor and takes up his fiddle and plays the hornpipe. Mike he start dancing like mad, not waiting to find out if the bricks was hot or cold, amusing the company who laughed till the tears runned down their cheeks. Then round goes Mike with his hat and I've known him collect more in a day than his master would if he'd worked for a week, and lots of drinks and nuts and biscuits for Mike thrown in.

Got on fine with catching the bricks, once I had got the way of it, and did not notice that the hot rough edges had worn away the skin of my fingers till I sees the blood oozing out, and Master say, "Gorn and git my old pair of gloves a-hanging in the shed." I was soon back with them but felt a bit awkard working in gloves. Was glad when evening come and I could git away from that job, catching seven pounds of hot bricks at a time coming down from above yer head, dust dropping in yer eyes, blood running from yer fingers, and hot blasts a-blowing in your face from the kiln.

Boys of to-day can think themselves blest they are looked after different. I got that which I worked for and precious little of it, but its not for us to choose. We has to come into the world when we gits the chance, doing our best for each other while we are here, so we may leave it without regret and go hence to where no man knows.

While I write this the wireless set is turned on near by, one of the most marvellous inventions for the welfare and civilization of mankind, and the announcer is speaking to the young generation at dictation speed. Had that happened to me when I was a boy who so badly wanted to learn, I think without doubt I would have been in a very different position to what I am. But no man can see round a corner into the future, and maybe human nature being as it is, if we had all had a different start we wouldn't have finished much other than we have.

The rainy days set in and the frosts begin to come which spoil the newly moulded bricks. It got towards the end of the brick-making season and instead of 2*s.* 6*d.* there come a week when all Master would give me was 1*s.* 8*d.*, because we had stood off half the week hanging about in the shelter waiting for the rain to clear. Begun to think I was getting near the finish of my job, and so it was and my Master tell me:

"Boy, shan't make no more bricks arter this week. Yew will come Monday, as we must clear up a bit."

So I come Monday and Tuesday and tidied up round about, and Master he tell me he can't find nothing more for me to do and I'd better find another job. I got ready to go but kept hanging about thinking I'd git my 1*s.* 8*d.* for my two days' work, but he tells me to be sliding off and be quick about it. I wont git no pay that night, he h'aint got it by him, he'll pay me arter a time.

I went off and kept thinking perhaps he'd think on it some day and give it me some time or 'nother, but he never did and a few year after I heard he was took ill and died and left no Will, so I lost my 1*s.* 8*d.* Not knowing which way he went, am doubtful if I shall meet him again.

He enjoyed himself while he was here
Went on the same from year to year
But where he's gone and how he fare
Nobody knows and nobody care.

But I still remember that 1*s.* 8*d.*, sixty year and more after, which show it's a bad thing to leave debts behind when your time come to put by your tools.

One Generation to Another

Folks allus say as they git old
That things look wusser every day;
They allus said so I consate,
Leastwise so I've heard my mother say.

When she was growed up a great big gal—
And went to sarvice at the Hall
She har'nt but one stuff gown to wear,
And not the littlest mite of shawl.

But now you can't tell whue is whue
Which is the Mussus—which the maid,
There ain't no tellin' with a gal,
When she's got her wages paid.

Will put 'em all upon her back
And look as grand as grand can be;
My poor old Mother would be stamm'd,
Her girl should ever look like she.

And t'aint the littlest bit o' use
To tell 'em anything at all;
They'll only laugh, or else begin
All manner o' hard names to call.

P'raps arter all it aint the truth
That one times wusser than another ;
P'raps I'm gettin' old myself,
And fare to talk like my old Mother.

I shan't do nowt by talkin' so—
I'd better try the good old plan,
Of spakin' sparing of most folks
And due' in all the good I can.

Whenever he see that fiddle he'd start dancing.

CHAPTER VI

My old man come home one night, come home one night come he
He see two boots stood in the door
He say what may that be?

Yew Fool, yew fool, what can't yew see
Them's milking churns what Mother sent to me.
Milking churns—what milking churns with spurs upon
I never can come home at night but what you start a' codding on.

My old man come home one night come home one night come he
He see a man lay in my bed, he say who may he be?

Yew fool, yew fool, what can't yew see
That's baby boy what Mother sent to me.

Baby boy? baby boy with beard upon?
I never can come home at night but what yew start a' codding on.

Harvest supper song.

ABOUT a week after heard my Father talking to Mother saying that his Master was taken very ill, so bad he didn't think the old man would git over it this time. A few days after sure enough he died and his Boot and Shoe business with him. True there was two in the family a son and a daughter.

The son was born tired, a complaint from which he never recovered; emigrated to America and what Uncle Sam did with him never was known to this day. So the daughter was left and could not carry on the trade, and there was an end to my Father's job. I felt I must find one somewhere, I was only eleven year old and had not made enough up to the present to put by for a rainy day, such as seemed to have come along.

It didn't matter much to me what it were and there was a Hay Trusser living in Ditchingham at the time, name of Bob Lane. He used to truss hay for the London Market or anywhere else that it was required. I come to hear he wanted a boy to turn hay bonds, so I goes along and gits the job at a shilling a week.

Next day was at work trussing hay at a nearby farm. My Master soon learnt me to turn bonds. I was left-handed at the time and naturally started turning the crank left-handed and got blown off that straight away.

"How the devil du yer think I'm gornter tie trusses oop with bonds all twisted left-handed? Now then, yer lump, keep yer left hand forrard and turn you the crank with yer right—pull towards yer, and keep stepping bakkards, and see yer turn quick—I'll see as how yer don't turn too much—I'll look out for that. Watch when I leaves off making and give two or three turns and twist it round the stake like this here, and larn to be quick about it. Yer ain't a-slippin' about at home—I'll make a man of yew, if I keeps yer for long enough."

And I thinks to myself no you wont—mopping up beer as yew du, but I keeps my thoughts to myself and arter a bit become an expert at turning hay bonds. Arter a few days he sezs to me:

"Boy, I wants yew to go along o 'me to Mendham and Weybread, as I've got a power o' stacks o' hay to truss there for Lenny o' London."

I goes along home and ask them if I can go with my Master and Father sezs "Yes, if I gits more money," and in the end its fixed as I gits two shilling a week.

Next Monday the horse was put into the shafts, the cart loaded with hay knife, crank, stakes, measure, stick, rake and fork, and off we go, me feeling a rare man going out to lodge and see the world, it not mattering to me that my pockets was empty, as I was always happy in them days and always hungry. Our pony had seen his best days covering not more than two miles an hour which give me plenty of time to look round, and when we gits through Bungay and Earsham, asks where we are now.

"In the cart, yew silly young ass, and where du yew want to be? Tarned over in the holl—shut yer mouth, boy, and stop yer prate, du yew du so I'll chuck yer out, takes all my time to keep the hoss in the middle of the road."

I thinks to myself this look like being a rough passage, but we kept jogging along and I keeps quiet and asks no more questions.

Arter a long time we comes to a house with a Dove painted on a board above the door and my Master sezs:

"Sit yew still and mind the hoss—I've got to go and see a man about a dawg."

I looks arter that hoss for an hour or more, not that it was much trouble, the poor thing was glad of a rest, but I couldn't think when Master was coming and wondered if the dawg had runned away, but it wasn't no such thing.

Presently out he come, staggering about, having found that there dawg at the bottom of several pint pots, and me having learnt something more. Off we go and gits safely to Mendham Lion, near where the hay was to be trussed, and he goes in to see about lodging, and the Landlady she say:

"All right, long as the boy sleep with yer," and that was soon agreed on.

I unloads the cart, puts the pony in the stable baits him and got all done, and come in and find him still unloading the earthenware and that he had emptied another quart. He sezs to the Landlady can she do something for the tooth, and she say she got plenty of bread and home-made cheese. My master ask for a couple of pennorth and one for the boy, which she brought and a drop of tea for me thrown in, so I has my first meal in a Public, being both hungry and dry. Soon packed what I got away and could ha' done with more, but my Master didn't think I had need to git fat—being round as a barrel himself thought he'd best keep me slim and nimble.

I sat quiet and listened to all the talk and after closing time Master say:

"Off wi' yer boots and let's git ready for kip," and upstairs he go. I followed close a'hind him feeling that strange and feared becos for the first time I was a-going to sleep wi' my Master. He tells me to undress and git inter bed one side which I did, dare not do otherwise. Scrambled in keeping well away from him and settled down amun the feathers all of a tremble. He follered and was soon asleep and snoring, but the smell and gases which come from him was so much I hardly knows if I'm in a bed or a brewery. There I laid and dasn't move and presently he starts dreaming and thrusts back with his elbow and catches me in the ribs. I starts agin all of a shake till he asks me what the hell is the matter with me a-duddering so? "Go to sleep and be quick about it." So I drops off and knows no more till morning.

Off we went next morning me taking my food for the day, a couple of slices of dry bread and half a pint of weak tea. My Master took no solid with him, his rations for the day was taken in a gallon bottle, he living on suction like a snipe and look well on it—near as broad as he was long. He only stood five feet two inches but could drive the hay knife down to the hilt without any trouble and a good trusser of hay he was for the London Market.

In them days a mort of hay went up to London for the carriage horses. We finished up at Mendham, and harness up and off to Weybread and puts up at the Golden Cross.

Lenney's agent had been down as we finished the stack and given my Master a couple of quid on account, so he was flush and sits by the kitchen fire and starts treating all comers. There was an old soldier started yarning and that tickles his fancy, and before long he was well oiled up, and more company come in and starts talking of parish events.

I sit in the corner and listen and before long hear something which come to mean a lot in my life. A man who lived near had just passed away into the unknown and took his secrets with him, and I remember well one man saying he had tried to discover the secret of perpetual motion and was an old fool for his pains, as he couldn't keep himself a-going let alone make a machine to do it. And another tells how he built a machine and got it to go, starting it off in his barn and if he hanter took his big hammer and knocked it to pieces or it would soon have bumped out the end of his barn. After that he never could put the pieces together agin and the secret was lost, and that just broke his heart in him and killed him.

They all had a great laugh at that and the subject was dropped, but not in my mind—a-sitting there and listening. Somehow I was all took up with the idea, thinking when I was bigger and could come by a bit more learning I would like to try and solve that problem. It seemed to draw me as it always have all my life since, spite of many a set back and many a bitter hour when all seemed no good. I have experimented on it for years—the fascinating problem of a perpetual motion machine—that is to say a machine that has the principal of its motion within itself. Whether or not I shall be like the old Farmer I cannot say. Perhaps I have wasted my time, but at anyrate it has added to my abilities and sometimes in my dreams I sees an engine running sweet as sweet with a long train over Brooklyn Bridge, New York, and knows that engine is carrying my secret. Whether I am as far off solving the problem as I ever was remains to be proved.

Off we goes next morning cutting up a four ton stack, Master in a hurry—as last night's doings had pulled a hole in the dough. Off come his coat and up go the ladder and he starts a'ripping and reaven the thatch off in a hustle, throwing down hay for making bonds. We turns ten pair of bonds and then he tells me to rake the ground up at the end of the stack and he starts cutting at the top end of the roof, me raking below.

His hay knife cutting through overhung the end of the stack and slipped from his grasp. I was down below and something made me step back as the knife flashed past my face, struck the spot where I stood a second before, and ran into the ground a foot and a half, standing upright quivering.

The hay knife weigh about twenty-four pounds and if I had not moved I'd have been split down from head to foot clean as a whistle.

Nearly drowned—cracked my head well nigh in two, and now near as two farthings to a halfpenny of being split in halves, seem to me I must be similar to the cat with nine lives. My Master was a bit shook up by that, near as frightened as I was, and almost come down with the knife and kept on saying, "I didn't mean to hurt you, boy."

After that he was more careful to keep the knife well down in its cut, and so we cut two tons before dark that day, and he measure up the stack and say we can finish the next night and git home Saturday, and pleased I was to hear we was getting home so soon.

At it all next day and finding Master was in a good mind I'd thought to ask him what the old ruin[1] was standing on the marshes, and he told me that was where the old monks lived. Never having heard of monks I asked what manner of people they were. He said,

"Same as others—two legs and a nose on their face, only they knew more. Ah, Bor, expect there be a lot o' canaries buried there."

"What are they?"

"Sovereigns, boy, Mr. Dimmock's man he was ploughing one day

[1]Mendham Priory.

and ploughed out a gold coin, and took it up to Mr. Dimmock. Guess there's a lot of money hid up there about. Wern't no banks there—that time o' day."

No more was said and we keeps on working till dark. Up early next morning—finish the stack about twelve and off back to the Golden Cross. When I had looked to the pony I come in and Master tells me the Landlady want to see me and she ask if I will clean the boots for her, and when I sezs "That I will," she say—"All right, start along then. I'll see how you gits along and then find you up summat for supper."

I pleased her well shining up the boots and she set me down at the spread table and a good feed I had, the first since I left home and I was hungry. I thanked her for her kindness and she give me some gays[1] to look at which pleased and contented me more than sitting in the Inn kitchen listening.

Next morning I got the old pony harnessed up and brought him round. When Master come out I gits in the back of the cart where I sits just able to see over the back, and soon we was jogging along towards home. About half a mile on our journey I heard a lot of dogs barking and as we got nearer see there were scores coming along the road; never had I seen so many dogs and was wholly stammed at the sight of 'em. Master tells me they was Squire Chaston's hounds which he keep for hunting and when I ask what they hunt he flies out at me and sezs—

"Bad boys, and if yer not quiet and don't give over with yer questions I'll drive in among 'em and chuck yer out of the cart—an they won't leave much of yew—no more than that ole wimmon in the Bible what Parson read about," which made such an impression on my mind I never forgot Squire Chaston, of Withersdale and his Dogs.

Years after I went to a Steeple Chase meeting at Bungay and the Squire was one of the riders in the Water Jump race. All was going well until his horse come to the Water Jump, and there I witnessed a scene what might seem impossible.

[1]Coloured picture papers.

His horse took the jump over the fence and the water and when he alighted on the edge of the opposite bank slipped—could not recover—made a half turn over and threw the Squire forward through space, arms outstretched and legs a'spread, alighting downward. The horse then turned completely over and for a second or two balanced itself on its back across the back of the rider. We

thought to see him killed but the ground was marshy where he lit and give way to the pressure, leaving an imprint into which he had been forced without much hurt. Two hours after he was walking down Earsham Street perky as a sparrer.

We got along but slowly with stops at all the Pubs along the way, and tired I got at looking at the outside of them. Mendham Lion, the Homersfield Dove and then the Buck, and the old horse never good for more than two mile an hour at his best and my Master slapping the reins on his back with a "Coom oop, Abigail!. Goo yer on, Abigail!" which made no manner of difference to Abigail until

We thought to see him killed.

he smell home when he stirred his stumps a trifle, and in the end we lands at the Three Tuns in Bungay. Now thinks I, I'll be getting my money and off home, but all my Master sezs is—

"Boy, I be going to wet my whistle, make yew haste home across the Common. I'll pay yer next week."

So home I goes and Father he sezs—"So yew got home agin—glad to see yer, boy. Have yer Master paid yer this time?" And when I tells him he h'aint and I left him in the Pub, he mutters he'll soon see arter that and off he goes. 'Pears Father finds him enjoying of his beer and he tells Father he'll be paying me next week.

"Next week be damned," says Father. "You'll pay me what you owes the lad before you leaves this house or I'll pay you with these bunches of fiverses and then wring yer head off yer shoulders. Four bob is what I wants and my boy don't go trussing hay with you no more."

Not many a man in them days cared to fall out with Happy Jack and my Master pays up and tries to look pleasant. Home come Father with the money and tells me I shan't go along with an old beer barrel like him any more. I can stop at home and he'll find up another job for me.

Well I runs round at home for a time and like most boys its not long before I gets into mischief with a pal of mine—a cousin—or anyway so he was called, but he was one of them what get left on the doorstep. Many a time I have heard my Father tell that story, of Bill and Susan who were married many a year and would have been rare pleased if a brack boy or a little gal had come along. One winter's night they was sitting over the fire talking of their private affairs, Susan putting herself about saying—

"Here's us tew a'sitting here—h'aint got chick nor child to keep us company."

"Well, that ain't my fault," says Bill.

"Nor yet mine," says Susan.

"Dang it!" says Bill, " must be somebody's fault." Then he smiles to himself and tells her 'praps the Lord may send a child when he sees proper, and they sits there knees and noses in the fire, Susan snivelling and the wind a'howling, both about as cheerful as a parson's black job, when a knock come on the door.

Outside a woman stood back in the darkness and a cradle was lying on the step, and she says—hurried like—

"Could your good wife mind the baby an hour while I go into Bungay and get my shopping done, seeing it's a wild night to have the child out."

Susan thinking it was a neighbour said—"Yes, and welcome," and only when they gets the door shut agin the wind and she take a look at the baby she don't think she know it, and ask who the woman was?

Bill he say he never looked, but its a funny thing they were talking of babies and one come through the door like a mouse out of a hole. Susan lifts him out and plays with him and calls him a rare boy and she wish it were hers. Time went on and they keeps a'listening for the woman and nobody come and they waited up till mid-night and nobody come, and they think its that wet and wild she wont come till morning, so they feeds the baby and takes it up to bed.

So it went on week after week and the woman never come back no more, and Susan and Bill got that set on the child they reckoned they'd rear him as their own, but it bother Susan he have no name.

"Doesn't seem as if he had a name," says she.

"Quite right, no more he have, Sue," says Bill.

"I 'ont part wi' him for any money now," says Sue, "but we must name him, shall we call him Bill, arter you?"

"Couldn't be better," says Bill.

"Funny thing," says Susan. "The boy seem to grow more like yew every day that pass."

"Ah!" sezs Bill, "And so he will—grow more like me than he will like you."

"And why's that?" says Sue.

"'Cos I takes him on my knee, look at him with a blink in my eye and make him laugh at a good joke—that's the reason why, Susan."

And with that she had to be content. So the boy grew up the very image and reproduction of the Good Samaritan who took him in off the door step, because said Bill, he would blink an eye at him and make him laugh at his joke. Anyways, young Bill and me was firm friends, up to all sorts of tricks as boys will be as long as man inhabit this earth, if they are healthy.

There was living in the Parish a middle-aged man who was nicknamed Long Pod, who could run like a hare and fight like a tiger making us look slippy if we went in his medder after apples or birds' nests or such like. He lived in a bedroom house with one living-room with a lean-to at the back for a pantry and the necessary Parliamentary building in the garden. Young Bill he sezs to me,

"What do yew say Garge, let's have a game with old Long Pod, git up on his tiles, put a sack over his chimney and smoke him out. Just had a look trew his winder and see'd him all hunched up by the fire—'spect he's asleep."

This please me all right and Bill tells me to stand below while he shins up the tiles and if the Bobby come along to start walking away. He'll know what that means and he'll lay flat till he's gone. He was on the lean-to in a crack and I gits a scrap of rope and ties the door bobbin so it wont open and stretch another bit across the gate. Bill goes along the tiles like a cat and pops the sack over the chimney sending the smoke down into the room in clouds. Long Pod soon wakes up and starts spitting and sneezing and makes for the door. Finds it tied, but he shakes and pushes and the cord being rotten gives, and out he comes and sees the sack on his chimney afore we had time to git clear away.

He rushes round to the back cussing and swearing and sees Billy, he lets fly at him but Billy ducked and tripped Long Pod up, and down he go on top of the boy who struggled out between his legs, run for it round the house and bolted through the gate. Up goes Long Pod and after him straight for the gate and over he go sprawling on the road calling for the Police. By the time the hounds were out the hares had disappeared into the misty dark and were seen no more.

It's hard to say what may happen in one's life time. That particular Bedroom House fell into my hands in latter years, and I have since taken it down but could not help thinking as I did so of poor old Long Pod—gone many a year to his long home—and the tricks we played on him, young varmints that we were.

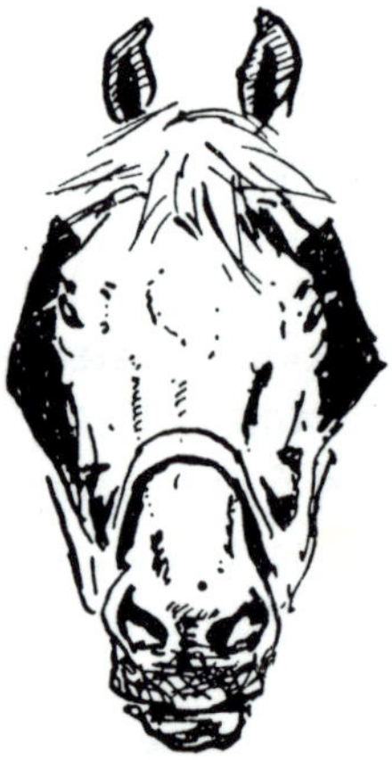

Gossip Joan

Good morrow, Gossip Joan,
    Where have you been a' walking?
I have for you at home
    A budget full of talking.
        Good Gossip Joan.

My sparrow's flown away,
    And will no more come to me;
I've broke a glass to-day,
    The price will quite undo me,
        Good Gossip Joan.

I've lost a Harry-groat,
    T'was left me by my granny,
I cannot find it out,
    I've searched in every cranny,
        Good Gossip Joan.

I've lost my wedding ring,
    That was made of silver gilded,
I had drink would please a king
    But that my cat had spilled it.
        Good Gossip Joan.

My pocket is cut off,
    That was full of sugar candy,
I cannot stop my cough
    Without a gill of brandy.
        Good Gossip Joan.

Let's to the ale house go
    And wash down all our sorrow,
My griefs you there shall know
    And we'll meet again to-morrow.
        Good Gossip Joan.

His great voice a'roaring at 'em to buy.

CHAPTER VII

Two birds flying high
Little boat drawing nigh.
Chinese temple there it stands
Shows the work of many hands,
Two men entering at the door
Some say three and some say four,
Apple tree with apples on . . .
Crooked rails, so ends my song.
Song of the Willow Pattern Plate (Traditional).

As was natural to a boy living on the bank of a river I had a great desire to have a boat. I had no money (as no more jobs had come along) nor could I borrow any, so I could not think where to get the necessary wood to make one, but necessity is ever the mother of invention, and so it was with me at that time.

I had my eye on some old rails that had once formed a fence across the meadow near our house. They were about an inch and a half thick and four inches wide, which I thought would surely make a box iron shaped boat.

The question was how was I to make it without my Father's knowledge, as the rails were his and I'd never get them for the asking. Had a brain wave and said to my young brother we'd clear a space in the middle of the faggot stack and build our boat in the centre, Father seldom went round there anyways. Collected the rails on the quiet but then what about tools?

I had no rule and only one small plane my grandfather give me, and we must have hammer, a saw and hook or bill as they are called. I was forced to borrow Father's, being very careful to put them back each day before he came home.

We could not make anything but a box-like boat of the wood we had, square at one end and pointed at the other, and had a terrible job to find up nails to hold the rails in place, but we got some out of old boxes, and somehow we got that there peculiar craft together.

Then come the question of paint, where was that to come from? No money—no paint—so we decided to tar it. Father had some in a pail and we must pinch some of that. So we did, and after that put some small stones in the pail so the tar rose to the height it was afore we took out any, so he shouldn't notice a good bit of it had gone.

Our liner was getting near completion, but we never give a thought to our bad workmanship and that the bottom of our boat was more like a sieve than anything else, full of holes. Realised at last that these must be blocked up so got some pieces of sacking and string and did some caulking for the first time in our lives. After a day or two when she was dry we got the faggots away one side and pulled and tugged until we got her launched on the flooded marsh alongside the yard, for it was a terrible wet summer that year.

She only leaked a little and we stuffed up the cracks, making her sound as a bell (as we thought) and pushed off on our maiden voyage with two short poles to punt with. We found before long we was Dry Land sailors and quickly come to grief.

The caulking did not last long—the water started a'coming in and as we were going over a dyke one place bursted. In rushed the water, fritting us so much we made matters worse trying to get to shore too quick and she started to fill and sink, lurched all on one side. I jumped, cleared the dyke and lit on the marsh where I could stand with my head just above water. My brother got left on the boat which was going down bows first, and in not much more than a second he was down in the middle of the dyke with his head well below but still hanging on to the pole which was sticking out of the water.

I gets hold of that and pulls for all I'm worth, and out comes Billy like a winkle on a pin, and we struggles along to higher ground like a couple of half-drowned rats, seeing our lovely boat come up again and whirl away down stream at a great rate.

Home we goes and Mother catches us and off we were sent to bed while our clothes dried by the fire, and when Father come in and see them he needs must know what we've been up to. He soon finds we have been pinching his rails and tar and was all for giving us a hiding; but Mother git round him telling him he was once a boy, and she be ready to bet none too good a one, and he laughs in his quiet way and lets us off with a caution.

The boat got stuck in the posts of the bridge and we cleaned her out and towed her home. Father comes and has a look at her and we asks him if he don't think we have made a good job of building her?

"Yes," says he, " And dang me if I don't make a better one. If you interfere with my things again I'll make it hot for the pair of yer." And with that he went and got his axe and smashed it to splinters for firewood, nearly breaking our hearts, but we dursen't say a word. He made us stand all the pieces up against the faggots to dry and so we did—large and small—more small than large, so that it would make good kindling for Mother's fire.

A couple of days later he sent us out in the evening to fetch it in and make a blaze which we did without a murmur, the flames all a-dazzle with the tears in our eyes as we saw our prized liner and all our labour passing away in smoke, as come to think on it much of a man's labour does during his life's work. Still, often it leave a good thing behind as well as the soot in the chimney, and that's experience. That was my first boat and I'm still a'building them and each one teaches me summat.

As I said, 1877 was a terrible wet summer, and I remember well Squire Jenny saying to my Father that it had rained solid for six and thirty hours, and we should have the worst flood ever known in the Waveney Valley, and so it proved.

It was the third week in June and all the vegetation at its heaviest so it held the water up for days. I remember it well for it was a Saturday night, and Father was off to get his weekly shave and asked me if I'd like to go along with him, which I did, jumping for joy at the outing.

It happened there was a man named Keeble, a Cheap Jack, holding a stall in the town—all sorts of household things and pots and pans—and I had a lot of fun listening to him juggling the crowd into buying his wares, mostly what's known now as "seconds" or flawed goods. Big red earthenware milk bowls, butter crocks, and willow pattern dishes like we had on the dresser at home with trees, and little men, and birds flying.

There wasn't much light in the market them days and Jack had set up a flare and I thought that and the crowd jostling round chipping him on his wares and his great voice a'roaring at 'em to buy, rare fun. Presently Father bought a little clock and tell me to carry it careful and not let it down and we set off home, the clock gripped hard in both my hands. I can hear it ticking now as if it were yesterday. It's still up in the bedroom and it still go.

Barely had we got into the house about half after ten than it begun to lighten—flash after flash—and thunder like one continuous roar of big guns as though it would rip up the earth. My brother and I were that scared we scurried off to bed, the lightning reflecting all the room.

The old house shook so terrible we thought it must ha' toppled over time and again, till we begun to think that the Last Day we heard about at school had come on us, and huddled ourselves in the bed wishing we was in the coal hole. One look I had and see the whole sky lit from end to end with blue fire, and the spire of Bungay Church near two miles away sticking up against the glare, and that was enough for me. After a bit down a mighty rain come falling as it were thrown out of buckets for hours on end.

When we come down on Sunday morning the water was rising rapidly, the marshes round the house looking like a great lake and the water creeping to the door of the house. Father sent us to drive the cow to the High Meadow which we did, though getting her through the flood water was a job. The Ferret locker was tied on top of a box in the cow shed and roped down and everything else put up as high as we could manage before we went to bed that night. Father calls out—

"Go to sleep, we'll chance the ducks," a saying of his when anything out of the ordinary was like to happen.

Next morning Father comes down and finds the water all around the house and opening the stair door calls up to Mother—"There's a rare mess here, we're flooded indoors," and stepping down finds he's up to his knees and our few sticks of furniture and carpets afloat—the hearth rug had sunk, being but an old sack that wasn't of much account, and riz later. We was soon downstairs in nature's clothes—it being summer time—and splashed round like a couple of Dive-and-Dops[1] enjoying the fun.

Mother calls out from above to have a look at her milk pans and see if they be all right, and so they were, not one overturned, floating on top of the water with the rims an inch above it. Father says, "Boys, gorn get yew a hay rake," and when I brings it he steadily drew pan after pan to the door of the dairy which was sunk about two foot below the floor of the house, done by the grandmother with her own hands to keep her dairy cool in summer. We got all the pans ashore and having some dry wood soon had a roaring fire in the grate six inches above the flood water and old black Betsy a'singing on top, and so we carried breakfast on to the upper deck, and a rare joke we thought it.

The water had got up to the pigstye which stood farther back on higher ground, and there was Susan the old sow to see to, who had a litter of young pigs, about a month old. The water was nigh up to their backs and they was waddlin' round shricken out their hardest. Father tells us boys to git 'em up to the medder with the cow till the water fall, but the puzzle was how to do it. Tried to carry the young 'uns one by one but the old sow near went mad, and would have had the seat out of our trousers in no time.

Then I had a brain wave, thought to myself if I got a tub we had for scalding fat pigs I could put them all in and draw it to a place

[1] Little Grebe.

of safety. Billy and I brings the tub along and th' old sow, thinking it was something to eat a'coming, draws up with all the little 'uns, and I grabbed 'em one after t'other and gits 'em all in, expecting every moment to be devoured. Flung a sack over 'em, and away I go towing it towards high ground, the pigs milling round inside so as to nearly wreck the ship, and old sow followin', after kicking up a rumpus yew could hear half a mile away.

The job over, back we goes to help Father. The water had come down so quick there had been no time to git all the stock off the Common, and six or seven horses were driven up onto the last bit of high ground sticking up above the flood. They had to go out to them in boats, halter one of the old mares and lead her through behind one of the boats and git the other young 'uns to foller. It was a hard job as they would go for a bit and then flounder into deep water where there was a dyke or holl, lose their legs and break back for high land, in spite of the men behind splashin' and hollerin' at 'em.

It was a cold, wet, dirty job, but if bad words could ha' warmed 'em they'd have been hot as fire. Kid as I was I'd heard some language in my time—little pitchers they say have their ears pricked, but never nothin' to beat what come over the water to me that morning. Some of it I can lay my tongue to this day, if occasion arise—they was pearls of speech and I h'aint never forgot 'em.

The good old ship never budged an inch and as luck would have it the water had got to the highest so started to fall. Mother had a merry job washing the house out, the river having left a mort of mud and a filthy stink, nigh as bad as a stinking eel. We having neither taste nor smell so to speak at that time of life didn't worry at that, and went out and took the dog ratting, there being many druv out by the water.

We found lots to see. The water from the higher land in its rush towards the river had made a landslide down part of the Bath Hills, and hundreds of tons of soil came down carrying great oaks with it ; as much moved in half an hour as fifty men could ha' done in a month.

A piece of them trees I have now for they were trimmed up and one extra large butt left, too tough for splitting. About five years later I was going up the river in a boat one sunny afternoon, hanging over the side with my line and hook baited with bunched worms, looking for eels laying on the bottom, when I sees what look like the round end of a tub sticking in the mud, and poking it found it was solid. A few days later I went up with Father's stack iron[1] which was pointed one end and had a good handle the other. I tied a rope on, drove the pointed end into the block, raised it and towed it home thinking it might be useful some day, as it was, for an anvil block, and am still using it at this present time.

Father come home that night full of troubles, the Snob's seat in his workshop and all the tools and bits floated up and laid helter-skelter all over the place so they'd take a week to get right-sided again. The beer barrels at the Pub over the way had been floating, and some it seemed had lost their contents. The coach-builder's yard about forty yard from the workshop had lost some of the carriages and carts which had floated away down stream with neither horses nor drivers, let alone passengers.

The farmer who had cut his grass on the high marsh and was cocked up ready to cart on the Friday had had it done for him by the flood, which made a clean sweep of every spear—just leaving a little hanging on the brickwork of the bridge lower down as a remembrance.

The silk factory was flooded out and much was spoilt. My Mother worked there as a girl for they employed about four hundred women, with a few men as overseers. They started work at six in the morning and worked till half after five at night, with an hour and a half for breakfast and dinner and were paid five to seven shilling a week according to the class of work. They were a rough lot, them girls and women, and used to stand along the dam come evening time and make a rare do with the passers by, so that some were feared to go along that way. We used to pelt 'em with snow balls

[1]A pointed iron about two feet long used in thatching to stick into the stack to secure bands to.

in winter when they come out on the road after work, and when we had got a few shots in they'd charge us from all directions and make a ring, pick us up by the slacks of our trousers and roll us in the snow, which was all took in good part.

In spite of their rough ways at the end of the week one of the men would go to the Bank in Bungay with a wheel-barrow, git all the money wanted for the wages and drive it home again along the road, and never had no unwanted help, which might not be the same these days.

Before I was very big the silk trade failed, the factory shut up, the machinery sold, and the building, after a time, was sold to the Maltsters. All the great windows were blocked in and to this day the silk factory is a home for John Barley Corn.

The year went on till November, my birthday month, for I was now in my thirteenth year. I had put in some more time at school, all my parents could afford, and had learnt the alphabet, the Lord's Prayer, and how to make a few figures. Also that the earth I was living on was resting on a foundation and well cemented down. Such things I have found quite contrary to what I was taught when a boy, when I was moving in darkness as it were. No one gave me advice or enlightened my path, but young as I was I had begun to realise I was only one atom among the millions and must think for myself.

I had also learnt to knit and was now able to make for myself a pair of mittens or socks, I don't say they were up to much, but they answered my purpose. I had often wondered how wool was made into yarn and when I went hay-trussing I found out, which show how one thing will open your eyes to another all through life—except for them who goes blind all their days, yet thinks they sees as much as the next man. May not have learnt much at school, but all my life have been out to pick up what knowledge I could and add a little more to my stock.

My clock struck twelve on a dull November day, the twenty-sixth of the month eighteen hundred and seventy-seven. I had another unknown journey to make, not knowing what I should learn, see and hear, but hoping I should be present when the clock struck thirteen and not gone down to the mole country. I was always hungry and decided I must git a job and be quit of my stomach gnawing at me, and thought I would try up at the Squire's, as the leaves lay strewn all over the walks and grass platts and would have to be cleared up by somebody. So I went to see the head-gardener. Luckily for me he was puffing and blowing while sweeping the same up when I come on the scene, and I sezs to him—

"Yew seem tew be in a muddle. Got tew much work a'head, hev yew. Can yew du wi' some help, Master? I want a job."

"Dare say yew du, Bor, but don't think yew are man enough for this job."

"What, du yew think as I can't sweep up a few leaves, that's ondly an old wimmen's job," sezs I.

"If yew don't keep clear of this broom end yew'll verry sune find out if I be an old woman or not—but take hold on this ere broom Shadow-works, and let's see what yew kin du." He didn't know that, small and thin as I was, I had been used to swing a scythe, and I took hold of the broom and swung it workmanlike fashion, clearing the grass of leaves until he looked at me fair stammed and mutters, "I didn't think yew had it in yew."

"No, Master," sezs I, "Yew mustn't allus go by appearances."

"So I find, boy, that 'ont du to du so at all times, but I don't want no lip from yew. Git here at seven o'clock to-morrer mornin' and I think I kin find yew a couple o' months work, if yew can do a bit of diggin' and will come for half a dollar the week. Can't pay yew more —take it or leave it—which yer like."

I thought half a loaf was a deal better than none at all, so I takes it on and sticks to it like a tripper. Didn't see much of the Squire, Captain Jenny, but he would give me a cheery good-morning, when passing. He was a perfect gentleman, one of the best but a prey to imposters, being at that time Justice of the Peace. More often than not he would walk to the Court House at Bungay by a narrow lane by our house, the shortest way. Some of the leg-weary and born tired, a complaint they never tried to cure, took advantage of this habit of the Squire's.

Have seen 'em many a time when I was a boy standing on the Common where they could see the Squire start from the Lodge on his way to the Court, and off they would go in haste up the narrow lane so they would be well in front and careful not to look back, limping and stopping every few yards to ease the pains. When he was within a

few paces they would drop down calling out in agony. He was certain sure to stop and ask what was wrong, and they spun a good yarn about the wars and soldiering, and how old wounds got in the Crimea played a man up something cruel.

The Squire was that kind-hearted he allus took pity on 'em and p'raps would give the old bounders two or three shilling at a time. They recovered from their infirmities fast enough, as soon as Squire dropped from sight. His was the kind of medicine they wanted and would straighten up and be off down the lane and across the Common slippy as you please and safe into the town by the other way, chuckling to themselves at their easy money. But the Squire knew how many beans made five, and though he give them a few shillings for their artfulness—it amusing him to see them hopping along, he was well aware it was a trick, as some found out to their cost.

Man is apt to think it is easy work deceiving of their fellow men, but oft times him as they are hoodwinking says naught but thinks the more.

I got used to my new Master and found he worn't a bad old sort, if yew done what he wanted and didn't contradict him, as he wouldn't

put up with that, not from anybody. We got on well together an' often talked about different subjects. Came to the conclusion he knew more than a cage of monkeys and it were best for me tew keep quiet and look after my work, and so I did, and held my job till the coming spring, and then was once more unemployed.

A Farmer near by had just drilled a twenty acre field with barley and no sooner was it in than the rooks come down like a cloud of blown leaves and helped themselves, so I off to the Farmer and offers to keep them thieving birds off for three bob a week.

To this he agreed and said I could take all the rabbits I could catch on the farm into the bargain, as he reckoned each rabbit cost him a bob to keep afore the year was gone. This pleased me all right but I tells him I h'aint got no traps, so he sezs he will find me a purse net or two, and let me have the use of the ferret which aint no good to him, as he hadn't got a gun.

Up we goes into the loft and out hops a couple of rats the size of rabbits and old Skinner starts cussin' and sezs—

"He'll lay a crown they been and spoilt half his things, the varmints."

Sure enough when we gets the net bag off the shelf it don't need no untying—the rats had eaten the bottom out and there warn't a whole mesh left in one of 'em. Old Skinner had a bit to say about that.

"Bust 'em, there aint er good net left, the bounders. Yew'd better take some 'er these along o' yew and see if yew can mend sum on 'em. I got er ball er string, yew kin have—then see how they knots are tied, happen yew kin make a new 'un or two fur yer self arter a time."

Thought to myself, here's a rare chance, took 'em home and patiently undid knot after knot and found out how they was tied. As usual the wrong way come first but not being in much of a hurry took my time.

Tried this way then that, then at last tied one the right way, kept on and made one after another but they di'nt come all the same size. Thought this 'ont du, must git 'em all alike.

Got a piece of wood to size then made my loops on that. Hung my starting end on a hook where I was out of the way of folks, and in a little time had learnt myself to make either diamond or square mesh, and manufactured half a dozen nets which I valued more than some folks would a fortune.

Away I goes next morning with the nets and the Farmer's ferret in a bag, the nets swung over my shoulder on a stick and me on top of the world, being at the time of life when I was full of know. Old Skinner storms after me, hollering at the top of his voice:

"Boy! Don't yew ferret ondly in the sand pit." And when I tends not to hear he hollers agin harder than ever:

"Boy! What are yew deaf in one lug and 'ont hear wur t'other? Mind what I'm telling yew and keep in the Sand Pit."

I holds up my hand to let him know I hears and keeps along, thinking by the old 'un's manner there was suffin' about the Sand Pit more than I knew of.

There was a bean stack standing near and a deep ditch with water in not far away, but the Sand Pit was a mystery to me as yet. A few minutes more and I was hiking round it—couldn't see the track of no rabbits, but something had been messing about leaving hundreds of small footprints which, I thinks to myself, might be the sand-martins which nested up the top of the bank. I blocked some of the holes, netted others, and popped the ferret in the mouth of a likely burrow. A minute or two later out come a couple of rats—one on top of t'other. Thinks I to myself what do this mean—no circus here, but found out afterwards the poor chap having a ride was blind. The good Samaritan seeing me bucked up, turned completely over—threw his blind pal—and did a bolt. A moment or two arter rats were running all ways, must have been hundreds of them—look as though the Old Man's ferret was going west.

I had struck a colony and was slashing right and left with my stick, some I hit but more I missed, not half liking the job, as I had never seen such a rowdy-dowdy crew in all my days, when stepping back too sudden down I goes heels over head into the bottom of the pit, turning a complete somersault. By the time I had recovered from the bump the rats were gone, the whole multitude vanishing into fields and hedgerows except the dead 'uns and the poor old blind rat which was still probing about.

Thinks I, yew shall have another chance, and I picks him up by the tail and drops him by the bean stack, where although deprived of one of the greatest blessings of life—the gift of sight—he could with his sense of smell prog for himself, and live in peace and quiet until Threshing Day when would come the Judgment for him and many another.

Set to work to collect my nets and found some were dragged off their stakes from the weight of rats which had bitten clean through to clear themselves. Others had gone completely, rats and all, so I was now like a ship in distress having lost all my rigging, wasted my hard work and my day, and it would seem lost the Farmer's ferret into the bargain! If he were dead and lying in the bowels of the earth I might as well give up the ghost also, I dursen't go back to old Skinner without him. He might only be full fed with juicy rat and have fell asleep, if so the only hope was to wake him.

I puts my head into the hole and bawled and hollered and rattled a stick as far as I could reach; having no rabbit to peg[1] 'twasn't any good thinking of that. After a few minutes was thankful to see the cat drawing towards me covered with blood and piping full of summat—young rat most likely. When he sees me he makes a bolt back down the burrer, but I gets him by the rudder and hauls him out, whereupon he uses his natural means of self-defence and sends out a stink that would ha' killed the devil. I pops him into the hay bag and goes and scares my birds until day end, having had enough of rabbit catching to last me a bit.

Old Skinner laugh till he near bust himself when I tells him what have happened and tells me that won't do me no harm—learn me how to go about it another time—and I thinks I wish I were a sharp one like old Skinner and knew all he did, then I could live by my wits and leave others to do the work, for I guessed he knew all about them rats, and was just playing it off on me.

[1] A rabbit split open and pegged down to see if the ferret comes out to feed.

The Lincolnshire Poacher

When I was bound apprentice in famous Lincolnshire,
Full well I served my master for more than seven years,
Till I took up to poaching as you shall quickly hear.
Oh, 'tis my delight on a shiny night in the season of the year.

As me and my companions were setting of a snare,
'Twas then we spied the gamekeeper, for him we did not care,
For we can wrestle and fight, my boys, and jump o'er anywhere.
Oh, 'tis my delight on a shiny night in the season of the year.

As me and my companions were setting four or five,
And taking on 'em up again, we caught a hare alive,
We took the hare alive, my boys, and through the woods did steer.
Oh, 'tis my delight on a shiny night in the season of the year.

I threw him on my shoulder, and then we trudged home,
We took him to a neighbor's house and sold him for a crown.
We sold him for a crown, my boys, but I did not tell you where.
Oh, 'tis my delight on a shiny night in the season of the year.

Success to every gentleman that lives in Lincolnshire,
Success to every poacher that wants to sell a hare,
Bad luck to every gamekeeper that will not sell his deer.
Oh, 'tis my delight on a shiny night in the season of the year.

CHAPTER VIII

John Barley Corn was a hero bold
Of noble enterprise,
For if you do but taste his blood
'Twill make your courage rise;
'Twill make a man forget his woe
'Twill heighten all his joy.
Burns

WHEN I was a boy Shoemaking was a going concern. Snobbing it was called at that time of day. As there was no machinery then for that kind of work very little made the Snobs think themselves of great importance. If any one wanted a new pair of boots or shoes made, or a pair mended, the only time to give the order was when they were down and at it, on their Shummukers seats. When on it they would work from morning till night to get a job done, but once any of them had made up his mind to do only so many jobs at a setting, they wouldn't do another stroke for any one —not even the King, but would rise from their waxy seats, reckon up how much money the jobs come to, lump 'em down on the Boss's bench (Snobs was all piece work) saying—that lot's so much,—take their money and be off. They used to say any one could tell a well-britched Snob from his elastic step and the way he could allus smell beer ahead!

Happen that I was the son of "Happy Jack," one of these famous Snobs, and early on in life was told not to speak about anything I see, and knew if I did I should near get my neck broke, so kept a bridle on my tongue. The Seven come to know they could trust me, and so I became their scapegoat.

Happy Jack was apprenticed to his waxy and leathery trade at one Matthew Corneys who carried on a boot and shoemaker's business on Bridge Street, Bungay. When he had served his time as a 'prentice and become an expert Snob he was made a member of the South East Norfolk Snob's Club who used to hold their meetings in an old brick stable.

They was known as Happy Jack, Calico Jack, Waxy Jack, Nosey Jack, Raggety Jack, Skinny Jack, and the unfortunate Burnt Ass. This last owing to the fact that one day during a drunken spree in the Public kitchen, when the snow was falling fast and a big fire

burning in the grate, he gets up off his seat to go outside, but instead of going forward he go backward like a moke and sit on the fire. There was such a roar of laughter from the other Snobs they made no move to get him off, and he sat long enough to burn the seat out of his trousers and some of his skin off as well, so was known as the Burnt Ass for the rest of his days.

These Seven Snobs worked, played, drank, fought, and poached together, all of which they was good at. What they did not know was not worth knowing, and all day while they were sitting on their waxy seats they would be planning for some mischief, but were generally smart enough to keep out of trouble.

On one certain moonlight night just after the shooting season had begun, four of the seven thinks they'll have a night out and git an unwary pheasant or two. They was talking quiet like and I was standing by when one of them sezs:

"Boy—would yew like tew go with us?"

"Yes, that I should, Bor."

"Well, so yew can. See yew du everything we tells yer and keep yer mug shut till yer told to split it."

Away they goes I follering close to their heels like a dog, till they tell me that they wants to put me on pimp, and when I asks what that is they say they will knock that inter me as we go along. After a short time we come to a big wood, and the chief of our gang tell me to stay there while they are gone to have a look inside, and not to go off the road.

"And if the Bobby come along and want ter know what yew are a-doin' of at this time o' night on the road start yew a-cryin' and tell 'im yew 'er lorst yer self."

Silent as cats they crawled through the fence after their prey and I was left alone, walking a few yards each way up and down the road. It was not long afore I hears the sound of steps coming towards me. It was a great fat Bobby on duty and as soon as he sees me he hastens his steps and seeing what was going to happen I down trousers. He pounces on me and sezs:

"Hullo, and what do this mean? That game wont du for me, now then, up with them trousers. How is it yew come to be here this time o' night?"

I keeps fumbling for this and that while the great old fule was a-standing over me, snivelling and saying, "I've lost me self, Sir."

"Don't know, Boy," says he. "Seems to me to be suffin' funny about this 'ere job, doubt but yer an artful young dorg," and the next moment one of his heavy boots come swack up agin the seat of my trousers. I catched the back of his heel with my hand, hanging on till he lost his balance, and swop he go on to the road nigh on busting hisself. I did not stop to see what happen next but bolted off back to our shanty, feeling sure he would not outstrip me—too fat for that.

It was a grand night with a light breeze a-blowing towards the wood. There weren't nothing wrong with the Snobs' ears and they hears the Cop talking and me a-clattering down the road, and there they was with the pockets of their frock coats bulging with pheasants. They decided to take a short cut across the fields, one saying:

"Du yew take my bards while I goes in front, and keep yew close to the fence and a nice distance behind. If I comes across any one I'll shew fight and yew'll know what's a' clock."

Off they goes, as artful as foxes and soon manages to git back to their shanty with a good haul and never a sign of Cop nor keepers. They see me and one of them held up his hand and scowled at me to keep quiet while they unloaded their pockets, me a-looking on. They moved an old chest standing in a corner, took up some bricks from the floor, scrabbed away the soil lifting a lid set in a wood frame that covered a hole big enough for one of the Snobs to hide in. In went the haul of pheasants and some more odd things that I did not understand at the time, but found out later.

They were old tins that had been used to keep thin sticks of rock in, which were sold at four a penny when I was a boy, about twelve inches long and two inches across the top. They made some small holes all round about an inch from the bottom, fastened the tin to a two foot stick, then socketed three or four more. The lot could then be carried with the ends resting in the coat pocket and when the coat was buttoned up no outsider would be the wiser.

When the Snobs had a mind to have a ramble at night during the shooting season this peculiar contrivance went with them, as they knew very well if they carried a gun and fired that off they would not get very far. Just before they started they used to put some rags in the bottom of the tin and sprinkle some sulphur on top.

Generally Calico Jack took the tin and stowed it away with some sulphur matches, the sort that had to be held at arm's length or you'd be suffocated, but they'd give a light in a second. My grandmother used to think they was the most wonderful things after she had been striking her flints for hours to get a spark into her tinder box, and I have often heard her say the man who invented the first match—something that would light by just rubbing it—had a good head on him, and, if she knew him, she'd give him a good hug and a kiss. She would have too, being one of them spit-fire old ladies good enough for anything in her day.

Was now getting on with my education and beginning to see things as they were and not as they appeared. Knew how Calico Jack and his company got their haul so quickly.

When there was a lot of birds sitting on the low branches all they had to do was light up the sulphur under an old coat and when it got going hold it under the pheasant. The silly bird sitting with outstretched neck to see what was doing down below, was soon knocked out and down he come, his neck was wrung and he was bagged in a hurry, for it was not the custom of the Snobs to let the grass grow under their feet.

If their ways were looked at in the right light they were made what they had become, getting only a bread and cheese living—the cheese hard to see sometimes—and also there is a saying, "Get old —get artful."

They was out night after night giving Cops and Keepers a time, and most occasions would get clear away with it.

I remember one particular night when I was out with them. The bricks and chest were back in their places, dust, rubbish and litter strewed about looking as though the chest hadn't never been moved for weeks, not even a feather laying about, and they tells me to light up another rush candle and started a game of cards.

All at once comes a thundering rap on the door of the shanty making the old place rattle. A voice from outside a-calling, "Put that light out—time yew chaps wur in bed!"

"Come in," calls Waxy Jack, "and have a sup o' somethin' with us."

In walks the Bobby casting his eyes round while he warms hisself at the fire, and Raggety Jack tells him to sit down on the chest and make hisself comfortable and asks if he would like a hot-pot.

"That I should," says he, and they tells me to make up the fire, take the cone-shaped pot that hung there, and put some fresh warm wood in, fill it with beer and put the small end in the embers till it begun to boil, then fill the Bobby's mug—and it soon began to warm his toes.

If his sense of smell had been as keen as his sense of taste he would have smelled all them there pheasants within a few feet of him, and had a feather in his cap and that would have been the break-up of the Snob's club.

After a bit, unwilling like, he says he best be off and bids good-night to all, but not to eaves-drop outside—the Snobs knew a game worth two of that. Up jumps Calico Jack and says:

"Think I'll have a sprint outside man, and stretch my legs," and goes along with him until he has a line on him[1] well up the road, then hurried back to the Shanty. Back he come and tells us all to clear off home and he'll sleep there with one eye at a time, as there is never no telling what Police and them sort of folks is up to.

Next day-morning the other celebrities met at the Shanty as was their custom before going to work, carrying their Snobs bags over their shoulders and doled out the night before's haul. Then they puts an old pair of boots or high-lows on top and away they goes one after the other, skip-jacking along and no folks meeting them but would think they had a bag full of jobs to do during the day.

No one took any notice of a Snob calling at a house with his shoe bag, merely thinking he was taking a job home. The Snobs knew well enough where to drop the feathered fowl, as no poacher what know his business goes out to get Long-tails not having his market fixed first.

So it went on time after time, they being like seven brothers. Not as the old version have it—what one have the other have to go

[1]To keep in the line of vision.

without—not so with the Snobs, they shared out all alike whoever did the catching, and if any one brass-nailed one of them he'd have to look out when he met the gang.

Burnt Ass was the tallest of the seven, standing head and shoulders over the others. He was rather too tall for poaching as he could not so easily get in among the bushes nor under low hanging branches as the others and was more easily seen by the Keepers, so more often than not he stayed at home and busied himself with other matters.

One night all had met at the Shanty and were having a game of darts when Burnt Ass says:

"I don't know what yew chaps think but 'pears to me this here's a lovely night for a ramble, shouldn't mind going out to-night to try my luck. What dew yew say, Nosey, shall we go for an hour or tew and see what we can git?"

Nosey say he don't mind if he du, and everything was got ready and off they goes. I remember well, him standing in the door of the shanty, a still sky behind him all pricked with stars, and thinking to myself what a grut long feller he was, my head scarce above the seat of his trousers. Looking up and down of him thought he was near long enough to take the pheasants off the perks with his hands, and could easily be seen stalking along the fences. He was a rare mark for the Keepers, and it was a fact that more often than not he had to go stooping when he was where he had no right to be.

On this particular night they had got well on the road and about two hundred yards from the corner of the Park where there were pheasants galore, and stooping down were creeping along a low clipped fence on one side, when Burnt Ass whispered to Nosey:

"Thowt I see the glitter of a gun barrel against the trunk of that oak tree."

"No more than I 'spected," says Nosey. "Too bright a night. Squat yew down close tew the fence and lie doggo."

"Look yew there—the Keeper's a-getting through the fence—shall us stop and chance it?"

"No fear, I ain't mug enough for that," says Nosey. "I'm off —come on, Long 'un," and away he goes.

The Keeper who had spotted them all along, hot foot after them, yelling at them to stop or he'll put a charge into 'em behind, and Burnt Ass who had crammed an acorn in his mouth to put the Keeper off his voice, slaps the waxy patch on his breeches as he runs and calls out:

"Shute at that yer . . . and hit it if yew can," for they had got the lead of the Keeper and were enough out of range to take no great harm.

The Keeper takes 'em at their word and let fly, and Burnt Ass copped a few on the very place he'd a-told the Keeper to put 'em, which made 'em double their pace to git out of it before the shindy the Keeper was kicking up brought help.

They had now come to the stile on the road side with a plank over the stream, a way they had often been before by daylight to plan for their night rambles. Burnt Ass, with his length and strength ripped up the plank and threw it on one side and gasps out:

"There yer are, Nosey—dang me, if that don't stop him—he is sure to bolt through, thinking we come this way. Crouch yew down here at the back of the fence and when he go flop in the water wrench the gun from him, then yew hull one of them bricks in the water so he'll think it's the gun, and run for it. I'll meet yew later at the Cross-Ways," and away he goes into the night.

Away come the Keeper splodding along, bucked over the stile, stepped on the plank as he thought and flop he go into the brook. While he was struggling to git out of his muddle, Nosey has his gun in a trice, hulls his brick and yells out:

"Look for yer gun in the mud, me lad"—and away.

It was a good gun they got that night but they took no risks with it but wrapped it up in sacking and buried it till the row had blown

over and then it went to a man who wanted a good 'un, cheap. Burnt Ass allus reckoned that was one of the best tricks they ever played the Keepers.

When they comes back to the shanty the rest was there, and I with them, listening with both ears pitched to the tale of what had happened, until I says summat and Calico Jack turns round and look at me with a piercing glance and says, slow and careful like:

"Shut yar mug, you ain't supposed to be heard, ondly seen, and if any one axed yew if yar heard us talking about a gun and yew split, we'll break yew and done with yew."

I knowed he means it and so did the rest, and I held my peace from that day to this.

Next day the weather set in wet and cold, finding out the weak places in Tom, Dick, and Harry's high-lows and boots making plenty of work for the Snobs, and poaching was out of the question for a week or two. The Snobs were cobbling all day and far into the night to get the jobs done. They were so full of work that I had to carry Happy Jack's dinner down to the workshop. At that time they were all at work for one master—a real good old-fashioned sort—one of the best in his day. He knew well enough that all the Snobs belonged to the old school and were moving in the same rut as their grandfathers, and found it was useless to try and make 'em mend their ways. They were all good workmen and behaved themselves at the workshop, so being a wise man he left them to do as they pleased when they were away from it. But one day there was a proper mess up, and it come about like this.

One Monday morning I was down with Happy Jack's dinner—a tin of smoking hot pig's head broth thickened with rice—and was artful enough to stop, as I knew Father would leave me a drop in the bottom. Skinny Jack was sitting next my Father getting his dinner cold that day, and carefully takes off the top of a sausage roll and lays it by, saying:

"I'll git the old woman to put another crust on him, Happy, must make spare ter make tew ends meet." Happy cocks an eye saying, "Look yew at that rat," and when he turns nips his sausage and it goes where it wont want no second crust. When Skinny gits the wind up they all laughs and says they will club together and buy him a pound and that will last all winter, if so his old woman will go on putting crusts on 'em. It was only a lark but Skinny gits right snaisty and raves at me for larfin' and says he'll stick me with his awl same as he did the elephant that come with the circus, which slapped his great trunk in at the front and pinched the cobbler's wax out of his hand, and then I won't forget it in a hurry.

"No," says Calico Jack, "no more don't elephants forget, and you'd best look out when the circus come again."

True enough come summer time, back come the circus and they brings the elephants down to the river, which run close to the Snob's workshop, to get a bathe and a drink, as they done afore. Now Skinny sits close aside the open front and it happen I was trotting along to keep up with them great beasts, as all boys will, and so see something more than I expected.

They all go past quiet as lambs, but the biggest pause, swing his head and lift his trunk as he pass the Snobs, as if he were a dog trying a scent. When they had finished bathing and drinking (and a queer sight it is to see, it is such a delight to them) they comes lumbering out and up the street again. As the biggest elephant pass the open front he swings his trunk round and swack goes a blast of mud and water full in Skinny's face, taking him so by surprise he goes heels over head in among the lasts, leather and old boots, the rest of the Snobs also getting their share of the splash. Skinny picks himself up in a rum pickle looking just as if he'd come out of a dyke. The others could not help but laugh and Calico tells him it sarve him right for being a peevish old beggar. The elephant hadn't meant no harm the first time, and he'd pricked him cruel with his cobbler's awl and he'd had his own back on him, and if his conk had been served like that he wouldn't have forgot in a hurry either.

Skinny asks him who he thinks he is a-talking to.

"Yew, a' course," sezs Calico. "Yar muddy looking varmint—if yew h'ant a' bin so snaisty and pricked that there elephant in the trunk we shounter bin in this 'ere mess."

That were enough for Skinny. He was wet and cold, his wind was up, and he lays on to an old boot what was handy and hulls it at Calico's head and it goes whump through the glass door what leads into the Boss's show room, amusing me and some more boys who were looking in at the window, enjoying the fun. Happy Jack yells out:

"Boys, mind yer top-nots," and thinking he'd quiet Skinny down he ups with a pair of high-lows that were lying tied together and slung 'em with all his force at Skinny's head. That about finished it and soon all the Snobs were fighting right and left, blood and oaths, leather and old boots, flying in all directions.

At the time that all this happen the Boss had gone into the town to measure a lady for a new pair of shoes, and when he come back and hear the din he sezs to us, "What's all this about?" I tells him he'll soon find out when he gits into his Snob's shop, and a black cloud come over his face—I had set the Boss's wind all right. When the old chap walked into his workshop he was wholly stammed.

The place look more like a slaughter house than a cobblers, the Snobs laying one here and one there with black eyes and broken noses, and boots and tools all over the place swamped with mud and water. He starts off and goes at 'em good and proper, tells 'em they are a set of rowdies what can't be left on their jobs five minutes but what they start rowing. Then he casts his eye towards the door and goes off again at the sight of that, and says he'll find out who started all the shindy and never have him on his place again.

Up jumps Calico Jack and says he'll tell how it all come about, so the Boss tells him to go ahead but speak the truth. "That I will, Master," sezs Calico. "I never was caught telling a lie yet."

The Boss soon realise it's Skinny what was at the bottom of the trouble and after a bit tells the Snobs it's no good thinking no more about it, nor going to the Circus folk who will make a laughing stock of the lot of them. They'd best shake hands and make friends and git going and clear up the shop, and they'd all have to pay three pence a week to make good the damage, and he'd say no more about it. The Snobs thinks to themselves there is allus a bill to pay for any shindy and this was worth the fun. So they sets to and puts things right and trade went on as usual, with many a joke about the colour of their faces.

A blast of mud and water full in Skinny's face.

The Old Grey Mare

Robin Cook's wife she had a grey mare,
Hum hum—hum hum hum hum.

If you had but ha' seen her, O lauk how you'd stare
Singing faldedal fiddledal, hy dum dum.

This old mare she had a sore back—
And on her back, I hull't an old sack
Singing faldedal fiddledal, hy dum dum.

She want for to go to Frumpletie fair,
Hum hum—hum hum hum hum.

A' though she warn't fitten to shew herself there,
Singing faldedal fiddledal, hy dum dum.

I'll give the ould mare some corn i' the fan,
I'll warrant she'll travel as fast as she can.

I'll give the ould mare some corn i' the sieve,
And hope an God husband the ould mare may live.

This ould mare she chanc'd for to die,
And dead as a nit i' the road way she lie.

All the dogs in the town spok' for a bon',
All but the parson's dog—he stayed at home.

I'll lay the bridle up o' the shelf—
If you want any more you must sing it yourself.

He laid back his ears and let fly.

CHAPTER IX

And now we haul to the Dog and Bell
Where there's a good liquor for to sell
In come old Archer with a smile
Saying Drink my lads 'tis worth your while.

Ah! but when our money's all gone and spent
And none to be borrowed nor none to be lent;
In come old Archer with a frown,
Saying " Get up Jack let John sit down."
"Two Suffolk Friends."

THE Master Boot and Shoe Maker was not a man of many words, but a great thinker with prominent forehead, piercing eyes and a keen sense of observation—could see what was going on the other side of a brick wall—when the matter concerned him without giving two looks.

He used to see me about the workshop and it seem I amused him, and one day he sezs to Happy Jack:

"Yer boy seems to have a bit a' grit in 'im, chip of the old block, ain't he, Bor?"

And Father sezs, "Yes, and I should want to know what wus a' clock if he worn't."

The Boss then asked Father if he wouldn't like me to follow him in the trade—boots and shoes allus being wanted I couldn't go far wrong, and Father sezs yes, but it seem to him that by the time I shall be growed nearly all boots and shoes will be made by machinery. But the Boss he wont hear of it that there will come any change in their time. So it was fixed that I start the next day and go round with Waxy in the old pony and cart taking home and hunting out jobs, as Waxy said the old pony would not stand while he got up the gardens to the cottage doors.

"The boy 'ont have much to du, ondly set in the cart and hold the reins while Waxy is after his business taking the money. I got a lot o' shop eggs[1] on the round he go, and I don't reckon Waxy's sharp enough on 'em one way and another about it—can't go on like this, all out and none in, it hardly pay for pony and cart, let alone Waxy's time. I reckon he stop too long at the Pubs, and if yar boy go round with him happen he'll git home sooner and I may git an idea where he go tew with my pony."

Happy Jack bucks off his seat and says he'll see what the boy'll say to it and away home. In doors he come happy as a sandpiper, as was his way except when the drink and the black tempers come on him. He take me by surprise telling me I can go along er Waxy next day on his round with the pony and cart, but I was pleased as punch to be off round the country on a trip.

Next day off I goes with Father to the shop, the pony was put in the shafts, the cart loaded up with all the finished jobs to take to their owners and up I gits by Waxy's side.

"Now then, Waxy," sezs the Master Snob, "look out and see yew gits the money for them jobs, and if they don't wonter pay yew, bring 'em back agin or I'll know the reason why."

Waxy sezs, "All right, they wont git away with nothing this day," flapped the reins on the old pony's back, rattled the stock on the spokes of the wheel and we were off at full speed, well under ten mile an hour. By the middle of the day we had got a mile from home. The old pony seemed to know every twist and turn—kept on a-looking—and every time he stop in front of a Pub Waxy stop to give him a breather and wet his whistle, leaving me a-sitting till I were fed up. I gits down once and has a look inside, and there he were going ahead with a lot of fishing men. I thinks to myself if I be going to sit till he gits that lot under the table I'm here till Doomsday, knowing from what Happy Jack used to say what holy terrors them fishing folk kin be.

At last out he come, and we do git along to some houses and leave

[1] Bad debts.

the jobs, and Waxy sezs he got the money all right and some more that was owing. So it went on till we had cleared the cart and not a bad debt among 'em. Waxy was now well britched with other folk's money and back we goes to the Pig and Whistle, and there were all them fishing folk with their blue jumpers, big long boots and rolling walk not half pleased to see him. They were soon putting it away—as their fashion is—you could hardly notice it were going, unless you looked careful, Waxy paying as he were the King (I had no idea at the time what was in the wind).

Well, they all gets properly oiled up and comes sky-larking out of the Pub, sees me a-sitting there waiting for Waxy and in a trice they has the old pony out of the cart and me on his back. They push both of us through the door into the Public kitchen, the pony going as sweet as if she were walking into her own stable, me on top with my head just clear of the beams.

They starts shouting to the landlord to bring Dick Turpin a pint, and a couple in a pail for the thoroughbred. The old pony was ready enough and soon found the bottom of the pail. They thinks that no end of a lark and fills it agin and the pony start pampling about, swinging his tail like a bass broom and the company laughing till they bent their two ends together shouting:

"Well, I'll be hanged if Waxy's old pony can't put down more beer than he can."

The landlord was patting the pony's neck and found a sore place on his shoulder, and when he touched that the pony thinks he had had enough of the entertainment. The beer was beginning to tell, he laid back his ears and let fly straight as a dart at one behind him who saw what was coming and tipped over in the nick of time, as the pony's heels crashed into a wood partition smashing it to splinters. Next minute he was out through the door, me laying flat against his neck and hanging on to the reins for all I was worth, through the yard and down the road where luckily for me there was a ford and the stream all swollen with the flood water. He didn't like the look of that so he stopped with all four feet set and over his head I go and splosh into the shallow. All the company come along a bit sobered by what had happened, and picks me up blaring fit to bust myself. There wasn't no harm done, and the landlord's wife cleans me up, while Waxy harnesses up the pony again—it being then about an hour afore dark. He sezs, Can I drive the pony home, he knows the way? He couldn't have asked me anything that would please me better but I asks him if he ain't a-coming? He says no, he got another job and it ain't no good me waiting, and fair startled me by saying if I did I'd be waiting months.

"I'm done with cobbling, boy," sezs he. "I be going to have a look at the briny with these lads here—tell the Boss I be gone to sea."

"To see," sezs I. "See who?" He blows out at me at that and tells me to git along home or I wont be back afore morning, he'll see me again some day, that is if Davy Jones don't tuck him up in his locker.

I landed home just afore dark and the Boss he hears me pull up the old pony and out he come. He asks where Waxy is and I tells him along at the Pig and Whistle with a lot of chaps wearing blue things what they pull over their heads, and the Boss mutters and grumbles about them blankety fishermen, and tells me Waxy be gone after the herring which I couldn't make nothing of. When I tells him Waxy took the money off the customers first he calls Father to hear what I have to say, and there was a rare shindy.

"The darned rascal," says he. "Know no better than to git in with a lot o' good for nothing seamen swilling beer at the Pig and Whistle on my money. Going after herring is he, blast him. Please God he'll be caught in the net by his gills first time they're out. Take yew the pony, boy, and bed him down—I'm done with outside work arter this—I'll sell the lot out next Bungay May Fair."

He was as good as his word calling in his bills and would do no more outside cobbling for the villages, the truth being he was getting an old man and was cut to the heart with Waxy's dirty trick, thinking the better he treated his men the more they turned against him, and he's not the first one to think that by a very long chalk.

The Snobs were now reduced to six, but the others soon find they could do without their missing link, and as far as the trade went he was soon forgot. It was a good time for trade, the Boss was pulling in the dibs, and begun to feel more cheerful—the sore place in his mind was healing up.

The winter wore along, the spring was near at hand, the birds was all a' piping, snobbing begin to get a bit slack and the Snobs could be seen getting their muscles up digging the gardens. When all the digging was done they would have two or three days' rest and go on the Randy and enjoy themselves, no work of any kind would bother them when they were that way.

But the first fine and still day away they'd all go in a body to plant and sow one another's gardens, till in a few hours all their crops were in. They had learnt the old ditty—"Help One Another, Boys, While Fortune On You Smile"—and the Snobs put it into practice, as all the town knew in them days. They used to say you never saw a Snob's garden but it had good crops. This was because with all their wild ways they weren't bakkard in digging up the land winter time and keeping the hoe going while the crops was growing, instead of standing about. They was never ones to keep their hands in their pockets—not in no way.

The sun was shining both side of the hedges and Bungay May Fair was close at hand, which the celebrities were looking forward to, thinking they'd have some fun and see the Boss's pony and cart sold, and take a hand in running up the price.

The day come, the old pony was fed up with all he could eat, brushed down, hooves shined, long hair clipped off. Then out come the beeswax, turpentine and brushes and Skinny and Nosey give him such a polishing as he'd never had afore. We served cart and harness alike and when the Boss come to look he couldn't believe it was his old pony and cart and begins to think it will fetch a tenner. They plans to let me drive, it as then folks will think it's a good quiet old pony what will take some old dame to market a treat. The Boss says to Nosey:

"Yew seem to be good at selling ponies and understand the hoss-dealing ways, take the turnout and sell it on yer own. Now then boy, start off and keep yer back straight and a tight hand on the reins, so she don't stumble."

Off I goes with Nosey driving through the town to the Fair, the other Snobs follering along behind, and we all gets safe to the Fair ground, where they was selling the horses and carts. There was all

sorts of how-de-row going on, the auctioneer selling this, that and t'other, and presently a voice calls out:

"Hi, Sir, can I put in a Lot?"

"Yes, anything you like—walk up, what is it you want to sell?"

"My old woman—seem plenty of folks about—chance of a lifetime to git shot on her."

Such a roar of laughter come from the crowd, the auctioneer thinks here's a chance to get 'em all in a good mood, carries on, and asks how it happen he wants to get rid of his old gal.

"Well, that's like this, Sir, when I married her she was straight as a lath, could get my arm round her nice little waist and give her a kiss, and thought she was an angel. Now, dang me, I can't git near her by a yard."

"Seems to me," said the Auctioneer, "She must be like other old ladies—gone fashionable—and taken to wearing the crinoline. Well, ladies and gents what am I to do? Must see the goods afore I can sell, and know if she be quiet in single and double harness, and a good cook."

"She be that all right, and know how to pack it away too. She and her great crinoline git in front of the fire—there's no chance for me to see it much less feel it—there ain't no room for both of us in the house, and that's a fact."

"Well," say the Auctioneer, "Here I have to offer unseen, one fat lady, who belonged to Prinny the Elder and was wed to him donkey's years since, being at the time, slim and genteel. A first-rate cook—she tastes her dinners herself—and has become so fat and puffed out she get wedged in the doorways of Mr. Prinny's house. For her comfort and his he feel sure she would be a good asset to the occupier of a larger house. Now's your time, gentlemen—how much may I say for the lady?"

A voice calls out, "Will you give a guarantee?"

"What guarantee would you be wanting, Sir?"

"That if I buys her she won't be rolling over in the night and overlaying me so I come out as flat as a pancake!" At that they all roars out and starts cat-calling and someone else shouts:

"Here be all the Snobs. Best git one o' them to buy her—she'll do well to wax his thread," and the Auctioneer have to bang down his hammer and call "Order," before he can be heard.

"Well," says he, "don't seem as if I can git a bid for your biggest half, Mr. Prinny. I doubt but what she has lost her young fluff and become an old flapper. Lost her glamour—old hins don't sell, yew know."

At that they all roars again and the Auctioneer get back to his real business, selling Mr. Prinny's biggest half being a sort of lark they has.[1]

After that before I know where I was they pushed me into the ring, and the Auctioneer begins his tale about the finest turnout he'd seen for many a day, and the pony so quiet a kid could drive him on Fair day and all the ring starts joking. They begins to bid and afore we'd been going long the turnout made fifteen pounds.

The Snobs were thunderstruck, but Nosey goes up and gets the

dough and the old pony was led away, me wondering what was going to happen next. I had no need to wonder—there was such a crowd of Sharpers round us asking Nosey and the other Snobs to go into one of the Booths and have a drink. As soon as all gets going the Sharpers started a game amongst themselves. In those days they called it "Pricking the Garter."

The Garter was a length of tape about four foot long, the two ends held in one hand doubled in the middle. The game was to find

[1]This custom comes from the old belief a man could by putting up his wife to auction legally dissolve the marriage tie and escape from all his obligations. Wives were "sold" in Carlisle as late as the year 1832, and other cases occurred at Birmingham in 1834, at Canterbury in 1820 and at Pontefract in 1815. The last case was at Dudley in 1859 where a man sold his wife for sixpence, though before this it had become a punishable offence. There is no doubt it was a custom regarded as an unofficial divorce. The reference to "Prinny" is of course a joke which evidently died hard. Prinny was the nickname of the Prince Regent who afterwards became George IV. (1820). He was famous for his preference for fat women.

the end of the tape when it was rolled up flat. The rolls and doubles forming a flat coil was laid on the table and it required a bit of skill to find the centre with a Pricker.

There were three artful Dodgers in the swim, two of them playing, and the other, supposed to be the cuter of the three, was winning every time, and getting the dough handed over to him with not so much as a murmur. The three Sharpers was working hard to get the lookers on into the net. Presently the winning Sharper says to Nosey:

"Here, yew, try yar luck. Yew can git an easy quid, it's quite simple; or let the boy have a go," and he hands me the Pricker.

The tape was doubled up afresh and laid down on the table, I pushes in the Pricker and gets the centre the first time, which the Sharpers made it easy for me to do, it being a trap set for a draw.

"There yew are," says the Sharper, "even a kid can do it," but when I ask for my quid what I've won, he laughs and sezs, "Don't bet with young boys, only old 'uns," and goes on to say:

"Come along gents—any of yew want a soft quid, I tell yew I'll put tew to one on anybody's shillings or pounds that there ain't a man standing near by that can prick the right loop the first time, and we will let the boy pull the ends to make sartain sure there isn't no swindling."

Well, they starts off in a small way with bobs and then crowns, sometimes winning and sometimes losing but keeping pretty level, and the drinks keep on going round. Presently Nosey who was getting a bit quarrelsome calls out:

"I'll lay yew five pounds I'll get it next time," and out comes a fiver of the Boss's money and plank down on the table.

"Done," says the Sharper, quick as a weasel, laying down his tenner so there was now fifteen Yellow Boys winking on the table. Nosey looks at 'em and then steadily at the maze of doubles in the tape, puts in the Pricker and sezs to me:

"Now, Boy, pull steady," which I did, the tape leaving Nosey's Pricker fast in the table. The tape was gone, and Nosey's five pounds as well. Before you could say Jack Robinson the Sharper calls out "Bad Luck," and sweeps the fifteen quid off the table leaving Nosey between the Devil and the Deep Sea, having lost five pounds of his Master's money and knowing he'd be laughed at for being a mug and have to pay it back into the bargain.

"Go on," says the Sharper, who knew well enough what was stirring in his mind. "Faint heart never won fair lady, nor the dough to buy 'em with my lad! Have another try and get who you like to pull the tape this time. All fair and above board and no deception."

Nosey swallers the bait—hook line and sinker—planks down another fiver and says, "Right yew are—two to one on that!" Made my fingers itch to see the table, having never seen so much money in my life. The Sharper with a face shrewd as a judge, wound, doubled, and twisted up the tape into a dozen and one turns, laid it down telling Nosey to take a good look and make sure and win this time. So he did, taking at least five minutes, knowing that he must win this time or be lost with the money. He made sure he'd got the right double and says to Skinny, "Draw it steady, lad."

He did so only to find the tape come away—Nosey had lost. Happy Jack who was standing behind the others saying little as was his habit but thinking the more, as was also the way with him, yells out:

"Blarst yer, Nosey, for a b—— fool, to let a lot of Scallywags like them Sharpers best yew," and the next second before the Sharpers could clear the table the Waxey brethren were on them like so many wild cats and there was a proper uproar. They soon finding out they was up against a party of fighting Snobs and one of their progeny.

I mostly had a bird's eye view of the Snobs' battle between their legs, but got a few blows in before losing my foothold and then went on doing my bit, as a dog would to help defend his master. It was only for a few seconds—the battle was short and sharp. The Sharpers were toppled over on their backs and their pockets turned inside out, the Yellow Boys dropping on the ground.

I started scrambling them up quick, as a hungry hen would git after corn, and slipped 'em down in between my ankles and the tops of my high-lows that were a pair of Father's left offs and not too good a fit, so there was plenty of room for all I could git hold of. The battle was over, Leather, Wax, and Hemp had won, but the Sharpers were just wondering how they were going to get back their ill-gotten gains and some of their own which had gone as well, when three burly policemen arrived.

The Sharpers spun their tale but the Snobs had as good a one to tell, and swore they were three of the biggest thieves on the Fair ground, and the crowd which was now thick as bees was all for the Snobs. The end of it was the Sharpers turned nasty and got marched off to the lock-up with the bracelets on, looking a pretty lot of forlorns. A lot the Snobs cared for such as they, nor for forty like 'em in them days.

What became of the triplets after that I could not say. By this time without a doubt they are landed in the happy hunting grounds and perhaps are Pricking the Garter as a reward for their evil doings in letting in honest men, if what they says is true, and we be punished by having to go on a' doing what we did wrong in this world whether we likes it or not.

Nosey called us all together and looks us over and finds there weren't no cripples among us. All were in good trim bar a bruise or so and a little claret tapped and dried on our faces, and off we goes to enjoy ourselves, Nosey telling us to keep together in case the Sharper's pals gets on to us.

I follers along behind and kept quiet as I was well used to in them rough times, especially when John Barley Corn was about appearing with his head in froth well above the top of a pint pot. I knew very well if I said one word amiss or as much as cast my eye in the wrong direction I was in for it, and would without doubt get the toe of somebody's boot.

Scarcely a week went by that I did not see a fight and a good one, showing the grit and spirit of them that lived in these parts those days. That's what built up the British Empire I am thinking, and we need diplomacy and integrity to hold it, as all the nations of the world are waking out of their slumbers in these highly mechanized times, and what will happen in the future in which we shall have no part, is hard to tell.

We goes along to the shies and I picks up a ball and the Showman tells me to go it, as he never knew a left handed one but what he was a sure shot, and anyways I can't fall out of my high-lows, which raise a laugh all round, but I knew he was talking to keep my 'tention off the nuts, let fly and got several, Nosey brassing up for the shots.

The Showman keeps on at me and says what will I take for my high-lows? I sezs "Twenty quid," and he offers tuppence. I thinks to myself if he knew what was in 'em he'd have gone a bit up on that. Along we go to the shooting gallery, and the Snobs like the look of the gypsy gals with shawls over their heads and ear-rings dangling, and they didn't let us stand looking long; they had a sharp eye for business and offers us a gun each with a knowing smile and:

"Try yer luck, gents—give yew an extry shot every time yew rings the bell," and one gits hold of me and says:

"Here yew are, boy, larn to use a gun, never know when yew wont want it, don't be bashful, Raggetty, nor shut both eyes when you fires."

I looks up at her holding the gun and thinks to myself her round black eyes shine like fireballs, and she could skin a flint stone if I could manage to hold it. Not having seen many gypsy folk before. I gapes with mouth and eyes at her till she ask if I'm deaf? I say, "I'm not wanting my ears brushing out," grabs the gun and lets fly and gits a bull's eye.

Then she tells me to do that again and I can have six free shots and supper with her in her van, knowing well enough I couldn't shoot and thinking to make a laugh of me. Sure enough she did and I gets my pecker up, turns on her and sezs I'd have her know my Mother didn't breed all the daft 'uns nor yet all the rogues, she'd best take her old gun and come along o' me scaring rooks and see how she'd like a job of honest work for a change. She give me a shove and tells me to clear off home and suck my milk bottle, and Nosey git me by the slack of my breeches and yanks me out of the booth, and says to me I'd best hook it, as they don't want no more trouble that day.

Soon as we had said farewell to the Fair ground and was on the way home, Nosey slouching along shoulders hunched up and grumbling away about what a fool he have been to git along of the Sharpers and lost his master's money till Father say it's true enough, the Boss thought he could trust him, and when he finds out Nosey's sold him a pup it wont never be the same no more. All the Snobs asks Nosey how much he is short and he says he's blessed if he know, but we'd best all go along to his Hall and find out how much we'd saved from the scram.

We come presently to a narrow lane—Nosey's Hall was now in sight. I looked it up and down and thought it had seen its best days. There was only one door, and Burnt Ass sezs to him:

"Why Nosey yew ain't got half a chance—no back door—if the Rate Collector make a call. You b'aint half as well off as Mr. Rat."

"How's that, Bor?"

"Why to slip out of, I mean. Did you ever know a rat to make a hole in anywhere but what he would make another one out, if he had half a chance."

Mrs. Nosey was taken by surprise, said she thought it were the Press Gang coming by the noise, but bids us come in and take a seat on the floor, as there weren't no chairs worth noticing. Nosey he bids her stand outside while we was talking and if she see any one a' coming to let us know quick.

Nosey then empties out his pockets and lays the Yellow Boys on the floor—seven quid—which mean there was another eight to make up, to what he should have had. He was properly done and sezs he'd sooner make a hole in the water than face the Boss with all that short, but Skinny tells him to shut his mug and put his head in the water butt to try out how he likes it, afore he talks so silly.

They all begun to fork out what they had, throwing it on the floor, and when they counted it, it was twelve pounds lying there winking at 'em. Father says, "Take what you've got, lad, and face up to it and tell the Boss we'll pay up the rest as soon as we can earn it."

I sezs nothing but starts pulling off my high-lows with all of them a' garping at me and shakes 'em and out rolls six sovereigns. I took 'em all by surprise, they couldn't think how ever I come by it, till I tells 'em when they were all having a downer with the Sharpers I used my wits and my fingers.

"Well, I'll be hanged," says Raggety, "the darn boy has licked us dorg hollow."

"Yes," says I, "I reckon I got you all out of a hole."

They was that pleased with me four of 'em picked me up and carried me by arms and legs out of Nosey's mansion and dumped me down with a cheer. Off we went home, the end of my first day at Bungay May Fair, and the best of the lot was I had two more Yellow Boys tucked away in the toe of Father's old high-lows.

I give 'em to Mother, and when she ask me where I got so much I tells her I picked it up on the Fair ground, which was true enough, and if she were wise she'd say nought about it, and empty her mouth to fill other folks.

. . . loaded with hay knife, crank, stakes, measure, stick, rake and fork, and off we go.

The Old Sea Horse

They say Old Man your horse will die
They say so and they hope so.
They say Old Man your horse will die—
Oh, poor old horse!

Then if he dies I'll tan his hide
(They say so and they hope so)
And if he lives I'll ride him again
Oh, poor old horse!

Old horse, old horse, what brought you here
After carrying sand for many a year
From Bantry Bay to Ballywhack—
Where you fell down and broke your back.

Now after years of such abuse
They salt you down for sailors' use
They tan your hide and burn your bones
And send you off to Davey Jones.

"*Sea Songs and Shanties*," W. B. Whall.

CHAPTER X

Who'er has travelled life's dull round
Where'er his stages may have been
Must sigh to think he still has found
His warmest welcome at an Inn.
(Shenstone) Cut on an Inn window.

THE May Fair was over and almost forgot and the Snobs were busy night and day after something or another, and we all found plenty to occupy ourselves. So the summer slipped away and in a few more weeks the shooting season would begin, and the Snobs began to wonder how they were going to get along, now Waxey had gone to sea.

"We'll manage some way or another," says Happy Jack with a grin. "I'll lay any one of yew half a dollar we ain't lost the lad, he'll be home afore long. The birds are making up, and he knows we'll soon be getting ready for the home fishing."

Sure enough a few days afterwards Waxey walks into the Snobs' shop where they was all sitting at work, much to the surprise of the Boss. Waxey was looking a bit shamefaced but tells him somehow he couldn't settle to the sea, and felt he must come and see how they were all getting on, and he's fair sorry for giving the Boss the slip. The old man looks him up and down and tells him by-gones is by-gones and he don't want to hear no more of that and he's glad he's back and looking so well.

"Yes," says Waxey, "being at sea gives you an appetite all right, yew could eat anything—Scalt Cat and a skep-er-greens. Not that one goes short, yew can have plenty herrin'—a dozen or more—if yew want 'em, no stint of herrin', but arter a bit I can't fancy them no more, and they never put no flesh on to my bones," which was true enough, he was near as thin as Skinny.

Well, he talks a bit and then says he must be going—he'll come in again afore he's off back to his boat—and he fixes up to meet the Snobs later on and have a drink, if they'd be at Old Sam's about nine.

The Snobs didn't want telling twice if there was any cheap beer to be had, and was soon finished up, thinking what was not done to-day could easy be finished to-morrow. Father comes scurrying home to spruce himself up, and tells me Waxey is back with plenty of money in his pocket and he's off to the Greyhound to meet him. I begs to go along too so Happy Jack takes me and Waxey slaps me on the back saying:

"Gord bless me, here's the boy. How did you git on when I left you at the Pig and Whistle? First-rate, I'll be bound," and I tells him "All right," but small thanks to him thinks I to myself. Waxey, the seafaring Snob, was the hero of the evening, telling us all manner of tales and all about the Ports he had seen, and how he had made friends with a Boat Owner, a good old sport, and he was coming over next week, and how he wanted to meet all the Snobs and how about getting up some racing? He's a rare chap for hoss racing *and* he got plenty of dough.

That was after the Snobs' own hearts—anything for a spree—and Sam the Landlord says he'll put in his two old ponies and a gypsy chap what was there says he's got half a dozen in his drove, real clinkers, that'll run with any man's, and it was all fixed for the next Saturday afternoon.

The next thing was to find the jockeys, Happy Jack reckoned I could be one, Skinny says he can double his legs up so they don't trail on the ground and he'll be another, and the Gypsy has two lads that ride like monkeys so we are fixed for four.

"Well," says Happy Jack, "if I can't ride I can fall off, and I'm a light weight—put me down for five." When they asks Nosey if he can't ride he says what do they think, he's rid his old woman's linen horse many a time, so he's set for number six, which 'ud be more than enough as some riders are sure to turn up if they hear's there is some racing on.

They tells me to be off and git Cock Robin to cry our Race Meeting. He was a character was Cock Robin, the Bungay Town Crier

—by no means a big burly fellow—standing upright his height would not exceed four foot nine inches and he always was upright, straight as a dart. He was a real professional at his job, his mouth opened from ear to ear and one was stammed to know where the noise he let out come from. The vibrations issuing from his little body sounded as if they came from a big bass drum. If he had owned the whole town he could not have appeared of more consequence, and many a time when I was a lad I have heard him crying in Bungay over a mile away across the Common. He also bought Rags, Bones, and Bottles, and wet or fine tramped the streets with his hand cart crying, "Here comes Cock Robin!"

Waxey give me three bob, the price of a gallon of beer, to wet Cock Robin's whistle, and I off to his roost and hammers at the door —he being turned in and wanting to know what I wanted at that time o' night, him just got into kip.[1]

I tells him my party of Snobs wants him to call a Race Meeting at half after two on Saturday, to be runned on the Common between the flying ponies of a Famous Gypsy and those of the noted Company of Snobs. This he promised to do during the next three days, giving good notice of the same, and be on the course with his bell to start all the races.

I was up with the lark—Saturday our Race Day—and there was no work for the Snobs. They had downed tools for the week-end. Waxey was getting ready for his Boat Owner and some more Old Salts—pals of his—that were coming by Puffing Billy, as we called

[1]Bed.

the train, which in those days had not been long running down the Valley.

Waxey and I met them at the Station. They looks round and says, "Bungay don't seem to be a very big town!"

"Big enough," says Waxey. "Yew can git anything yew wants

here—such as new tops or bottoms[1]—a pint of beer—a black eye or a punch on the nose—same as yew can at Yarmouth."

Then he introduce me as Heel Ball,[2] the Jockey, what is going to ride Green Hemp,[3] the Snobs' best pony in the second race. They all laughs at that and smacks me on the back and we go off to the Common where the people was drawing in large numbers.

Down I go to the paddock which had been rigged up by willing

[1] An old saying "Go to Bungay to be re-bottomed," supposed to refer to the old industry of copper bottoming boats carried on there.

[2] A ball of resin and red ochre wax, used in shoemaking, to polish heels.

[3] Green hemp. Balls of green twine—six or seven strands are used together waxed to stitch leather.

helpers, and there I sees the young gypsy riders and their ponies and I sezs to them, "Dew you ride to win or lose?"

"Whichever way there's most to be had," say the black-eyed gypsies.

The Snobs were busy picking out their ponies for each race and Cock Robin making out his list as starter—four runners in the first race, Nosey and Skinny riding against two of the gypsies. Up they

gets and trotted round two or three times all the crowd laying bets. Presently Cock Robin gets 'em into line and off they go, Skinny's mount running in among the crowd of folks his long legs swinging just clear of the ground, causing roars of laughter which upset the pony which rears up and Skinny slid off aft, and went down flop on his back, every one thinking he had cracked his head.

He was soon picked up and carried off to the paddock, where his friend the Boat Owner give him a drink of rum and milk out of his flask and he was soon on his feet again. Meanwhile Nosey was getting round the course and won the first race by a head and a half.

The Old Salts faces was all smiles, but others were hanging their ears.

Presently Cock Robin announced the second race in which I was to ride Green Hemp, and Father and two of the Snobs the other ponies, the gypsies not riding at all which puzzled me for a bit, until casting my eye on Cock Robin about to ring his starting bell I sees his hand flat on the top of his head, and knows that mean I'm to ride to win, and it don't matter what happen to the other mounts—this having been arranged previous. Down come his bell with a sweeping clash and my mount was hitting the turf in an instant, and she being the better pony and me far the lightest weight was soon fifty yards ahead of the others and getting near the fence we were to jump, with a dyke of water close up the other side.

It was every one for himself—I had to clear that jump though I liked the look of it little enough, and the others would if they could—that did not trouble me.

Gingering up my mount and laying well forrard, keeping my knees close, I hoped for the best and that it wouldn't be a broken neck.

We cleared it somehow, me lying on the poor old girl's neck and saved myself by clutching a good handful of mane, but we were over and running up the straight turf, the old pony blowing like a grampus not being used to these doings, and got past the winning post. A few seconds more and in came Father thundering along amid roars of laughter and cries of:

"Yar—boy—har licked yar, Happy Jack!"

"Yes," says Happy, "don't mind that—all in the family."

I was picked up by the Boat Owner and the Old Salt and I was glad to think I had beat the old man.

I asked after Waxey and Raggety Jack and it seems they was coming along having had a spill at the water jump. Waxey's horse lit on the edge of the water and sent Waxey flying yards ahead flat on his stomach sprawled out on all fours on the grass, looking like a blown toad. His horse followed head over heels on top of him and he was now like a toad squashed, but fortunately for him the

It was every one for himself.

ground was soft and he was waxey by nature as well as name. If it had not been so his bellows would have lost their wind. He was soon picked up and placed in a hand cart and wheeled back little the worse.

Raggety Jack was more fortunate, he fell off his mount sideways, went flop into the water and had an unwanted bath. Presently I sees him coming along spitting the mud out of his mouth, and his clouts hanging about him, making me think of many a broody hen that I had ducked in the river. His mount hadn't stopped to see what had become of him, and was feeding contentedly on a patch of grass half a mile away, which suited it better than the racing business.

Seems I don't recollect much more about the Snobs Race Meeting, possibly something to do with the milk and rum the Boat Owner give me to celebrate my winning the race. But I do remember one of the Old Salts riding in the last race.

He must have weighed fifteen stone and he was properly canned before he started, but go he would and the crowd cheered him yelling, "Go it, Briney," as he went down the course. His feet were about trailing on the ground, and the pony had no fancy for his rider and swerved round so the Old Salt was almost off and clutched at its tail which made the crowd roar again and the Boat Owner calls out:

"Keep going, lad, you've got a good hold of the tiller—steer the ship into port!"

He did not trouble his mount long. No sooner was he down to the bottom of the Common than he rolled off like a sack of potatoes gasping his inside were near jolted out, and there he lay groaning.

We couldn't get him up and was forced to take the hand cart, put him in on some hay, and wheel him back rattling, bumping and bouncing in the air, for the old cart had no springs. Not that that troubled our seagoing Jockey who was soon asleep and snoring, the crowd all asking if he were hurt much, and others saying, "He's a' breathing that heavy should think by the look of him his innards are crushed, por fellar." But all that was wrong with him was the Brewers' Sleeping Sickness.

The Snobs thinks they have had enough, and Cock Robin rings his bell and gives out that owing to the accident to the Old Salt, him still lying unconscious and might even end with an inquest, the last two races will not take place. The crowd was soon on the move and in a few minutes the course was clear.

We had to think of our invalid who had to be back on his boat

that night, so we wheels him up to Dr. Brewer's Surgery at the Horse and Groom near by, and the Landlord come out and sezs:

"Hullo, chaps, what-er yar got in yer cart? Where'd yer pick up that lot?" And when we tells him what have happened he laughs and sezs, "I should think the pony was glad to git rid on 'im. He must weigh near sixteen stone, seem to me the poor beast was hurt more than he. Run the cart round into the back-yard and shoot the old fellar on to some hay, that will help to shake him up, had too much of John Barley Corn—by the look of him, I knows what he wants."

With that he gets a mug and some water, a quantity of common salt and a dash of vinegar to give it a colour, and shakes the Old Salt up and tells him to drink it down—it will make a new man of him in less than half an hour—or his name isn't Dr. Brewer.

He bolted it down wringing and twisting his face all shapes, saying it taste a bit salt to him. The Landlord with a wink tells me to stop near him in case he want anything, and sure enough in a few minutes he start a' groaning and saying he's going to be sick.

"What on land," say I, but he just give me a look and tell me to "fetch a bucket and hang on to his head," and I does so and tells him "there's plenty of room in the pail," just to hearten him like. Presently I hears a laugh and there is the Landlord a' looking from the window to see how his tonic is working.

"Never knew my mixture to fail," sezs he, "you'll be a new man in half an hour." But the poor Old Salt could only lie and groan.

Well that evening ended in a proper spree and the end of it was the Boat Owner and all his company missed the nine o'clock train back to Lowestoft. They was in a real stew as the boats had to be out on the tide in the morning, but presently they finds up a cart and ask the owner if he will drive 'em over.

After a lot of arguing he agrees for two quid, as he says he wont take the job on unless he's well paid first. This is agreed and we all gits in—they having a fancy to take me—the Boat Owner growling the driver and his hoss are a couple of old soldiers. He and Waxey goes on the front and the others behind and me on the floor, mostly the place for dogs and parcels.

Off we go jogging along at about three miles an hour and I think it looks like being a long trip—shan't git there afore daylight at that rate. All was going well till we come to Watch House Hill and the driver says—

"The old hoss will have a rum job to draw us lot up here."

"Yew wants to du a bit of tackin'," says the Boat Owner, "same as we du at sea sailing into the wind."

"Well," says the driver, "we bean't out at sea nor yet against the wind, yew sea-going folk think all such as me duffers as don't know how to git a lead up a hill—reckon I didn't open my mouth wide enough with this lot a'board."

The Boat Owner grabs at the reins being a bit short in his temper and wanting to git on.

"Give me hold on 'em," sezs he. "I'll show yer yew stupid ass, pull the hoss across the road like this, first to the left and then to the right."

"Dang yer tacken'," shouts the driver, "don't 'spose yew knows there's holls[1] both sides 'er this 'ere road—keep clear of the holls I tells yer!"

He was too late, the Boat Owner starts to turn, the horse pulls too hard on the reins, the heavily loaded cart runs backward and one wheel drops into the holl, the driver snatched the reins and in an

[1]Ditches.

instant jumped down, but the three Old Salts went toppling heels over head into the ditch. As for me I rolled up against the tail board which prevented me going with 'em.

The Old Salts was lying in the ditch cussing and swearing amid the mud and water and brambles, but I soon scrambled out of the cart none the worse for the kick up, and laughed till the tears run down my face to see the pickle they was in.

"I'll tell yew what I thinks, Mr. Boat Owner," says the driver. "Yew may be all right tacking at sea but yew ha' made a proper mess trying it on land, my old woman would ha' made a better hand at it. If I had known what yew was up to I'd ha' put my pig net over the lot of yew, and kept yew in the cart that way."

The Old Salts scrambled out and the air was blue with what was being said, but no one was hurt, and they sets to work getting the cart out, the driver hanging on to the horse. I and the Boat Owner took hold of one wheel, the two Old Salts the other—the Boat Owner called "heave," out she come and the driver eased the shafts down on the horse's back.

"What about the belly girth," sezs I, "have any one got some string?" The Boat Owner sezs he'll soon show 'em how to splice, and will put two together same as they do ropes at sea.

A bit of string found up we soon discovered he was an expert at the job of cutting out and tying in, the girth was mended—all put to rights and the horse led to the top of the hill. The Boat Owner waddled along grumbling—

"He didn't know there was so many ups and downs in the whole county as there seem to be on this . . . road."

"Dar say not," sezs the driver. "Yew live and larn—walk on a bit, it'll save the old hoss, long way to Lus-toft this time o' night."

"So it seem," sezs the Boat Owner, "and we pays for it tew, what would yew think, Driver, if yew had paid a fare by road, rail and sea and then had ter walk? Yew'd soon begin to grumble, I'm thinking. Reckon yew and that tarnishin' old hoss 'ull be the death of me."

"Stop him," I sezs, "and let's be getting on board. We shan't be there afore morning as it is."

Up we all got once more and the Driver brush the old hoss along saying we are not above two mile from Beccles. The Boat Owner he know Beccles well and they starts talking about old Sarah Ann what keep the Cat and Fiddle Inn, an old friend—if one can put it so, of more than one of them—had many a spree with her when she was young—and it does not take 'em long to make up their minds to pay a call.

The driver whips up the old hoss who thinks a stable's not far ahead, and off we goes rattling and bumping over the stones, making such a din at that hour of night heads come out of windows a'wondering what wild lot is a'coming. We knocks up old Sarah Ann who asks the Driver what on earth brought him there with a crew like that in the middle of the night? But when she see the Boat Owner her face was all smiles and they gets joking about the times they had years ago.

"Don't seem to me only the other day," says Sarah, and the Boat Owner sezs it seem to him he have come to the time of life when he can do with seeing her again—she don't look to him much different to what she allus did, and she laugh pleased as a woman always will be with a bit of butter, and tells him to give over, she's the Mother of seven sons and six daughters and has done with all that nonsense, and asks how long we be thinking of stopping?

The Boat Owner say he isn't in no hurry, and she tells one of her boys to come and play the fiddle while she get a cup of tea for the company with a drop of summat to liven it.

The boy start playing dancing tunes and the gals were quickly on their feet and pulled us from our seats and soon all the company was spinning round the room till the Boat Owner sezs he can't stand no more of that, he's getting too heavy for the job, and flop down. Then in come Sarah with the drinks having a good eye to business, and all started lowering down the pints.

All was enjoying of themselves when the Driver calls out—

We'd best be getting a move on if we was to be in Lowestoft afore daylight, and Sarah say, if they don't soon be clearing out of her house she will be having the police after her.

So the driver goes out to see to the horse, the others to the backyard, and I see the Boat Owner standing in front of the fire fumbling first in one pocket and then in t'other, while a change come over his face. It turned red as a cock's comb and where there had been all smiles he looked like the devil ripe for mischief, then without a word walked out into the street.

Sarah makes up the fire and took up the old kettle saying she'd no doubt we'd like a cup of tea with summat short in it afore we went to warm up our crops. Out she goes to fill it, and a minute later I heard the daughter laugh and say,

"They'll never think of that," and something splash into the water, and presently back she come and put it on the fire. At that minute in comes the Boat Owner and she says she's just getting a cup of tea.

"None of that old woman's drink for me," says he, "seem to me missus there's summat wrong in this house, I fancy yew 'er got some thieves about."

"Not that I knows on—let me find 'em out doin' anything wrong, I'll sune roust 'em," says she. "Best conducted Public in the town, and I'll thank you not to miscall it."

The Boat Owner brings his fist down on the table with a crash that made the cups dance in the saucers and lets out at her—

"So that may be but I'll tell yer straight some of yer party har had me fur fifty quid to-night, and I'll thank yew to find out where it is afore I leave this room, yew runty old bitch."

"Yew drunken lot o' devils, coming to a respectable house and kicking up the hell of a row at this time o' night. I treats all on yar well and then yew got cheek enough to swear I robbed yew. I'll let yew know I'm honest as yew are, and so 'ull my folks. Yew ha' lost yer money at the Snobs Race Meeting—I know well enough they 'er a Rum Click—would rob a blind Grandmother of her breakfast and then call her an old fule—yer a dirty lot of swine, the lot of yew . . ."

The Boat Owner and his pals started a'hollerin' at her and there was a pretty shindy going on when in come two Bobbies and want to know what all the noise is about, and why we are all on licensed premises at that time of night. Every one starts telling their own story and at last they tells Sarah they will have to search the premises.

"Look where yew likes, Gents," says she, "only be careful when yew goes into my Lodgers' bedrooms, and don't disturb 'em, there's one or two ladies as might take it amiss. One thing I can tell yew, yew wont find no loose money lying round up there!"

So they looks round in the cupboard and find nothing and begin to question the Boat Owner as to if he can swear he had the money when he come from the Race Meeting, and Sarah says it was more than time we was getting out and the house shut and they had best take their cup of tea and be gone. She passes it round, the Old Salts taking their share, but they were very quiet, thinking more than talking.

Sam the driver, was artful enough to have kept outside till called for, but he soon had the old hoss coupled up, we gets into the cart, me in my old place under the seat, and off we go joggin' along.

"I don't know, Old Hoss," says Sam, "Seems as though yew-er half asleep, shall hetter wake yew up," and rising from his seat, whip stock in hand, he gives the mare a welt on the ribs. She bolts forrard and at that instant both traces broke, the tugs slipped off the shafts, and Sam clinging to the reins went flying from his seat into the hard road. Down went the cart breaking both shafts, the Boat Owner and the two Old Salts pitching out head first with me on top, which was a bit of luck. What them sea-faring beauties said about the Snob's Race Meeting, the driver, and Sarah Ann I need not repeat, but it was good hearing.

Sam still lying in the road calls out to us to hold the old hoss, that he was pulling his arms out.

"That would not be much loss," says the Boat Owner. "What I can see of it this blankety job's your doin'. Talk about drivin' us to Lus-toft, we could ha' walked it in the time, and I'll have that two quid back I was fule enough to give yew."

"Yew great old Blow-Broth," says Sam, "it would take a better man than yew tu du that." The Boat Owner collared Sam by the neck, put one knee on his chest and starts picking his pockets, with Sam yelling blue murder and one of the Old Salts stuffing his fist in his mouth. That soon come to an end as round the corner come the police again, and before I knew where we was they had arrested the Boat Owner and the Old Salts and off with them to the Lock-up, having had enough of them for one night. Finding Old Sam can't stand, they rigs up a stretcher and carts him away to the Station as the best way out of trouble and ask me where I come from. When I tells them they say I'd best be off home to my Mother, and in no time I was left alone.

I stood a few minutes thinking what I had best do, and thought I'd see if Sarah Ann would let me stop till daylight.

There was a rush light still burning in the kitchen and they had been much too excited to lock the outside door. She looked up sharply as I come in and I heard her say to her daughter—

"There's that perishing boy back again, thought the door was locked . . . put the money away and the kettle back on the fire. What are yew doing back here all alone . . . where 'er them others?"

I told her what had happened and asked her if I could stay till daylight?

"No, that yew can't," said she. "Seen enough of yew already, look to me as if we shall all get locked up if we have much more to do with that lot. Clear out, and git back where yew come from as best yew can, or yew'll git my toe up against your backside."

She locked the door on me and that was the last I saw of that Click. There I was outside in the dark, it being all hours and me having to pay the price of my six mile free ride.

I don't remember much of how I got home that night, nothing

but a'goin' along with my eyes standing well out from their sockets and my ears pricked up, and, thinking had I wings, I would have taken to them. As it was I had to trust—like Old Sally[1], with her full eyes set back fixed on a pursuing enemy—to the fleetness of my feet.

Seemed to me as if I were miles from anywhere on that long dark road home, half scared out of my wits with the thought of Ghosts, Demons, and Devils, every time I heard an owl hoot, saying as they do—"Who-o-o are you-u-u."

Having got down Watch House Hill I tried to take a short cut over the marshes and came a cropper down a bank. When I picked

[1]A hare.

myself up I found my knee was out of my trousers and my jacket in rags and I'd lost my cap, but that did not worry me, as I was only a mile from home. I got across the marshes and landed on the turnpike and soon come to the long lane which led to our shanty, a narrow path with just room for one to walk, the hedges meeting over the top, and in a minute or two was home and the door shut.

Happy Jack was in kip and hollered out what was I a'doin' of, and I told him what happened and how the others had all git locked up afore we were half way there.

"Tha's no more than I 'spected, thowt they'd make a mess on-it. Don't want to hear no more er-bout that, git you off to kip."

So I went and slept the hours round, thinking I was lucky to have got home alive and no bones broke, and that I would give the Snobs company a wide berth. Which I did, not wanting to become a Snob and sit nose and knees together on a waxey seat from morn till night and night till morn.

The Ploughman's Song

Our Master said, "Rise my good fellows, come rise with a will,
Your horses want something their bellies to fill,"
When four o'clock comes boys, up does he rise,
And into the stable merrily flies,
With rubbing and scrubbing, I will swear and vow,
We are all jolly fellows who follow the plough.

When six o'clock comes boys, at breakfast we meet,
Of beer, bread and pork so hastily eat,
A piece in our pocket to take us along,
All through the day come right or come wrong.
So trampling and whistling I swear and I vow,
We are all jolly fellows that follow the plough.

Then we harness our horses and away we all goes
And trip o'er the plain as nimbly as does.
When we come to it so jolly and bold,
We see which of us the straight furrow can hold.
With share and with coulter I swear and I vow,
We are all jolly fellows that follow the plough.

Our Master came to us and thus he did say;
"What have you been doin' boys all the long day,
This field should be ready to harrow and sow,
'Tis working not whistling that makes the corn grow.
You have not ploughed an acre I swear and I vow,
You are all lazy fellows who follow the plough."

I stepped up to him and I made the reply,
"We have all ploughed an acre and that is no lie,"
He turned him around and he laughed at the joke,
Saying "It's past three o'clock boys, and time to unyoke.
Unharness your horses for I swear and I vow,
You are all jolly fellows who follow the plough."

CHAPTER XI

Never, never, let your gun
Pointed be at any one!
That it may not loaded be
Matters not at all to me!
Nursery Rhyme.

As the old saying is, where the one is there must the other be also, and so it was with an old catcher known as Eel Joe, a sloe-eyed old varmint who made his living catching eels—he did not trouble how or where he got them. His pots were a kind of wicker-work basket, open at one end and about three feet in length and six inches across, and were baited with worms.

His lines or "liggers" as he called them, were strong pieces of cord seven or eight yards long with one or two stout fish hooks made fast on one end and baited with young birds heads, or anything of the sort he could get hold of. The other end was fastened to a small stake, and fixed at a suitable spot on the bank, the line being left all night. Many a time I have seen him drawing in his liggers with a four or five pound eel securely hooked, me looking on with a wistful eye thinking he would lay his pots in my Mother's pantry were there eels to be had. He had 'em laid within twenty yards of our house as it was, and I have seen him take from them a good sized pail full of eels day after day and felt real angry, knowing there were hundreds of other places he could have laid them. Struck me we were Sammies to let him do it and determined to make some eel pots for myself. When I asked him to show me how to do it he grinned at me and said:

"What Bor! . . . shew yew how, that 'ont du tew shew yew how to make pots, yew'll then be takin' away my livin'. Best thing yew can du is ter find out, same as I did. What's the use of having brains if yew can't use 'em. Yew got to look out and prog fur yar self. No good thinkin' folks'll carry yew, corse they 'ont."

I stood looking at him shoving rushes through the whole length of the worms for baiting his pots, it made my blood run cold to see him and I said—

"Poor things, that must hurt 'em something cruel."

"That don't hurt 'em, Bor . . . must git my living."

Yes, thought I, don't seem as if yew trouble, not about hurting anything or anybody as long as yew get an easy living. Dare not say so but thought it.

I was now determined to make some eel pots for myself as Eel Joe wouldn't tell me how to start but to find out for myself. I thinks, yes, so I will, soon as you're gone home I'll get one of your pots and have a good look at it, and see how it's made.

After having taken all the eels out that he had caught the night before, his custom was to see if any of the pots wanted repairing, and if they did he done 'em at once, then they was laid in fleet[1] water until

[1]Shallow.

the afternoon, when he would, with the massacred worms threaded on rushes, bait each pot.

He took four rushes and passed them one by one through the wicker work of the pot below the spikes at the top end, then tied them together from the outside. As each one was baited he put it in his heater-shaped boat ready for layin' out just before dark, near the banks of the river. He would lay them with the mouth, or trap entrance, facing down stream in shallow water with gravel or sandy bottom. Being set to find out what I could about eels I asked him what difference that made where they was laid?

"Don't yar know, Bor," says he, "eels clean thar selves in shallow places where the bottom be sandy or gravel stones, and there's another thing I'll tell yew, and don't yew ferget it. Eels and fish when they are on the feed allus' feed up stream. That's the reason why I lay my Bops with their mouths facing down stream, then they lay riddy for the eels to go in and take the bait. They tug and pull to get the worms off the rushes, and if they goes to turn and git out the same way as they come in the sharp spikes prick 'em and they bolt through the long cone-shaped part of the trap which opens and lets 'em through, then closes again. Ivery eel what goes through there has my name on it. All I has to do is to take the plug out and shake 'em in my pail. That's the reason I puts that long stick through when I be baiten' of 'em, to shift any weeds and make sure the traps are clear. Now do you begin to see?"

"Yes," says I, "it du seem there's a lot more to catchin' eels than I thought of."

"Ah," says he, "that's so, there's a lot to learn and yew be only a pup as yet."

When I tells him I can't be that else I should have four legs and a tail to wag he laughs, looks at me with a twinkle in his little piercing black eyes, and says I don't want no tail, my tongue wags overmuch as it is, and if I live to get as old as he is, and weather all the storms he has, I may begin to know a thing or two.

"How old are you, Joe?" says I.

"Sixty five and been catching eels all my life, and there ain't any one as can tell me more about 'em than I know. Don't care who he is nor where he come from. You'll allus git more eels on a sandy or gravelly bottom where there's willows and osiers growin' on the bank. That's the reason I make my pots of that sort of stuff. I very often have tied up a bundle of osiers and sunk 'em in the river and arter a day or so chucked 'em out quick with er crome[1] and got er stone er eel that way."

I had now learnt all I wanted for a time and was looking forward to the moment when I should be laying pots of my own make, which I felt would not be long if I was left alone, so that I could get on.

First I got a quantity of osiers suitable for the purpose, and laid them in the sun for a day or two to toughen so they would be better for working. I then took nine good-sized osiers, peeled and trimmed 'em and flattened the thick ends, cutting them to a skewer-like point, and so had the nine ribs or mainstays ready to start. Now come the difficult part, how was I to make a cone-shaped mouth or entrance, with spikes pointing inward.

I started to braid the nine ribs together to form a round about six inches across and made a very poor hand at it—my braiding osiers were much too thick, and it looked as if I was trying to imitate cobble stone paving. I unbraided the lot, thinking well, that's only one failure, and by it I was gaining experience, and I had not spoilt the ribs or stays so I did not mind. I got another lot ready for braiding, cutting them much thinner and made a fresh start, but found it a difficult job to hold the nine ribs in place while I was forming the entrance or mouth of the pot. However, I kept trying and trying, and after a time I managed to braid up to the outer edge of the entrance.

My next job was to turn over the ribs to form the baiting part of the pot. I gave each rib a twist so that it loosened the grain and they would easily bend where wanted, and then bent them all over to-

[1]Crome—an instrument like a fork, with a long handle—the prongs bent over for dragging weeds from dykes.

wards the middle or waist and kept them at equal distances apart, they forming a circle of about three inches across and bound them with string to keep them in place. Then I started to weave over and under the ribs from where I had left off, and slowly but steadily got it finished to the middle.

The next thing to do was to put in the trap. I now wanted nine thin pieces of willow wood about an inch wide and nine inches long —the thickness of thin cardboard—and from about one third of the

length I began to cut the edges away towards one end, and brought that to a point. I then cut the other end—had now two tapered ends, one three inches long, the other six. The three inch end I pushed in between the ribs and wicker work, carefully putting them into position close together, forming a cone-like trap that would easily open and let an eel through, and once it was through, close again to a point, leaving no chance for the eel to get back again.

Now the trap was made the next thing was to set all the ribs at right angles and weave all round so as to leave plenty of room when the ribs were brought over for the eels to swim round the trap. Not easy, but I persevered and got all the weaving done over the bend, and it was now straight away work to the tail end. I left a hole about two inches across into which I fitted a long willow wood plug, tapered at one end for a good fit.

There you are, Eel Joe, thought I, as I looked at my first eel trap with pride, I made a trap arter all; but when I come to put in the water it floated, the osiers being dry.

What was I to do . . . couldn't wait a fortnight or three weeks while it got saturated with water like Eel Joe's, so got a couple of old bricks, weighted it down, and laid it in fleet water just afore dark, baited with a dead frog. Soon as it was daylight I was up after my pot, taking the crome I had made for the job from the handle of a pail partly straightened out and bound on a pole.

When I was drawing the pot ashore with my wonderful crome I could see the tails of several eels 'pearing through the wicker work, but as I drew it nearer the shore to land it, eel after eel dropped into the water, and by the time I had it in my hand there weren't an eel left in my lovely pot. They had got out again by getting their tails in between the wicker work of the pot (which I had not put close enough together). The eels had left holes big enough for me to get my fingers through.

I was now finding out what Eel Joe had told me . . . talking was one thing—doing is another, and was now wiser than when I started, knowing that the eels wedged-shaped tails and the slippery surface of their skins was a natural means for them to make their escape. If any one examines the formation of their tails they will find out they are on the principle of two inclined planes, base to base. With its muscular strength and fins the eel can exert pressure on the water at an angle and drive itself forward at a great speed—a natural principle of movement.

It had not occurred to man until about the year 1832 that he could use the same principle in a spiral form, until the impulse of some genius made a propeller whereby ships can be driven from shore to shore of the ocean. By the principle of the inclined plane he can soar up into space, and now makes himself a thousand and one devices for his use.

Experience teaches wisdom. I did not lose heart even if I had lost all my eels, but looked upon it as the price I had to pay for learning. I got together a lot more osiers suitable for the ribs and the wicker work, peeled and then dried them in the sun a bit, and as some were too large for weaving, split them in halves with an old knife. I found that was a slow process and wanted some other scheme quicker than that; so I sharpened up a piece of hard wood about three inches long to a wedge or chisel-like edge about one inch and a half across its cutting edge. On trying it first one end of the osier and then the other, I found the best end to split them was from the top, for the grain of the wood runs in parallel lines with the pith of the osiers, and found I could get three out of some osiers.

As it happened I had a piece of hard box-wood, cut a length three inches long, rounded it up at one end to about two inches then tapered it off to about one at the other, then cut out three equal tapered pieces. I then had three cutting edges on the small tapered end in tripod form and had completed my new device.

I trimmed the small end of an osier, split it into three with my knife, took what I called my triple splitter and found with care it did the job well, cutting the osier into three equal pieces. Was now getting on like an old house a'fire.

Was doubtful about starting my second pot having found my first awkward to begin, but had a brain wave and made a mould or templet[1] from a piece of board three quarters of an inch thick, the size I wanted. I bored nine holes to fix the ribs and form the mouth or entrance with corresponding slots on the cutter edge to fix the ribs in position when brought over, and made it in two halves so I could get it out when the wicker work was done.

Then I made another templet for the middle part near by the trap and was now ready to begin putting the ribs in their places. That was soon done and I began braiding under and over the wicker work

[1]Templet. An instrument used as gauge or guide in bringing any piece of work to the desired shape.

of osiers, and in about an hour had the entrance made and was ready to bend the ribs over that would form the first half of the pot. Having done that, tied all the ribs in their places and went on with the wicker work up to the middle of the pot where the trap was to be put. I now bent the ribs over to form the back end, tied them down to another templet, cut off the ribs the right length, put in the wood plug and

worked my wicker work round it. Then I drew out the plug and finished off the wicker work by braiding in reaved osiers and had now completed my second pot. The osiers were all wove close and tight this time, if an eel went through the trap he was mine. I laid it in the dyke to get soaked with water and thought well—one ain't much—I'll make a dozen.

Next day was up with the lark and at my job until owl's light at night, and in about three weeks had about a dozen pots made, which I was not ashamed of, as I reckoned they were as good as Eel Joe's.

I had already made myself a heater-shaped boat something after the manner of Eel Joe's. It looked more or less like an old-fashioned laundry maid's box iron that she smooth down and take the ruts out of clothes with. Was soon aboard my liner loaded up with eel pots feeling as proud as Johnny Gant. I never had the pleasure of knowing that celebrity, but understood he was a seven stone man propped up with unprofitless pride and as artful as a wagon load of monkeys.

When baiting my pots one afternoon who should come along but Eel Joe, shuffling and muttering towards me with his little black eyes on the flash, and says in a quick hasty voice—

"Now I know where my pots go tew, I kept on lose-en-on-'em, one or tew at a time, reckon I know who the thief is now."

"Yar can think what yew like, Mr. Shove-at-the-Wheel," sezs I, "Hain't stole yer old pots, I made all them merself."

"That's a lie, I know, they looks zactly like the new 'uns I lost."

"Werry likely too, took the patterns off yours and made a dozen for meself."

"Well, yew-er made a good job on 'um. What-er yar goin' to du wor-'em?"

"That's my business, not yours, but since yar askin' I'm a'goin' to lay 'em and catch eels. I'm not a'goin' to let yew have the lot, arter what yew said that I'd been a'pinchin' yar pots. Yew reckon yarself so high-and-mighty, and think that nobody done know anything only yew and can't make an eel pot. Tell yew what Mr. Know-All, yew can take yar pots and boat and slide off, we kin git on werry well wi'out a selfish ole varmint like yew."

He give me such a look I thought as how I was going to get a clout on the head, but he think better of it and cleared off. A good riddance he were, too, and I could lay my pots without fear of them being pinched. Now and then I lost one or two by laying them too near in to deep water or on the edge of a hole, so they rolled down out of reach, but not many—and I went on catching eels for many years and very paying things they were, always having a good market.

The way to get the biggest catches in the shortest time is by babbing. For this I wanted another handier boat and set to work to build one. I had saved up a few shillings to buy wood but the question was what about measurements. Soon I thought of a plan.

I walked boldly into the yard at Bungay, where the boats were hired, and took one I liked the look of for half an hour, rowed it up stream and soon was round the bend of the river and out of sight. I had not got a rule of any sort but took all my measurements with a piece of string, and soon got the length, breadth, and depth, made sure they were right and tied a knot for each, and was back again with my boat well within my time.

I went home and made a start and once going was so interested in it—while building—that I worked at it all one day, then lighting two candles about seven to go on the early part of the night. Was so much engrossed in what I was doing that I forgot even my own presence, and went on working until I found the candles were growing dim and going out, and when I come to look round found it was daylight. I was surprised to think that I had been working fourteen hours, and thought no more of the passing of time than I should have done had I been asleep.

The boat finished I was ready to go babbing. Any one who needs a good bab for eel catching must have one long darning needle. If that is not at hand he can make one with a piece of fine wire, turn one end to form an eye and bring the other to a point with a file. Then he must get about a yard and a half of worsted so when the eels bite at the babs their teeth hang in the wool, the eel give a pull and the babber with a quick steady lift, land the eel in the boat or bath he must have with him, or an old umbrella does well at a pinch.

Thread your worms (large earth worms are best) on the worsted, tie the two ends together and coil them up into a bunch about four inches long and tie them together in one place with a strong piece of small cord about five feet long. Then weight with an old iron nut or a piece of lead of about an ounce, with a hole in the centre. Pass your string through and let it slip down on the top of the bab, and fix to a hazel stick about five foot long. Then you will be ready for some sport with those queer, amphibious creatures, which seem to be on the feed to any extent when the wind is from the south or south-west.

Their natural element is water but they need to clean themselves, and do that on gravel and sandy bottoms and in among the roots of willows and osiers close to the water's edge, where the roots grow out in bunches and look like chimney-sweeps brushes.

Choose a warm still dark night, a freshly-made bab, water about four feet deep as close to the shore as possible, and if you are babbing from the shore take a stool to sit on. Place your bath or umbrella handy, so as to get the right swing of your bab to land the eels where you want them, for when he feels he is out of the water he will loose the bab in a moment. If he lands on the grass he will be back in the water again before you can start looking for him. Be sure to keep the bab clear of the bottom, letting it touch gently now and then, as if it is laying there you will not know when the eels is biting and pulling your bab to pieces.

The most I ever got at one sitting was a hundred and seven, between twelve and two one dark night in July. Eels prefer darkness when they feed, why I cannot say, but when the moon come up and sailed out over the Common I got no more bites and come away home, the bottom of the boat covered with eels.

Eels are migratory and will move by night when the atmosphere is warm and wet, wriggling out of the river into the low-lying marsh land into ponds, dykes, and ditches. I have sat sometimes on nights like this quietly by the river and heard hundreds of them making a sucking noise, with their heads just above water, moving among the reeds and rushes after anything that can be eaten. Seem to me that eels have neither taste nor smell, and are but scavengers like the crocodile.

I remember one poor fellow that was drowned a little way from the house, whether accidentally or not I must leave. Anyway, about six weeks after his body was found entangled in some bushes hanging over the river so they held the body against the stream when it come up, until a man fishing come on it by chance. When drawn ashore it was found to contain a large quantity of eels.

There is one peculiar thing about them, they will not bite when the wind is blowing from the east or any cold quarter, also they are very much affected by heavy rains and thunder storms which bring soil into the river. The change in the water upsets the eels, and they swim down stream near the bottom for a night or two.

The water Miller, or any one accustomed to their habits, set nets

across the river made fast each side with a heavy iron chain, which goes across the bottom of the front of the net to keep it down. A top line runs along the top of the net which need not be level with the surface of the water, as it is sure to be pulled down by the force of the stream, and, when about a foot below the surface, will allow the floating weeds to pass and not block up the net and wash it away, which have happened many a time.

When this net is properly set it tapers off to a tail-like point about twenty inches long into which the eels collect and can be tied with cord before taking them out. The longer the "poke" is the better, as it can more easily be drawn ashore or into a boat. He who undertakes to catch eels in this manner know very well he must always be near and handy to keep his net clear of weeds . . . they are few and far between who have made a fortune catching eels with a net of this kind.

I remember very well one day Father telling me and my brother to go and have a look at his net set by the bridge. We felt ourselves great men pulling up the poke, and thought at first a log of wood had got into it, it was so heavy, but soon found it was a great old eel about three foot long and weighing about half a stun. We carefully got it out and put it in a deep bushel skep and covered it with a sack, pleased as punch to think we had got the biggest eel we had ever seen in our lives. We were just putting the net back in position again when to our surprise up go the sack and out come the eel, over the top of the skep, tail first, and like a flash splounced into the river, we hoping it would go down stream and into our net again, but no such luck.

We dare not tell Father we had got a whopping great eel and then lost it, or he would have threshed us till we were black and blue, so keepin' very quiet we went indoors—thought to ourselves what the eye hath not seen the heart does not grieve for.

Father look up and sezs, "What yar got, boys?"

"Nothing," sezs we—and he goes back to his pipe.

"'Spect they done runnin'," sezs he, "tain't no manner o' use arter the third night of thick water."

We thought we was well away with that, but before night I was in trouble of another sort.

Father had an old muzzle-loading gun and like most boys getting on in their teens I longed to have a shot. I had been warned not to touch it, but my fingers itched. That evening Father went off, as he did most evening, on affairs we knew little of and often found it best not to guess, and I had my chance and took the gun out of the cupboard by the fireplace where it was kept. Not thinking it was loaded —as there was no cap on—I got a cap out of the box which lay handy.

I put it on the nipple and took the old barking-iron outside to have my first shot, with only a cap as I thought. Levelled the gun at a small plum tree near by and let fly and can thank my lucky stars I did not aim at any living thing, much less one of the cats or Father's old dog, for off it went bang—a full charge of shot into the plum tree, cutting it in halves. Not prepared for the kick—and she kick like a mule, that old gun—over I went heels over head. Was more frightened than hurt, but where the stock struck my shoulder I was black and blue for weeks.

As it happened Father weren't far away, hears the gun go off, come up behind me and see his plum tree blown in half, and me with the gun. He come on with that quiet way he had, saying never a word, caught me back of the collar and started to measure the length of his broad leather strap across my poor thin little behind, till I was a mass of bruises fore and aft, top and bottom, learning me the lesson not to interfere with other people's things. I never touched the old gun again and after a time it disappeared, Father having lent it to a miller he was friendly with.

I had had enough of monkeying with guns and thought I had best keep to the game I knew.

It happen money was a bit short at that time, and any one of us who have been hard up know from experience that hunger and thirst are bitter thorns. Many a time through no fault of my parents I have gone hungry to bed, and remember only too well that I have had to rake and scrape a few rags and bones in order to get the coppers needed for a loaf of bread. Between all of us it was just a thumb piece, the rest of the meal made up of swedes, turnips, or anything eatable that came to hand. We filled our pods[1] and were content with what we got, mostly believing what we were told—that good things come to them that wait.

When it come to it that we did not see butcher's meat more than once a month I thinks to myself—

"Yes, wait and go on waiting—till Doomsday in the afternoon,

[1]Pods—stomach. A puppy distended is said to be "poddy."

suffin' must be done or we'll be half starved. Must git a move on and look out for myself."

Had now found out that if I had an aching tooth or an empty stomach I knew where the pain was or the maggot bit better than any one else could tell me, and so I become a mid-night warrener.

On a heath not more than a mile away there was a warren about 100 yards in extent covered with furze and bracken with a line of hillocks in the centre honeycombed with holes. At the time I thought these were natural, but afterwards found they were barrows in which our ancestors disposed of their dead. If I had known I should not have been so brave, being only a nipper at the time, but I knew there were hundreds of rabbits there which made my fingers itch and my mouth water.

Had been told by a farmer that forecasting was as good as work, so took his tip and set to going over the purse nets that had got all bit up with the rats in the sand pit. Found this time it were a tedious job making the mesh with my fingers so made myself a netting needle of elder which is a hard, yellow, close-grained wood with plenty of spring in it. This answered the purpose well and in a few days once more had a score of rabbit nets ready.

Now had all I wanted except my Father's ferret which I must borrow. I picked a still star-lit night, slipped out of the house when all the rest were in kip, took the "cat" out of her locker and away across the fields and soon got to the warren.

Quiet as I was the rabbits heard me and thumping with their hind legs (as their habit is when scared) made for the burrows, which suited me well. Set the nets over all the likely holes and turned my ferret in—she was a white one, being easier to work at night than a polecat[1]—and chanced my luck, thinking the first rabbit that I got I would tie a string on one of its legs and drag it round the hillocks, so if the cat came out the other side she would scent round on the trail to where I was—otherwise it was easy to lose her, especi-

[1]Polecat. Polecat ferret, which are dark in colour.

ally as she wern't coped[1], ferrets working better with their muzzles free.

In a minute or two out bolted a rabbit from a free hole and then another into one of my nets. I was glad, and soon put paid to that as it was creepy standing there under the stars doing nothing, with no sound on all that big place except a little sough of wind in the furze, and the whoo-whoo of an owl in the wood by the railway behind me.

The ferret come out a moment later, and I slipped her into her bag while I drew the rabbit all round the hillock on the grass and then turned her in again. Soon there was a proper pampling[2] inside the warren and the rabbits started bolting in all directions, some out of un-netted holes, others two or three into the same net dragging the stakes away and rolling over and over. In this way, although some escaped, I got five more, and they were soon at rest with their fathers.

The ferret had not shown itself this time so I stood quietly waiting when I heard something shuffling in one of my nets, pounced on it in the usual way and give a yell that should have raised up them old bounders in the barrows if they were waiting on the Judgment call.

It was a hedgepig coming out to take his nightly stroll, and well I knew it when I gets hold of his spikes and turned it out of the net with a fling and a good send off with the toe of my boot. I had need to be careful now with the blood running from my fingers as if I picked up the ferret I was likely to be badly bit. A minute later round the barrow come my ferret loping along the trail I had made, she having come out t'other side to what I was working, and I carefully gets hold of her quick at the back of the neck, as the smell of blood madden 'em.

Thought I would have one more try and turns her in again a bit further along. Nothing happens for a while and I huddles down

[1]Coped or cooped, muzzled—from Anglo-Saxon "Cops"—a fetter. Ferrets unmuzzled are apt to kill and suck a rabbit and lie up, but when muzzled often not keen to work.

[2]Pampling. To pample is to trample lightly. Possibly from the Old English "pomple"—to stumble.

under a furze bush to wait as it was getting chilly. Presently I heard a shriek quite close at hand that sound for a minute like a child, and give me such a start the hair lift on my head, until I realised I weren't the only one hunting that night, and it was a stoat as had fastened on a rabbit near by. Once on the trail they are so set on their prey they take heed of nothing, and will come almost to one's feet when the blood lust gets them.

Just after that out bolts another rabbit and after it the ferret. Thinks I, I have now got seven and wont risk losing the cat, so I slips her in, ties up the bag tight, and puts her into the pocket of Father's old frock coat I had pinched for the evening's outing. It had what is called poachers pockets—the ferret went in one the nets in the other, and I slung the rabbits on my back and off I go, some hanging in front and some behind.

I got round the second barrow when I heard something blowing and saw a short distance in front a white object. It gave me such a fright I dropped the rabbits and lay down flat, with my ticker hammering against my ribs and the blood drumming in my ears. After a bit as nothing happens I has another peep, and see it's naught but an old white horse grazing as had seen me and given a snort. Felt about as wise as Waltham's calf which went nine miles to suck a bull, or, as the meaning is—a proper fool.

Shouldered my load again and them as has carried rabbits across ploughed fields and over fences (which is the way I went), and a ferret and nets into the bargain, knows they can be mortal heavy, and I was not sorry to turn into the yard in the early hours of morning. Put the ferret in the locker and gave her a feed of the rabbits guts, hid up my catch and away to kip, no one the wiser as I had not seen a single soul saving the white horse, and the rabbits carried no names on their tails.

The Farmer and the Maid

An old Farmer came from the Northland
Of him I have to tell,
By a fair Maid's house he took his stand,
Many a mile from his own home land.

"Come forth" he cried "to a Bridegroom bold,
For I will marry thee,
And carry thee to the Northland cold,
Set by a darksome sea.

"First gather ye up your Father's gold,
And all your Mother's money.
Bring two of his nags to the Northland cold,
Two nags for you and for me."

Then up she took her Father's gold,
And some of her Mother's money,
From her Father's stall two horses bold,
To ride so fast and free.

She mounted up the milk white nag,
And he ups on the Derby Grey,
They rode till they come to the broad water's side,
Three hours before it was day.

"Fall off fall off your milk white nag,
Deliver him up to me,
I think he looks too rich and rare,
To rot in the salt salt sea.

"Pull off pull off your silken gown,
Your petticoats one two three,
For they also shall not sink down
To rot in the salt salt sea."

"If I must pull off my silken dress
My petticoats one two three,
Then turn you before I bare my breast,
Pray turn your back to me!"

She cried again upon his name
"Oh, turn your back to me,
It is not fit for a man of shame
A naked woman to see!"

So he turned his back his broad backside
And was viewing the grass so green,
When she seized him in her hands so small
And flopped him into the stream.

He swam high and he swam low,
Until he came to the side.
"Reach out your hand my pretty fair maid,
And you shall be my bride."

"Lay there! lay there! you deceitful man,
Lay there in the stead of me.
For six pretty maids have you drownded here
But the seventh has drownded thee."

Then she mounted up the milk white nag,
And she led the Derby Grey,
She rode till she came to her Father's hall,
Three hours before it was day.

CHAPTER XII

All you that stand before the fire,
To see you sit is my desire;
That others may, as well as you,
See the fire and feel it too.

Since man to man is so unjust,
None can tell what man to trust;
I've trusted many to my sorrow,
Pay to day, trust to-morrow.
Painted over a fireplace in a house at Mulbarton.

AUTUMN COME round once more and there were no more eels to be had, but I was out to earn a shilling if I could.

Had my eye on a hurdle and rake makers near by that had been carried on from father to son for generations—employing about two men all the year round. If business was brisk they might set on a green hand for a time, trimming the bark off poles for hurdles, rake handles and scythe sticks. Special orders would always be given not to trim any pole with a crutch on the end of a suitable size for an old lady's linen prop.

The Boss of this hurdle makin' business was known by one and all as Old Chips, and he was another one of the old school. If he set any one on for a few weeks and they cut the bark off themselves instead of the poles, he would not care a hang, only say—

"Shave the bark off the poles, that's what I pays yer for," and curse 'em for not being more careful. He would have laughed at the thought of "Workmen's Compensation."

On old Chips's hurdle making yard I had often cast a wistful eye. Thought I should dearly like to git a job there and learn to make hurdles and rakes for the farmers round about. One day in the spring time, watching from the gateway what was goin' on inside,

I could see coming along the road a double shafts wagon drawn by a pair of horses, loaded up with young ash poles and other hard wood such as nuttery. I stepped clear of the gateway and as it turned in along come Old Chips at the shuffle, saying,

"Glad yew-er here wur them poles, Bor, thowt as how I should have ter send someone else arter 'em."

"Dunno hew'd ha' been fule enough tew ar gone arter 'em—got to go near up ter yer ass in mud ter git at 'em. One of the master jobs ever I had in my life—'spose yew don't know where they cut the ten acre fell this year? Well, Bor, I'll tell yer, right the fudder side er the Hundred Acre Wood and arter I'd loaded up and started to drive out I hain't got above fifty yard when in go the wheels up to the hobs."

Old Chips look over the horses steaming up like a cloud, big hammer-spotted[1] greys they was, and the wagon cluttered with mud, and go grumbling off, saying the team-man should have made two load of it instead of dragging the guts out of the hosses. The team-man gave him a black look saying—

"He's like a good many more on 'em—think he know every thing, and such as me know nothin' for all he only makes wooden hosses for ole wimmen to hang the duds on, and never touched a live hoss if he could help it. If I han'ter got 'em in one load as he told me he'd 'er swore holes trow-me, and 'praps told me to take my hook off ther place. If yew want to stop on it yer gotter bite yer tongue, that's a sure thing. As t'was I had to git a couple of trace horses to give us a haul."

Back come Old Chips in a better mind, tells the team-man to come along and get a drink. He throw some sacks on the horses to keep them warm standing, and away they goes over the road to the Pub. At the last he looks back and ask me if I kin do with a job. I tells him that's what I'm after.

"Well then," sezs he, "help my boy Dukey to unload them poles, and mind yew du what he tell yar, then p'raps I might give yew a job another day."

[1]Hammer-spots. The dappling on a horse from Anglo-Saxon "hama."

I had now got a start—to help his boy Dukey as he called him. Dukey standin' head and shoulders over his Father, such a height as I could easily run a'tween his legs. We started to unload the wagon. There was no need for Dukey to git on it, he could stand on the ground and reach the lot, which he did, lumbering the poles down in a hurry, saying—

"Pick up the small 'uns, boy, layen 'em up tidy in a heap over there, and be careful to keep the big ends one way." I chucked off my

cap, slid out of my jacket and slipped into that job for all I was worth.

In about an hour Dukey and I had unloaded the wagon and laid together in separate heaps all the poles that were suitable for hurdles, rakes, hoops, and broaches[1].

"I dunno, boy," sezs Dukey, "Dad and that there team-man are a long while havin' that drink. That the worst o' him, when he git to a Pub, never know when to come away. Reckon one of these times I shall find him grown to ther seat. Look you arter them hosses—I'll gorn see where he is."

The first to come out was the team-man and he'd ha' been a lot better with a good deal less than he'd had, and the beer having gone

[1]Broaches. Rods of sallow or hazel sharpened at each end and bent in the middle like a hairpin, used by thatchers to fix their work. From the French—"Broche."

to his legs he had a shot or two and couldn't git up into the wagon. At last I gives him a leg up, hands him the plough line reins and off they goes, one of the men standing near saying he weren't in no state to take a wagon and hosses up Bridge Street. But Dukey laugh—

"He'll come to no harm in a month er Sundays, did yew ever know a drunken man as didn't light on his feet," said he. After a time Old Chips drew out, looked at the poles, then sezs to me that there wouldn't be no more work that day and to come again to-morrer, and I went along home real pleased with myself.

Next day I got up early and along to the yard arriving at Old Chips' breakfast time. Out he come patting his stummy and sezs, "Well, I er got a good inside lining, Boy—packed away a dozen white herren'[1] and a round or tew er bread, orter dew suffin' on that lot, shan't git no more afore night. Now we'll see what yew kin dew—brought a saw?"

I told him I h'aint got one so he sezs he'll see what he can find me up, and told me to get two trestles as was handy and set them alongside each other, which was quickly done.

We then started laying on poles to be cut up for hurdles. Out come his rod the length of the hurdle and a notch cut on that give the length of the ends, allowing for the end that would be sharpened up for fixing the hurdle in the ground.

"Now then," sezs Chips, "yew want to screw yer nut when cuttin' poles." I looked at him and laughed.

"Yew don't seem to understand me, boy, that's like this, yew want to measure twice a'fore yer cut once then yar 'ont spoil the stuff. I don't waste nothin'. All the short ends are split up fer rake teeth, and ones about eighteen inches long are split to the right size for rake bows or stays. Yar know what I mean, don't yar? If not I'll sune

[1]White herring. Fresh herring, to distinguish them from cured herrings, bloaters and red herrings.

show yew, hand us that rake—dew yew see these two small pieces, them's put there er purpose to keep the head on, worn't for them the rake won't last twenty minutes. Now yer knows what rake stays are and any piece long enough to make teeth—lay it to one side."

I did not want telling twice, looked out and kept clean ones on one heap and ones with knots on another. Presently Chips looked round.

"Where yar got tew, Dukey? What's the good er me gitten this youngster ter help us if yew are gornter fiddle er-bout half mornin' cleanen white herren'. Yew kin dew that there job ter night. Wonter git this stuff cut ter sizes now t'is fine weather, then we shall have plenty er work under cover time it rains."

"Right," calls Dukey, "I'll be there in a squint."

In a few minutes he was on the job, sleeves turned up, telling me if I got busy carrying the cut poles away and stacked them up in the work-shop I shouldn't find much time to put my hands in my pockets. Dukey was right, he kept me going, knowing his job inside out. In about three hours the load of poles—large and small—were all cut up, some for hurdles, others for rake heads, stays, teeth and handles; thinner rods for broaches and hoops for herring tubs. They were all cut the right length and packed away. Then Chips asks me if I think I can do a bit of shaving, and I tell him I don't know about that as my whiskers are not grown yet. Chips laugh till his great belly shake.

"Wait a year or so, boy, then yew wont have no trouble. That's not what I meant—see that there thing with a round handle each end, that's what we calls a shave or draw knife, best tool on earth bar none to clear the bark off wood. Put that piece in the vice, screw it up tight and I'll show yew. This is how it is done. Off come a strip of bark as long as myself."

He then handed me the draw-knife and I soon come to it, though not as quick as Chips, and pleased him so he claps me on the back and sezs he'll make a tradesman of me afore he's done, as I has the makings.

The next job was to split up all the stuff that had been cut for hurdles. They were laid on the trestles and he showed me how, if you want to split a big pole or a small stick, you must allus start at the small or top end, right across the centre of the pitch and in between the knots, if any. The wood splitting tool is a blade about two inches wide and eighteen long, with an eye at one end, set at right angles to the blade and fitted with a strong handle about two feet in length.

I had to hold the big end tight against the chock, he then placed the splitter on the small end, and giving the blade a light tap with a wooden mallet the pole was split down the centre at least a foot. Then with two or three wrings of the handle, down its whole length.

I had to be quick laying them to one side and placing another on the trestles always with the small end next to Chips. He was splitting away with the eye of a hawk, at such a rate it was all I could do to keep going and clear of split stuff and put fresh ones on the trestles. If by chance I did put one the wrong way he would whip it up and twist it round at such a speed I had need to look after my top knot or get it knocked off. Then came the last one and Chips looked up at me said,

"Well, boy, that's the one the Cobbler threw at his wife." I looked puzzled at that so he tells me that years ago there was an old cobbler who had a row with his wife so he ups and hulls the bit of wood at her what he made the boots on, she being an aggrevating old Mawther[1]. The piece of wood is called the 'last' and from that day to this it has been a by word. With which he packs up and tells me to go along home and he'll go across to have a look at the Black Dog and see what he's barking at.

Next day Chips sezs he got an order for a couple of score o' hurdles and they got to be made quick. In those days there was no such thing as boring and morticing machines. All must be made by these expert craftsmen by hand, they finding much contentment in the work and mastery of their tools.

"Full speed ahead," says Chips, "I'll mark 'em out and yew go on

[1]Mawther—literally girl—corrupted often to Mother, from Danish "Moer"—unmarried girl.

pointing the ends which drive in the ground, Dukey, then I'll start the boy boring."

Out come a shell auger looking as if it was the one Noah use when he built the Ark, and picking up a gouge and mallet Chips say he supposes he'd better show me how to start. He takes the auger and with two or three turns it was well in the wood. I felt a bit awkward at first, but crowding away with all my might soon got my first hole through. I did not mind if I could keep just ahead of Dukey who was to finish the mortices off, and as soon as one set was ready they would be putting them together, which would give me a chance to get on with my boring.

The rush was all caused by an afternoon sheep farmer finding that he wanted hurdles in a hurry, and put off doing that which he could have done the day before, and was in a muddle to get a field of swedes fed off and the land manured so he could get to his ploughing. Old Chips was quick to the rescue as his way was when he saw his money, and the farmer was satisfied.

The days went on and the next job I learned was how to make scythe sticks. We first picked out poles of the right sizes and as clear of knots as we could, cut them off to the right length, cleared them of bark and trimmed any knots down level.

"Now," sezs Chips, "I'll show yar, Boy, yew must git 'em all the same size."

He then took hold of a funny sort of shave. It had two long handles and a hole in the centre the size of the rings of the tacks[1], and on the side of the hole was fixed a steel cutter at the right angle, so that when the tool was slipped on the shaft and turned on it, the cutter would cut it to the right size. Then the rings for the tacks could be slipped on and fixed where required by a wedge. Chips did one to show me and then told me to hand him a draw knife and he sharpened one end of the stick to a point. This is done so that when a scythe is stood on end to be sharpened with the rub, or hone, it shall not slip.

[1]Tack—local name for the handles on the scythe stick, from the Dutch "tacke."

Next day, some odd jobs finished, Chips told me to go and fill the big copper in the yard with water, light the fire under and get the water boiling as soon as I could, and be careful I kept the copper lid down tight and let no steam out. He had beat me this time but that started me thinking. On looking round I found there was a long square box near by with a tight-fitting lid, and underneath the bottom of this wood box or steam chest was fixed a tube that led to the copper.

In about half an hour I had steam up and Chips was quickly at the Cook House Door, his shoulder loaded up with scythe sticks. The lid was whipped off the steam chest, the scythe sticks and a couple of bundles of rake bows or stays popped into the steamer. That killed my cat to see wood steamed in this way, a thing I had never seen before. Could understand steaming Norfolk dumplings but not wood.

The lid was put back in its place and fastened with a cross bar.

"There yar, Boy——" says Chips. "Keep a good fire goin' and in about three hours they'll be ready."

I was still in the dark—could not make out what all this steaming was done for, but kept quiet having found out long before questions was apt to git rough answers, and I should find out in due time. Chips comes back after a bit to see what sort of stoker I was, and finding the fire was roaring away and the steam hissing out says—

"That's just what we want, the meat 'll soon be off the bones."

"Yew ain't a'makin' broth," sezs I.

He smiled and scratched the top of his head and walked off, but in a short while was back with Dukey. The lid was opened, out rushed a cloud of steam, Dukey collared hold of one stick and drew it out smoking hot. Chips laid hold of the other end and in an instant placed it between two bars fixed for the purpose. Dukey passing his end over a bar at right angles so he could get it under the other one, slipping it along to right angles with the frame; the scythe stick took the right curve, and being left in the 'stocks' for a few days they dried hard and remained the desired shape.

Next came the rake bows or as some people call them stays, but that does not matter. These slim strips of wood surprised me when steamed, seemed as lithe, limp and tough as leather, and I was racking my brains to see what Chips had schemed up to keep these small pieces the shape of a half circle, but had not long to wait.

The bundles were taken out of the steam chest then laid crosswise on a long trough with a circular bottom, the right width and depth for rake stays. All were spread out side by side—steaming hot —and a long heavy piece of timber rounded to fit was placed on top and by forcing the timber down into the trough the strips were held in place to get cold and harden. This was one of Chips's schemes of mass production, and opened my eyes to what can be saved a man in labour by using his head piece as he was meant.

We then started to make a quantity of hay rakes, Chips cleaning, boring for stays, and tapering the ends of the handles on which the heads were fixed while Dukey got the heads to size, boring and tapering the hole in the centre to fix the handle in, and six each side of that for the teeth, thirteen holes in all. My job was to find all the short pieces that would cut up into lengths of six inches, and clear of knots, to be split up for teeth.

Chips, seeing I had a skep full says—"Think yew'd better start splitting now, boy—'spose I'd better show yew how to go on." He picked up a bill book, placed a length on what he called his splitting block, laid the bill hook across the pitch and with one blow of his wooden mallet it was in halves, then quartered, and while I should still have been thinking which way to split it next, it was in half inch squares—a dozen teeth for a rake.

He left me to try my hand at it, telling me to be careful allus to split from the top ends, as they rive better that way. After a bit I got into the way of splitting them to size and in an hour or two had the skep emptied of the blocks with very little waste which pleased Chips. He told me to start rounding of them up at one end so they come about the length of my little finger and then they would be ready to drive into rake heads. I had a mould for this, a piece of wood with a hole in it, and if the teeth fitted tight I knowed they were not too small. I started rounding them up, hacking away until my fingers were stiff and sore but I took no heed—wired away into the job—and got it done, surprising Chips when I told him I had finished the lot, and he bid me lay 'em in the sun spread out so that they would get dry.

When we had enough teeth finished I was turned on to help

Dukey bore the rake heads. A gadget called a templet was fixed on the top of the block with twelve guide holes the right distance apart for the teeth of the rake, and they were bored quick enough with a brace and bit, once one had learned to press even on the brace and not let the bit wobble about. Before very long the six dozen heads was finished and we started to put the rakes together, Chips fixing the stays through the holes he had already bored, so they was then ready for the heads.

"Now then, Boy," says he. "I want yew to be puttin' the teeth in the heads. Lay hold on that there head, put it in the vice, near one end—bottom edge up-ard and screw it tight. Hand us a tooth and I'll show yew how to drive it in. There's one thing you must allus be werry tickler about, dont yew drive 'em in with the flat side forrard, but allus drive 'em with the square edge to-ards the handle side of the head, the rakes 'll do their work best when the teeth are set with the edge of their square forrard."

Then he gives me another templet and told me to lay it on top of the teeth and keep it close up against the head, then make a mark on every tooth and trim the ends where they are marked so they come all the same length, for if they be uneven the rake will not run easy.

After I had done two or three of the heads I found setting the teeth was quite an easy job, and going steadily, found I could keep ahead of Dukey who was putting the heads on the handles, and soon there was piles of rakes stacked ready for Haysell and Harvest. When they was finished Old Chips stood and looked at them and then at me with a twinkle in his eye—

"Well, you harnsey-gutted[1] little squit, never say I h'aint learnt yew nothin'—du yew du as I've shewed yer, yew'll git a job as will last yew a life time, as long as there's men and horses as needs corn and hay."

I thought on that later and turned it to my own account, but little did he think few would be troubled with hand-made rakes or aught else within twenty year.

The next job as I was put onto was making bundles of broaches for thatching. That was an easy job. I had only to cut off the lengths about two feet from nuttery poles and they were then split down the middle making two. Some of the larger ones made three and four.

After the splitting was done they were tied up into fair-sized bundles and were then ready for the thatcher. When they were wanted they were laid in water two or three days to soak, which would soften them for raven, that is to say twisted round near the middle without breaking. The two ends which had already been

[1]Harnsey-gutted. Lank and lean like a hahnsey or harnser, otherwise a heron.

pointed could now be brought together, passed on either side of the hay bonds and forced down into the thatch. Thus it acts as a huge staple keeping the bond and thatch in position.

Then we made herring tub hoops and I was puzzled at first, wondering how Chips would bend the stuff round to make hoops the right size, but I soon found out. Out come his measuring rod, poles the right size were cut and split, cleaned up a bit and flattened at both ends. Then Dukey brought out what I thought was a wheel made of wood about three inches thick with an iron plate about a foot long fixed on the outside rim. Two pieces of wood were nailed on the opposite sides of the wheel about six inches beyond the edge of it with holes bored in line through both. Into these a peg was fitted which could be drawn out when required. It was a templet. A length of nuttery was slipped under the peg, the end passed over and under the pegs and then fixed at one end, a wedge being put tight under the peg. The rest of the length was then brought round the wheel, the two ends lapped one over the other, the other three nails being driven in and home (being turned on the inside by the iron plate), and before you could say Jack Robinson, Chips and Dukey had the hoop off the wheel and it was finished. So it would go on till a hundred or two was done to complete an order. As Chips said a lot of gold did not hang to that job only a few red herring, but still they came in handy in the winter with taters, meaning there was not much profit in tub hoops, but many littles make much.

Just about then I got a soaking one day coming home. Mother was out and I didn't trouble to shift myself into dry things, but pottered about after my own doings and caught such a cold as kept me from work a week or two, ruttling and tissacking, till Mother was fair crazed with hearing me. She had a cure for that which was hard to beat.

She'd choose a juicy white turnip, cut it into thin slices sprinkle the bottom of the pan with brown sugar, lay some slices of turnip then more sugar—one above the other—and let it stand and drain for some days. Afterwards the syrup was bottled off and we used to get a spoonful about every three hours it tasting rather like treacle. It was a rare powerful medicine and kept us boys running, but it broke up a cold.

It was drawing on into winter by the time I was well again and I kept fretting to get back to Old Chips and the yard and, one grey day in late November Mother said I'd best be off, there weren't no peace with me grizzling round about. So I doesn't waste more time but away as hard as I could set legs to the ground. I found all as I had left it and Old Chips in the yard. He looks me up and down for a bit and then says:

"Well, boy, so yew be come back, thought yew must be making for the mole country—bin away so long. We be getting slack—hurdles, rakes, scythe sticks, broaches and hoops is all finished, dont know what I kin find yer to du, yer'd best be lookin' after another job, I'm thinking. We done very well in that five weeks you was a' long of us. I 'spose you wants somethin' for yer trubble—here's five bob—can't afford no more."

It was a bitter cold morning with a mizzle of rain blowing into the yard, and soaking through my jacket, and I stands there and looks at Old Chips with two half crowns held out on his palm telling me to git out, and I feels like blubbin'. I had been happy working in the yard with him and Dukey, and I had a fancy for the job and now it was all finished and I got nothing but a shillin' a week. Chips see my face and start blustering:

"Think yerself lucky to get what I gives yew," says he, "can't afford no more, there ain't a lot of money knockin' around just now and five bob's five bob. Come spring time things may be better. Now git off afore I helps yer."

So I takes the money and was gone like a shot in case I got more than I asked for, feeling little as it was, he could not take away from me that which I had earned. I did not trouble him any more the rest of his life. He was a hard man and a hard drinker which made him snaisty tempered at times, but he was born and bred to his trade and a good one to learn from.

Back I goes home, cold and miserable, wondering what I was to do next. Mother hears the click of the half door and come through from the front room to see who's coming.

"Why, boy," says she, "back a'ready, what's come to yew—changed yer mind with the weather?"

I stood there like a zany looking at her, knowing if I said a word I'd be blubbering and was shamed—great boy that I was, but I holds out my hand and she sees the five shillings Old Chips had given me and it come to her what had happened.

"Given yew the sack has he, the old varmint, and five shillings for all them weeks of work—no more'n I expected, only yew was that set on going I thought yew'd best find out for yerself. Yew are hardly fit anyways—thin as a shotten-herring[1]—yew's growing up, and boys is kittle cattle them times—it wont dew yew no harm to be home for a bit. Come yew into the fire and stop frettin' yer self."

I swallered back my tears and went to sit by the fire and watched Mother at her mending—it being too wet for her to be about. I can see her now with Grandmother's Rag Bag that the old-fashioned folk of fifty years ago kept their pieces of cloth in for repairs, when ever they were wanted. A history book it was of all the things she'd ever owned, but then she had to make the best of all the odds and ends and not waste a scrap, whatever the sort or colour, as long as it would patch a hole or mend a rent, for cloth was dear and hard to come by—like most other things.

But she had thrift and a contented mind. Looking back I think that winter I come to learn the value of them two things from her, for I was poorly till the spring and spent many an hour at the fireside—Black Betsy singing on the hearth and the cats thrumming away in tune with the old kettle—Mother at her mending and the wind battering on the end of the house till it shook, but we was warm and snug enough.

We had need to be contented at home for village life at that time was much more isolated than it is now. The only intercourse with

[1]Shotten herring. Herrings which have spawned.

the outside world was by horse and cart and horseback, and they who did not possess either had to hoof it, and by making use of their legs became good pedestrians, and by the practice of walking healthy, hearty and robust. Not like many of us at the present time who—if they could—would ride their bikes into the pantry to fetch a spoon.

Many of them without a doubt helped themselves at times to their neighbour's goods, but on the whole they led a pure and simple village life. It was not difficult to buy goods, as every village over far from a town had its General Stores, and many of the goods sold were produced at home. There you could get a pound loaf for a penny, a two-pound loaf for tuppence, and a stick of rock as long as your arm for a halfpenny. New milk was a penny a pint, skimmed a farthing, tea was a luxury only obtainable by the rich. I knew of old ladies who rather than be out of the latest fashion burnt a crust of bread, put it into a cup, filled it with hot water added a dust of sugar and fancied they were drinking tea. Many of them had a pig in the sty—those that did not work for the Squire or large farmer, that was not allowed—for what reason I must leave. Those that kept one fed it on waste from the gardens and acorns the children collected during the autumn. When killing day come round, the meat was jointed out, and the hams hung in the kitchen chimney to be smoked by a wood fire and cured for future use. It was the custom then for the butcher to take the pluck for killing, to be eaten afterwards as brawn and chitterlings. Fry 'em and eat 'em with sugar, mustard and vinegar, and they was reckoned a good dish; less you was one of them whose stomach turned at innards.

Many of the old folk brewed themselves a good drop of beer from malt and hops, and also from horehound that grew in their gardens. Horehound beer when made good would drive the corks out and burst the bottles. Most villages had their own windmill and ground their own corn, very often making the meal into bread with no bran taken from it, so the people were more healthy as it is more laxative than the fine flour of to-day.

The Village Public was the working man's Parliament, with the

Sessions on Saturday evenings and nine times out of ten the Miller was chosen as Prime Minister—the Speaker either the Village Tailor or one of the Snobs. Sometimes the members would use their tongues too freely and the result would be a rough house, but all was handy with their fists those days—fighting was a lot thought of, and a little blood lettin' cooled hot heads.

It was true our Fathers and Mothers were illiterate, could but spell out a few words and just made a mark for their names, but they cultivated a wonderful memory. Could tell tales by the hour together and seeing life as it really was they lived and let live, being in the truest sense broad-minded. What the ear hath not heard nor the eye seen the heart does not grieve for.

Man has now achieved his aims and put to his own use most of the natural forces of the earth and is using them—so it seem to me, who am growing an old man—for his own destruction.

Looking back at myself—a little lad sitting by the same hearth as I sit now, watching my Mother at her work those winter days—it seems another world, so great is the change in men's lives.

Old Thyme

Come all young women and maids
That are all in your prime,
Mind how you weed your gardens gay,
Let no one steal your thyme.

Once I had thyme (time) enough,
To last me night and day,
There came to me a false young man
Stole all my thyme away.

And now my thyme is done,
I cannot plant no new,
There lays the bed where my old thyme grew,
'T's all over-run with rue.

Rue is a running root,
Runs all across amain,
If I could pluck that running root
I'd plant my old thyme again.

CHAPTER XIII

Now Lammas comes in,
Our harvest begin,
We have done our endeavours to get the corn in;
We reap and we mow,
And we stoutly blow,
And cut down the corn
That did sweetly grow.

The poor old man
That can hardly stand,
Gets up in the morning, and do all he can,
Gets up in the morning, and do all he can.
I hope God will reward
Such old harvest man.

Traditional.

A BIT after I had done with Chips what should come into my possession but a large quantity of odds and ends of willow wood. Some were long enough for rake handles, and there was any amount that would make heads, as this wood is very light, tough and serviceable. There was about the place plenty of hard wood that would make teeth. I determined to make a quantity of rakes and try my luck hawking them. Naturally I had critics but that made little or no difference to me, I persisted in my undertaking and got six dozen rakes made.

Next thing that occurred to me how was I going to carry the lot about from farm to farm to try and sell my goods. Well, as it happen I knew an old man called Bill, and knowing he had a dicky and cart and would help at any time he could a lame dog over a stile, thought I'd ask him if I might borrow the turn-out and go round and sell my rakes.

One fine morning just before Haysell come on I went along to see Bill. He was never to be seen except wearing a sleeved weskit, an heirloom that had been left him by his Father or Grandfather. Whether he was rolled in it at his birth I could not say, but that weskit seemed to be part and parcel of the old man himself, and he was never to be seen day in and day out with it off. I should not doubt for a moment he slept in it cold winter nights, and when ever it got torn hedging, or worn thin from chafing he would have it mended as soon as he was home, asking his good wife Susan to put on another patch.

As I come along the door of the cottage stood half ajar and the old couple was a-settin' in the sun Susan trying to mend yet another tear in the famous weskit. They nods to me and then gits on with the job in hand.

"Take the dratted heavy ole thing off, can't yer," says Sue. "Yew'll have lies told about yar if I mends yar things on yar back. I h'aint got nothin' in the patch bag the right colour neither."

"Don't keep praten that 'ont du the job," sezs Bill with a wink at me. "Don't make no difference to me what the colour is so long as it keep out the wind."

"Sit yew still Bill—don't I might prick yew."

"Yew 'ont dew that my ole weskit's too thick for that, go yew on and git on with the job."

Sue said no more but picks up her needle and starts crowdin' it through the stuff with all her might, while I squats on my hunkers on the step in the sun and watches them. Presently she starts again.

"Wonder how many more times yew'll want me to put patches in? I'll tell yer what I think on it, Bill Bor, a heavy stinkin' ole weskit like that there orter be barnt, that 'aint wholesome."

"Don't yew run on such squit as that—reckon that'll last me as long as I live. Money wont run ter buy a new one, yew knows that very well. Du what I want yar and don't say no more."

"Well, of all the weskits I ever see in my life if that don't top the lot," said Sue, when she had finished the patch. "Put me in mind of Joseph's coat what I've heard folks read about in the Bible, that was all colours and patches, I should think master must laugh fit to split to see yew."

"That don't matter, he don't pay no regard to what I puts on my back, as long as I gits on with my work and earn my money. I'm going to wear that as long as I live, and when I goes that goes with me, and if I be fust yew see yew buries me in it."

"I s'pose yew must have yer way," says Sue.

"Yes, I must," says Bill with another wink at me. "If yew don't du as I sezs I'll harnt yer. Now Boy what may yew be wantin'?"

I tells him that I come to borrow his Dicky and cart if he would lend it me to take my rakes round to the different farms.

"Yes, that I will, Boy, wur the greatest o' pleasure. Yew'll find the old Dicky a bit slow, but if yew gives him his time he'll du the job arl right. Yew kin have him and yew kin give me one of yar rakes for the use-on-im."

Next day I picks a good rake for old Bill, goes and fetches the Dicky and cart, loads up my rakes and seating myself on top, off I go steadily crawling along, slow but sure.

The start was good but it nearly ended in disaster, as while going slowly along the road I heard such a rattling of heavy wheels and thundering of horses' feet I wondered what on earth was a' coming. Round the turn in the road come a wagon and a pair of horses which had stampeded. Fortunately old Ned was pickin' the cleanest part of the road as most Dickies do, and was to one side, and the wagon went past like a flash just plucking the edge of my rakes. Some went flying into the road and me with them, lighting on my rear, and by the time I had picked myself up all was quiet as if nothing had happened, and old Ned was pulling at the grass by the road side. I scrambled up my rakes in a hurry, some of 'em were broke but that I did not mind as I could mend 'em.

It was Ned and the cart I had borrowed that troubled me most, but I was cheered to find there was no damage done except a bruise the size of my hand on the side of my sit-down-upon. I reloaded the rakes, took my seat on top as before, and started off again. Away we went drawing along well on the side of the road, and presently come to a farm where it look like doing business. Out come the farmer, takes a look at me and the turn-out, and says:

"Hullo, Boy, how long ha' yew been in the rake makin' business?"

I tells him how it come about and asks if he wont buy a dozen or two, that he can have 'em for fifteen bob a dozen. He says that's a deal too much and he'll give me twelve shillings and not another brass farthing. Nor would he, and thinks I to myself I ha' got a thin shelled egg here, and had better handle it careful, so lets him have a dozen rakes for twelve shillin'. He picks 'em out and pays me, and off I go to find another customer. I found several that day and gets sometimes a shilling more and sometimes only as much, but I had one stroke of luck.

Ned was getting tired and the sun was hot so I lets him stop in a drift[1] and take a mouthful or two of Doctor Green. The only thing that mattered to Ned was his belly, and that must be filled. I was setting in the hedge packing away some flap-jacks my Mother had given me, when jogging along come the farmer in his gig, his

[1]Drift. A track-way to fields or to an "off farm."

face all smiles having done well at market. He pulls up, looks at me sharply and says:

"That's a good lot of rakes, Boy, where are yar off tew with 'um. Just what I want some good rakes, but I see yew got some broken ones."

I tells him what had happened and he listened a bit and then says he'd take three dozen and the few broken ones cheap, as he could easy git 'em mended and he give me fourteen shilling a dozen. Out come his Long Melford[1] and he pays me and away he go. I shakes up old Ned (having now nearly cleared my rakes) and makes for home, thinking he might stir his stumps a bit faster with no load. But no, the same old stroke, so I lets him go his own rate feeling sure we would get home some time afore night, and so we did, landing back just afore dark. I put him into his stable shoved the cart under cover, thanked old Bill for the use of his turn-out and was off for home, feeling rare proud—with my pockets full of dough.

When summer come round once more I thought I would try and see if I could get a job harvesting. Have found the best policy in life is to forget and forgive—and so it was with me and Farmer Cribby. I thought he might need a man to help get his corn up and went off early one morning up to the farm, knowing it was the best time to catch him. I could hear him afore I got there, shouting to his men from the stable door, and when I gets round the stacks in the rickyard could see his hat was pulled down well over his ears, and knew there was thunder about.

"Who's Master here," storms Cribby, "me or yew? I het-ter find the money so 'spect I am. I'm goin' to start harvest when I thinks proper. No sooner, no later."

Not another word was said, the men went after their work and Cribby turning round sees me standing there and asks me what I want. I tells him, and asks if he can do with me over harvest.

"Seems I knows yew," sezs Cribby, looking me up and down,

[1]Long Melford. A long sheep or pig-skin purse portioned off in the centre, "one for the rook the other for jackdaws," i.e. gold and silver.

and when I minds him how he runned us off the swede field years ago, he laughs.

"Jack Baldry's boy—chip of the old block, I shouldn't wonder. Yew wanter go harvesting, Bor—yew ain't big and strong enough for that—might take yew as three-quarter-man." I stood and stared at him and said, "I've never heard of a three-quarter-man afore."

"H'aint yer boy, yew'll find plenty o' them knocken about if yew keeps yer eyes open. I was lookin' fur a harvest hand not a three quarteren. I'm payin' my men six bob a day for harvest, and if I gives yew four bob and a tanner that be three-quarters what they gits—now kin yew see it? Kin yew swing a scythe?"

I said I could and after a bit he agreed to take me on and try what I could do. I started the next Monday morning, frail basket in my hand, with a strap round my waist made from an old horse's rein, and a rub bag from a bit of a leather buskin. Rub and scythe I was forced to borrow from my Father.

Off we go—seven of us—to a barley field, the teamster, or Lord of the Harvest being the first to set in cutting, the rest following and me last but one, with many a joke about three-quarter-men getting their legs sawn off.

We had grand weather all through that harvest, but when the first wheat stack went up, Cribby (whose bite was not so bad as his bark) took me off mowing from dawn to dark, which was hard on a growing lad and put me with his handy man Old Bill. Bill did most of the thatching. It was my job to serve him, and it was he who taught me most of what I know.

First we got a heap of wheat straw near by each stack in readiness, but it was laid down all higgledy-piggledy. Before it was ready for thatching it must all be carefully shook out with a fork on to a separate heap, and well sprinkled with water while the shaking was going on, then left to soak for a while.

We then shook some hay up and give that a sprinkling of water. This was for making bonds the length of the stack and used for binding down the thatch. Each one was wound on a stick pointed at one end and this point would be stuck in the stack near at hand while the thatching was going on. We made four of these bonds, two for the top, one for either side, and two for the bottom of the roof about a foot from the eves. We then pointed up some broaches which had been soaking in a tank for several days.

Bill had made himself a thatching comb as he called it, about two feet long, fitted with three-inch teeth two-thirds of its length, the remainder rounded off to form a handle. With this he combed the thatch down after putting it on. Up goes the thirty-staved ladder and layen well up the roof I sezs:

"What are yar gornter begin that end?"

"Yus, that I am, Bor, dint-yar know I wus left-handed—we're a couple of left-handed Dicks working together. If yar ain't done thatchin' er-fore you best pull and yell-um the straw and bring it up to me, I'll lay it on. When yew gits a minute or tew to spare keep yer eye a' liftin' and see how I fold one lot under the other to keep the water out and make it fence."

Bill knew the tricks of the trade, for he was an old hand at the game. I was a young 'un and must serve him, the hardest job of the two and a back-aching one at that. I had to climb a thirty-staved ladder with a load of wet thatching straw held between two thick sticks tied together at one end with stout cord, forming a kind of hinge; the other two ends (when in use) were joined with a loop, which could be slipped over. This arrangement Bill called his bailing sticks, a name I did not soon forget, carrying them up that there ladder a hundred times or more, on my back.

Next morning all preparations done Bill says:

"Now we'll slip in and git this stack thatched while the weather holds, don't like the look of them there Noah's arks,[1] I'll very sune knock into yar head the difference between pretendin' tew du a job and knowin' how tew du it, and if yew don't du as I tells yar I'll very sune upset yar apple cart."

I knew what that meant and said naught but started to pull the

[1]Noah's arks. Certain type of clouds.

straw at the bottom of the heap and got enough to make one yellum.[1] When the straw was pulled the next thing was to yellum it—soon did that, putting my toes under the edge of the pile and leaning well forrard was down and at it.

I drawed and combed the straw bakkards and forrards with my hands towards the front of my legs, and found there was enough for a yellum. When done it was laid on the bail, more straw pulled and two or three more yellums made, laid on top, the hinged stick swung over and tightened down by my knee and the loop slipped on, keeping the bail together. Then on to my shoulder in a jiffy and up the ladder I go with it in a crack. Bill collared hold, took off the bail and chucked the sticks down.

"Ain't the fust time yew-er served a thatcher, Bor, I kin see."

"No, that it ain't—I sarved Noah when he thatched his ark."

Old Bill cocked his eye at me and chuckled sayin':

"I thought by the looks on yar yew was a bit antique, but not as old as that—of all the lies I've heard in my time that du top the lot, yew young varmint."

"That's no lie, Bill—don't yew remember old Farmer Noah what used to live about here, a good old fellar he was, and when I'd done with hay trussin' he give me a job, helpin' him to thatch a shed what he used to call his pony's ark."

"Artful young pup, yew be," sezs Bill, "let be havin' some more yellums up—stir yar stumps and let's see if yew kin keep me a' goin' and I'll tell yew a tale of old Noah.

"He was a just man but thought a lot about his beer—and beer was beer in them days—would just about sell anything he had to get it, even his Grandmother if any one would ha' given him a pint for her which ain't likely, dirty old mawkin she were. Used to go out he did, winter evenings to the Pub near by, and get as drunk as a fiddler, coming home all hours as best he could, a singin' like a nightingale. Some times he'd bring a drink for the Old Woman, sometimes not, but she used to sit up for him till midnight and

[1] Yellums. Bundles of straw (as much as can conveniently be carried under the arm).

more, so I should judge they were a loven' couple or she would never ha' done it, but I don't doubt there were times he got the rough side o' her tongue.

"Be that as it may one night he was later than usual, and the Old Gal bein' tired, ups, and shifts herself for bed and lay there a' listenin' to hear him come in. When he do come along he thinks to himself—dang me, I'll have a game with the old 'un to-night, and what du he du but pick up a brick and heave it into the well back of the house so it make a mighty splash and start a' hollerin' fit to wake the dead, 'Nancy—Nancy!'

"The old Lady she hears the racket and up and out of bed in her night clothes and all, and out through the back door to the well, sure as fate her Noah had been and fallen in. But the time she took a' doin' that, Noah, he run past the end of the house, through the front as quick as a lamplighter, and lock that and the back door as well (pleased as punch to think he'd got the old Gal outside). And he bein' a bit 'on' goes on a' laughin' to see her shivering and shaken in the garden, and sticks his head out of the winder at the back and calls:

"'Nancy out and Noah in—what do you think o' that now? Nancy out and Noah in!'

"But she start to give him what for, sayin':

"'I'll give you Noah in when I gits inside.' So presently he give over the joke unlocks the door and nips up to bed and a' covers himself up snug, thinkin' what a spree he'd had with his old Woman, and soon fell off to sleep.

"But she was a' shiverin' and a' shakin' and warmin' herself down below by the fire a' sayin' to herself:

"'Nancy out and Noah in—I'll have him in—where he can't get out in a hurry, or my name's not Nancy Price. I'll larn him not to lock me out on a cold winter's night, catchin' my death as like as not.'

"And what du she du, but gather up some strong thread and a sack needle, and a ground ash stick a good three feet and more, as he had cut out of a hedge little reckoning he'd be the first to feel the weight of it.

"Well, when she had got everything fixed she step along to the bottom of the stair and listen to make out if he be asleep, and sure enough she hears he a' drivin' pigs for all he's worth. So up she goes and looks at him, and when he stops she sit down and wait a bit, and when he start a' driving them pigs again she ups and folds the sheets over him—and bein' a good hand with her needle in half no time she have him properly trussed up for all the world like a chicken, not able to move leg or wing, and all ready for his throshing.

"Then she pick up that ground ash and lets him have it good and plenty—a' singin' out as she goes, 'Now I'll git me own back, you old drunkard—Nancy out and Noah in—Nancy out and Noah in—how do you like it this way about—Nancy out and Noah in?'

"It warn't long afore he was a' hollerin' for mercy you may be sure, but the more he hollered the more she lets into him.

"'Who's got you trussed up in bed?' says she. 'I'm boss in this house and I'm a' goin' to lay you by for a time till I'm sartin sure you've larnt it, then I shall know where you are.' He goes on a' hollerin' that she would be the death of him if she didn't lay off it with that ground ash. But she tells him that don't matter to her for says she:

"'If I was to put you under ground I should soon find another old man as good as you, so du you see you don't come home no more like you did to-night. Du yew du yew may start a' singin' a different tune to what you think, same as yew are doin' now. This 'ull larn yew to play Nancy out and Noah in with me." With that she let him out, and he as sober as a judge by that time, nor as far as I've heard did he ever play that trick on her again. Just show that what I've allus said is mostly right; wimmen be kittle-cattle, but when they sets their minds to a thing it mostly come out the way they wants, even if they have got to take a ground ash to help 'em."

I listens and laughs at that tale but had now got my work cut out. Had not much time to see how he put on the thatch but kept my eye open every time I went up the ladder.

Cribby come along presently and told me to go across to the backus and get a gotch[1] of beer to wet our whistles, which I did. Coming back, just as I was a' goin' through the gate to the stackyard a great old sow what was rootin' about took into her head to break through and make a dive 'tween my legs. The old bounder took me properly by surprise, and away go the gotch smashed to smithereens and away I go across her back, till she make for a gap in the hedge

and leave me in the brambles. I picked myself out thinkin' I was in for trouble, but Cribby and Bill laugh till they near split themselves, and Cribby still a' shakin' went off and fetched another can of beer and a couple of mugs.

When we had wetted both eyes we felt better and went on full steam to get our stack finished afore dusk, which we did, and found time to cut the eves and rake up.

Next day Bill started to teach me the trade on a stack with upright gables, which is a bit more tricky than those with rounded ends, showing me how to start at the bottom corner of the roof, hanging the straw well over to form the eves, pressing the top end close in. How to lay the yellums over-lapping, double the loose straw with

[1]Gotch. Jug.

the comb and drive in the broaches so all was in line, straighten the straw with the comb and twist the bonds on to the broaches, driving 'em tight so all was ship-shape, bottom and top, and finishing off as I went, Bill serving me.

I soon tumbled to the way of it, the weather held fine, and by the end of the week all the corn stacks were safely thatched. Then, as it happen there was a weak place on the barn roof, and Bill was set to mend it. That was reed-thatching, which is quite a different job and takes a lot of time and patience to make a neat and tidy job of, when a bad place is gone down to the rafters.

I worked all that autumn with Bill, he teaching me his art, and many a time in the years since I've been grateful for his patience and craftsmanship, as there is not so many these days can turn their hand to thatching.

Bill was a good friend to me when I was a boy but he and his missus had a hard life. When he was getting on in years he suffered cruel from rheumatics and lumbago, so that some days he could not get about or go to work. I made him an eel skin belt to bind tightly round his middle, as the eel, being full of phospherous, is a champion cure for lumbago.

Bill was a rare strong-docked[1] old fellar to git around, but Father he had scores of eel skins hung up for making garters, and belts, and all manner o' things, and having taught myself to braid years before when my pigs were shackin', I set to and braided him a belt six inches wide and left the ends for tying. He was rare pleased with it and it eased him a lot. At that time there was no old age pension and old folk had to work as long as they could crawl, or else go to the Spike or workhouse. Bill and Sue could not bear the idea of snuffin-on-it in the Spike, and kept their home together till the last.

During the sharp winter of 1881 poor old Bill was still at work tending cattle and doin' odd jobs on his master's farm. That year the bad weather set in early, the turnips had not been got in for the winter, and Bill being at every one's beck and call was told to go down

[1] Thick-set.

to the field with a pick and git up some turnips ready for carting. Off he went and while labouring at them turnips the cold struck him, and he lay down for the last time, with the pick in his hand. When they found him some hours later he was dead and cold.

They picked him up and laid him on a hurdle pulled out of the fence and went steadily trudgin' along over the snow till they come in sight of his cottage. Sue sees them coming and run out to meet her old mate, seeing from the way his feet fall that it was all over. She didn't say a thing but bids 'em bring him in and lay him in the front room and go and tell the Woodman to make a box.

That was done, and when he brings it it happen that Mother and I were there. Sue told us with the tears a' running down her face how it were.

"It's no more than I 'spected—he allus would have his way, so t'was no use me talkin'. I wonter had him go to work that mornin', he weren't no ways fit, but he sezs to me he wouldna' take no harm with his thick old sleeved weskit, and now he's gone and left me, and me fifty years his bed-woman."

The Woodman carried in the box and came back and said quiet-like to Sue:

"Yew h'aint laid 'um out. Go yew and put a night shirt on to 'um."

Sue look at him a minute and then say:

"No, that I sartainly shan't, Bor. Bill allus tell me if he die fust to put him away in his old weskit, don't he'd harnt me as long as I live. He 'ont rest if I 'ont, and I shouldna' feel right in my mind when I come to go in on top.[1]

So Bill, still in his old sleeved weskit was put into the box and the lid nailed down, and I see the last of his kind old face.

I fretted for him for many a day, as is the way when young. Death seems a terrible thing then as 'tis meant it should be, to keep us in mind we have but a short time to live and work. As the years

[1] "Going in on the top"—refers to the custom of the double grave, that is a grave dug two feet extra in depth so a second coffin can be placed on the top.

go on we thinks but little of it when it comes to other folk, unless they be nigh us, for it always seems it will be other folk and never us. In this man deceives himself and at the last is unprepared, not having done one-quarter of what he has set his hand to do.

THE ART OF SCYTHING

He's happy whom experience schools
To learn the comradeship of tools.
I like to swing a scythe myself
Well balanced on the right hand tack.
A thin-ground blade, tight fitting wedge
That holds the ferrule to the back;
A grass-nail firmly in its place
Will blade and stick together brace.
To keep the point above the ground
The scythe should lug down at the heel.
A hazel bile that's strongly bound
And best of all—good tempered steel—
Completes a cunning tool all round:
There's rhythm in the mower's swing
And music in the morning ring
Of the rub on the steel
From the point to the heel,
With a tap and a slap
And a dexterous twist
Of the labourer's wrist
As he sharpens the edge,
Then tightens the wedge
Of the right hand tack,
Then tucks in the rub
In the belt at his back.

Ernest Edward Smith (Master Builder, Cromer).

Note.—The function of the "bile" is to sweep the mown grass across to the swathe, leaving a clear track for the mowers' feet.

CHAPTER XIV

A Fowler in pursuit of game
Observed a Dove and took his aim
In hopes to kill her on the spot;
But instantly before he shot
The adder round his ankle clung,
And struck him with her venomed tongue.
Thus villains while their wiles they lay,
Some harmless neighbour to betray,
Into unthought dangers run
And justly are themselves undone.

Old Rhyme.

TIME pass, the spring come round again. I was getting along into my teens and looking forward to the time I should become a man, thinking what I should do.

I got to wandering off alone as growing boys will, stirred with feelings they don't know the meaning of. Once clear of the house I lay for hours on my back in the grass looking at the sky, watching the small single clouds floating overhead till my eyes were all of a dazzle and they faded away into the blue. I did not understand why it was that a skinny little brat like me had come into the world. Was it ordered or only a matter of chance, and why did every new thing seem familiar—as if I had seen them before—that was a problem beyond my powers to solve.

My head was like an empty nut shell, the kernel not matured. I had no troubles, cares nor worries, except those that were so much part of each day one did not notice 'em, I had believed what I was told right or wrong, year after year—knew no better.

But now my mind was a' startin' to grow same as my body was changing, I began to doubt many things I was told, finding it was best to think for myself. That I should have to look after myself and not expect my parents to nurse and cuddle me all the days of my life. I had rid myself of the marks of the cradle and the days of the old coach cart, with its upright bars through which I could peep when being bumped over the stones. I began to see it weren't no good allus leaving it to other folks. I should be left in the lurch, struggling along behind with never a bit of cheese to put on my bread.

Not that I wanted more'n my share. I was not when young nor am I now possessed with a dishonest greed for gain, money never has stuck to my fingers and I reckon I'll die near as poor as I was born. It don't mean much to me, if I have enough and a little to spare, for there's a lot of the best which come to a working man that money don't buy, if he can keep an even balance of body and mind. But looking back I realize it was then I began to see a man must have a trade.

I'd learnt a bit of this and a bit of that and the use of woodworking tools. I'd found out how to use my hands and make things for myself. I'd tried a mort[1] of jobs but not learnt myself to do one thing well that I could keep on a' doin' and would allus bring in a wage, like Father's snobbing. So it was not long after I took a fancy to learn carpentering, and it come about this way.

There was an old Carpenter by name of Sam Deeping, or anyhow that was the name he went by. I do not know if he ever married but he was a good tradesman and also possessed other qualifications, if it was only drinking beer of which he was very fond. Would dust anybody down and run a mile to get a pint.

He got into the way of walking by the footpath over Bungay Common to the Duke of York at Ditchingham, put a pint or two on the slate, then back the same way. When he got near our house he would stop and have a yarn with Father. I used to draw up close with my ears set forward to hear Sam telling Father how he "got on," saying with a chuckle:

[1]Mort—from Icelandic "Morgt"—much.

"What's the use er-gettin' old if yar don't git artful?"

"Living in a shanty back of Castle Hills arn't you?" says Father.

"Well, what with paying the rent of a house there weren't tuppence left for a pint, so I give the landlord the slip one night and that's how I'm comin' across the Common now and then to the Duke for a pint or two, and tew git into that bloke's ribs if I can—Anybody can git beer by payin', it's an art gettin' it without."

"I'm wholly stammed how yew got cheek enough."

"What yew think I knocked about the country for all these years—for nothing," sezs Sam.

"No, that's a sure moral you h'aint," sezs Father, and off go Sam Deeping across the Common to his shanty. He came past several times after that, dropping off all at once. No doubt he had filled the slate and found out the poor dog Trust was dead. But I used to mess around with him when he did a job and took a liking to the trade, being handy with my fingers. After a bit I started on the building and carpentering as apprentice, and mentioned one day to my mate it was Sam Deeping who first put me in that way.

"I know him well," says he. "One of the best of tradesmen but fond of his juice and has an oily tongue. One of the biggest dam' rascals I ever worked with, wouldn't trust him no further than I could see him."

Sam had been away from Bungay several months then, but I met him one day and he told me the place sort o' haunted him, and he had heard an old bloke had a house to let in Quaves Lane, and he was going over to see if he could hire it. So he did and this was the way of it. Being Sam he could no more go straight than a footpath can keep in line—'twasn't in his nature.

He went to see the owner just after breakfast thinking to catch him in a good mood, and when the old gentleman asked him his business told him he wanted to hire his house in Quaves Lane.

He had a way with him when he chose, and soon, after a little conversation gits the Blacksmith's daughter (as we calls the key) and permission to take the house at two shillin' a week, and go off to finish a job the other side of the town.

He got it done in good time and asked for his money, but his customer having met him before asked for his bill, and Sam said he never made bills—never having been to school in his life—and old Rosepink said he never paid without. So Sam promised to git it made out and off he go to his favourite Pub. There the Landlord made out the bill for him to:

Mr. A. Rosepink,
Corner House, Beccles Turnpike.

To Sam Deeping:

Jobs done to shed.
Cutting and contriving
Labour, nails, and driving
Fitting up to tew by four,
Tew and sixpence and no more.

and back goes Sam to old Rosepink who have a good laugh at his bill and pays it, making Sam make his mark as he cannot write, and telling him he be Deeping by name and deeper by nature, they bid each other a pleasant good night. Back goes Sam to the Pub havin' a half crown in his pocket and drinks old Rosepink's health saying:

"May he live till his ears trape the ground—and I live to see 'em."

When he came to the surface he told all the company he had had a good day—earned half a crown and hired a house.

That made 'em gawp and one asked what he wanted a house for —never been known to stop in any place long enough to live in one.

"Never you mind that," said Sam, "I have hired it and paid a month's rent in advance," and he swings the key between his fingers to convince them. One spoke up and said that's what he wanted— a good house cheap, and it came to Sam all in a flash how he could make an easy quid.

"I bin in lodgins that long—don't care much if I move in or

not," said he. "Let it to yew if yer likes, stands at the end of Quaves Lane, but yew'll have to pay me the rent for a month, as I had to shell out for good faith—the old man not knowin' me."

There was a laugh at that as others did, but the man knew the house and had a liking for it, and Sam pushed him over another pint and clenched the bargain. His pal paid Sam the quid then and there, in case he should change his mind, he having a mind to move.

What with one thing and another Sam was getting a bit tired out, so he bid the company good-night and went home to his diggin's, and laid in his bed thinking what would be the best thing to do about his landlord. Presently it came to him he'd best clear out of the town after a day or two, having a quid to carry him, and let his sub-tenant git on as best he could when the old bloke went after the rent in a month's time.

Which is what happened, and a fine shindy there was when the old man turned up and found the wrong tenant, and the tenant found he'd paid a quid for a house that should have been eight bob, and looked like having to pay that on top into the bargain. They went at it hammer and tongs and the tenant started swearing, but the old gent he said he could swear harder than most and set out to prove it, suggesting Sam's pal had better pay up and stay on as tenant. In the end they both agreed they was daft to have anything to do with Sam Deeping, who never so much as owned a pint mug much less a house—and the tenant paid up the eight shillin' with a curse, wishin' Sam might fall from the next ladder he got on to and break his damn' neck. With which the landlord heartily concurred and went his way.

Sam had hoofed it to Norwich, but hadn't been there long when he was spotted by a hay dealer from Bungay, who was going with some loads to the barracks. Knowing Sam was of a roving nature he was not surprised to see him, had a pint or two and went his way, but Sam thought he'd best shift. No doubt he still carried on the same old game and about a twelvemonth later made his way to Harleston. He heard of a builder who wanted a carpenter and got the job, givin' great satisfaction for he was a craftsman all right, and had now good work could he but stick to it.

Somehow after a few weeks he got the old cravin' to come back, bein' only seven miles off. So he finished up his work April time and tramped to Earsham. Being spring, and things in the building trade busy, he got another job with a builder who put him in the way of gettin' a little house by the railway crossin' with a tidy garden. From there he slipped over to Bungay and looked up his pals.

Things had blown over, he only came into Bungay evenin' time and all went well. He got his pals to give him a hand diggin' the garden and he scrounged some carrot seed putting the whole lot down in carrots, which he thought he could sell to his landlord against the rent, the landlord havin' a pony. None of 'em in Earsham had realised that Sam had two sides to his face and was out to dust down whoever he could.

The months went by, the landlord came along for the rent, and Sam spun a yarn about havin' to send his old woman money Haddiscoe way, and havin' had no reglar work for months, and being a bit short wont the landlord take the carrots instead of rent? As it happened they were a tidy crop, about twenty rods, clean and sound, and landlord agreed, gave him a receipt for the rent and said he'd have 'em cleared in a few days.

Sam was on the right side again but go straight he could not. He slipped over to Bungay that night and Father was in the Pub. He had taken me along with him and we passed the time of day with Waxey who was keepin' the company on the titter with his tales—he havin' a lot o' new ones since he'd been seafarin'.

There was a French boat had been lyin' at Yarmouth a week or two back, berthed alongside Waxey's craft. It happened he'd picked up a bit of the Froggie's lingo, and suggested they should come a stroll into the town one night and have a jollification. If they had but known it was safer for mice to go walking with Tom Cat than for those as were not acquainted with Waxey Jack to go on the spree in his company.

Off they went and after a bit found themselves in the bar at the Three Mariners where the Ladies of Yarmouth made it their business to take a fancy to the Frenchmen. The drinks went round and soon they started dancing. The Froggies joining in were gripped round the waist by the Yarmouth Ladies, and were soon in such a whirl they were puzzled to know one end of themselves from the other. It seemed the Ladies found they were not light weights, sat down for

a breather and refresher. Soon, strangely all had a call elsewhere, the Frenchmen finding that all of them except one had been relieved of their purses.

They all turned on the Landlord, jabberin' like a wagon load of monkeys. But he had no wish to understand their lingo knowing well what was a-foot, and bundled 'em all out, calling "Time gentlemen, please," and Waxey was left to do what he could. He calmed 'em down and took 'em back to the boat and said he'd have the loss cried first thing in the morning, and for very shame and fear the

Ladies would have to give up the purses—only they must each pay a shilling for the crying.

This, the last one who had any money left did for the lot of 'em, and next day the passers-by heard the Crier going up and down the "Rows"[1] crying:

Johnny Crampoo's lost his purse
He who's found it's none the worse,
He who lost it let him seek it
He who's found it let him keep it!

That job was soon over—and Waxey went back and told the Frenchmen:

"That was well cried, that was—yew 'ont hear nothin' for a day or tew—dew yu have a bit o' patience and them there purses 'ull tarn up. Yer bound to git 'em some day or t'other."

The Frenchies, born innocent it seemed, thanked him politely for makin' known their losses and went back to their boat, full o' hope, which was all that was left except memory of their evening out with Waxey Jack.

All had a good laugh over that, though boy as I was it seemed somehow doing the dirty on the Froggies—they not understanding how Waxey was fooling 'em. But he had that way with him when he chose, a look and a manner that kind, and them sad monkey eyes in his head as you'd think 'ud never deceive yew in a month o' Sundays—till he'd larned yew.

Sam Deeping allus had a fancy for Waxey and they got talking, and Waxey said he'd better come along o' him and go as ship's carpenter—he could git a job easy as fallin' off a log. Sam said he'd a mind to then and there. The only thing that stopped him was he'd not got the ready to take the train as far as Yarmouth. He thought a bit and said would the Landlord give him a couple o' quid for his

[1] Yarmouth Rows. Very ancient alleys which still exist. At one time there were about 200 of them, the width of the alley-way between the houses varying from 3 to 6 feet. Access in any sort of cart was only possible by the old "trollies" which are believed to be an adaption of a cart used by the early Britons.

carrots, as good a lot as he'd see'd for a long time. Landlord having seen 'em a week or two back said he was agreeable for thirty shillin', if Sam 'll git 'em up he'll come over evening time and cart 'em.

Sam agreed and said would he bring in his few sticks to the auction yard—as he'd as soon be quit of 'em. So it was settled. Sam had another pint and was off homeward bound wondering what he'd do about his landlord. Thought he'd go and sleep the night in the house and go to work next day, git up the carrots evening time and slide off after his friend from the Fleece had fetched 'em, all of which goes to plan.

It was early before Sam Deeping had finished all he had to do—the cottage was empty, his sticks gone with the load of carrots, and a streak showed in the east where the sun was comin' up. Sam locked the door and put the key under a brick near by, and see'd a bit of chalk lying agin his hand. He thought a minute then picked it up and wrote across the door:

"Sorry to say dear Landlord it's cheaper to move than pay rent." Provin' he could write when he wanted to.

Next day the news was out that Sam Deeping had flitted and when the Landlord came to look he found the message—the carrots gone—and the house and garden swept clean as a whistle. He cussed a bit thinkin' anyways he might ha' left the carrots.

"Damned rogue," sezs he, "if that don't top the lot, but what kin I du. If I called the perlice it'll be sending good money after bad. I'll wait a bit and keep quiet, may be he'll be back afore long, and when I catch him I'll play hell up with him so he 'ont know hisself."

The months went by and the Landlord bided his time. Sure enough one day in the winter Sam Deeping had enough of the briny and came back to Bungay, as was his way. The news got round. His Landlord waited for him one night and though gettin' on in years he'd been handy with his fists when young, and Sam's wind had gone down a pint pot with John Barley Corn long ago. He was a sorry sight by the time the shindy was finished and came staggering into the Fleece so his own Mother wouldn't ha' known him.

"That's a rough way to pay yer rent," says he, "thought as how the tarnishin' old rogue was a' killin' me, it's a wonder I weren't picked up for dead. When I gits over this no more hiring houses for me. Afore I even knew who he was I found myself heels over head—he was one tew many fer me—thought my last hour had come."

But he didn't find the house was with him this time—they told him straight out he only got what he asked for and it were lucky it weren't jug on the top. Sam cursed 'em and soon saw the bottom of a pint pot, then several more, and was turned out that night properly canned up and slept by the roadside. So it went on for some weeks, till his money was all spent and his doings known through the town. His pals had all deserted him, and he was left alone gettin' a crust where he could, but no one would trust him no more. He became an outcast and when the New Year came he was found dead in an outhouse back of Castle Hills. He had passed away to the unknown, where each man must be judged on the work that he has done, and where there is no rent to pay.

I felt sorry—there was a good side to Sam and he taught me a lot in his day being a clever tradesman, but I was about the only one as gave him a thought. With the others, who had once laughed at his slippery ways, it was a case of:

So where he's gone
And how he fares
Nobody knows
And nobody cares.

Sam Deeping found I was a handy lad to serve him at any of his jobs whether it was taking a house down or just an alteration or improvement, and it was this way I learnt how houses were built in the old time.

I remember well one old oak-timbered dwelling which he had some jobs to do—framing a new door and taking down a partition. We found the entire original house had been framed with stout uprights, and well braced and the spaces in between filled about two inches apart, and then bound tightly with withies made from small elm, ash, nuttery, osiers, or any wood that would rave. After the raving or twisting it would become so supple it could be tied in a reef knot if required.

The poles were then filled in with plastic clay and the whole termed wattle and daub work. Mostly the rooves were reed thatched, as both this and clay lump walls must have a big overhang in the eves to prevent rain softening the wall surface.

Twine and cord makers were few and far between, the builders had to get for their job what was near and handy, and used a lot of bramble cut green, the thorns trimmed and left to season for a time, then they would toughen and rave well. I have found it many times in thatch and wattle work in a good state of preservation.

The clay lump made a good warm house and some stand to this day if the water has not been allowed to get to them. The bricks were perhaps much the same as the Israelites made, about fourteen inches in length, nine inches thick and eleven wide and it would take two people to lift one on to a wall, they being put into position with a layer of plastic clay. The clay was puddled by man power and mixed with short cut straw, or sometimes a horse was used to tread it. It was used a lot for horses' stables, cattle shelters and the like. Wattle work was a lighter form of construction, suitable for houses and barns and buildings not so likely to be kicked by horses.

Without a doubt brick-making and the brick industry would have been carried on centuries earlier if it had not been for the superstitious idea of burning coal, which was considered a crime. Our Fathers looked on coal with awe, dreading the burning of it thinking they and the earth would be enveloped in the smoke, not so much as dreaming that it would become one of the natural resources of mankind and one of the greatest.

These old houses and barns, built of timber and rough cut poles covered with plastic clay, were much warmer and more comfortable than most of us imagine. When I have been working taking down these old fabrics of the past I have thought to myself, "One buildeth up with pride in the work of his hands and another cometh and taketh down that which he has built" centuries before. So is the way of the world and I used to picture to myself these old craftsmen whose heads did not ache any more, nor their hearts fret.

Nevertheless what they did has paved the path for the succeeding generations and gave birth to what we call our modern times.

Besides teaching me the finer side of wood-working (for there was little Sam could not turn his hand to and make had he a mind) he taught me to know the smell, and feel, and look of wood. To pick green wood from seasoned, to choose an elm plank, and you needs an eye for wood to pick elm, for if cut wet it will wring and twist all ways, and built into a stair will creak and complain every time the weather changes. For all that it is a fine wood for cart-wheel hubs, has a pretty grain and takes a polish without wax.

Also that alder, a soft short-lived tree, is treacherous to burn for it smoulders and flies and throws the sparks all ways, but is one of the best woods to work into hat blocks and the backs of brushes. It was alder wood burnt to charcoal (he told me) and mixed with brimstone and saltpetre that made the first gunpowder.

That to make mill wheels you must pick the best seasoned wood, ash or oak, sound and free from blemish and use pear wood for the teeth. That most fruit wood makes rare pretty chairs and such like, and is champion to burn with a clear hot flame. There is only one thing will fill the house with a sweeter scent than pear and cherry, and that is Scotch fir.

It was working with Sam that I learnt that woods is like folk, every one has its own virtues and failings, every one wants living with and knowing, if you are going to get the best out of it, and every one has its own particular use for which it is most suited in the scheme of things.

Man has found it all out in the course of centuries and applied it to his own advantage. He made carts, and later aeroplanes, and anything that must have whip and take strain, of ash, although in these days its place is taken a lot by hickory, which is really young walnut imported from abroad.

Oak is used for all things requiring great strength and endurance which must last long in water and all weather conditions. Oak seems to grow best in the cold heavy soils, and to draw from them the power to withstand damp and weather.

He also taught me a lot else about small wood, such as spindle tree which is scarce more than a bush, and bears crops of pink berries filled in autumn time with orange seeds. How it will split to a sharp hard point so that it goes by the name of "skewer wood." The use of birch tips gathered in winter time for brooms which will sweep better and cleaner than any other twig you may gather, and that white birch is the best thing for mangle rollers. How every twig and pole will bend and rive according to its nature, and the use of nuttery and willow and osier to bind and hold.

This way, and many others which I have tried to tell about, show how, when I was a boy, men and women too, learnt to use what grew by their hand for them to pull free and costing nothing. How what they had maybe was rough but mostly made of seasoned wood and fashioned by a craftsman skilled in his work, who knew the worth of what he put his labour to. Now the young folk have much that looks very fine and shiny, but they wonders why their doors stick and split and drop so that they won't lock no more, and the window frames are that soft you can stick in a pen-knife up to the hilt, and the rain beats through all ways. Why the drawers of them fine suites jam till they nearly pulls the whole chest on top of 'em, every time they opens it. They thinks that every thing grows in the shops and know naught of quick grown foreign timber unseasoned and hulled together, doors and windows sold by the gross to a size, and all the botches covered up later with putty and paint and a slop of varnish.

There's craftsmanship still to be had for those who can afford to pay for it, but it seem to me that many working men and women these days have lost the use of their hands. That them fine schools which should teach 'em fills their heads with much which don't yield a deal of profit, and makes 'em helpless as a clutch of new-hatched biddies, which must be cooped, and scratched for, and run under the feathers at every little wind that blows.

THE ANCIENT CRY OF THE RADISH BOYS OF YARMOUTH

Moredosher, moredosher,[1]
Come here, yew-raw,
Spring redosh,
Come two bunch, ee yow-who.

Come you that got money,
Whilst I a' got none,
Buy all my spring radishes,
And let me go home.

Come all yo' pretty maids,
That used to buy any,
For here's your spring radishes,
Two bunches a penny.

[1]Moredosher. Corruption of "more radishes." A very old ditty sung by the Great Yarmouth Radish boys. About a hundred and fifty boys used to be employed selling radishes in the streets.

Come all yo' old women,
Be joyful and sing,
For here's your old radish boy
Now come agin.

Here I am,
Both weary and tired;
For here's my last pennuth,
And I don't care who buy it.

CHAPTER XV

Ho! first come cowslips, then come daisies,
First come night and then come day;
First come the new love and then comes the old one,
And so we pass our time away.
Twenty, eighteen, sixteen, fourteen,
Twelve, ten, eight, six, four, two, none,
Nineteen, seventeen, fifteen, thirteen,
Eleven, nine, seven, five, three and one.
"Twenty Eighteen" English County Songs

IT was just about this time that I set my hand to what my heart has been set on all my life—one of those great secrets of the universe which moves always onwards, everything travelling on its appointed course, to come one day to the complete circle which, so it seem to me, all creation is shaped upon.

I know now as I did not know then, that there is nothing known to man which does not move, even that which seems immovable like the rocks and the soil in the depth of the earth and the hard transparency of a crystal. Motion is the secret of the universe second only to the secret of life itself. I had to wait many a year before I really understood the length and breadth of the problem, which, in my ignorance I thought that I could solve, though I still think it possible, man having within him that divinity which set him far above all other animal life.

When a boy I was very fond of engines although it was little enough I saw of any, but I would run miles to see machinery in motion. I did not then understand the power of steam, it was a wonder to me, as was the story I heard that night in the Public kitchen of the man who reckoned he could make his engine run on nothing, when I was but a little lad travelling with the Hay Trusser.

I had never forgot it and now I was getting along in my teens the urge to make what I dreamed of come over me.

I lived in my mind with crank-shafts, fly-wheels, cylinders and pistons, springs and the balance weight, spindles, and likewise the pendulum for company. I turned and sorted it over so to speak, and one day on an impulse of a moment thought I had solved the problem.

By using the triple crank shaft, mounting it on a wood frame with a cross piece of wood on the shaft with weights on each end it would, I thought, act as a fly-wheel. I had nothing for the weights and wondered what I could do when an idea struck me.

Not far off down the river was the Butts, a shooting range under the hill where the Volunteers used to practise rifle shooting, with a great earth mound to take the fire behind the targets. That, I thought must be full of lead, and first chance I got I was away down the river in my boat, and seeing there was no red flag to show they were shooting, was soon busy digging away in the earth with no one to trouble me and found all I wanted.

My next job was to make a mould which I did out of clay, and waiting my time until Mother was out one evening I took a small saucepan of hers for a melting pot. I put my bullets in, stood the saucepan over the kitchen fire and the mould (which I had made after several attempts and was at last satisfied with) on the hob, so it should be near and handy.

At first the fire was sulky but some dry sticks soon cured that and I had it snapping and crackling, and after a bit my lead bullets started melting.

This being my first attempt at casting metal I had no idea what would happen. I started pouring the molten metal into the mould with my head thrust well over the top to see what was doing.

The mould was wet clay, and no sooner was the lead in than out, as the moment the molten stuff touched it steam was generated and blew the hot lead sky high with a bang and splurged all over my face and head. Mercifully I shut my eyes in time or I would have been blinded. Down went the saucepan and I was tearing away with both hands trying to get the burning stuff out of my hair. A good deal of it came off with the lead, my face was covered with burned patches, and altogether I looked a pretty beauty. As to the lead, some had gone into the fire, some was still hanging to my hair, and the rest was spattered round about but none left to make my crankshaft.

I made shift to clean up the mess and Mother when she came home cleaned me up pretty thoroughly with her tongue, but give over when she saw my poor burned face and set to doctoring it with an ointment she made of pig's lard and healing herbs. After a bit my skin stopped smarting and healed over, not much the worse. I had come to the conclusion however, that a lead crankshaft would not stand the strain and gave up that idea.

My next try I made a crankshaft of wood which was soon done. I then made a suitable wood frame, fitted wood bearings and mounted my crankshaft with a wheel from an old-fashioned coach to act as a fly-wheel. Then I connected up my crankshaft with levers made of wood with weights attached, this being more or less a compensating arrangement in which the forces were equal and opposite. I had now found out that it was the same distance from Land's End to John o' Groats, and in the manner of speaking I had arrived between the hearth rug and the door mat, and although this second attempt came to nothing I did not lose heart.

What with hard work and willing experiment in every minute I could spare, my mind had come more used to dealing with the difficulties. Also I had managed to get together a few more tools and had learnt to use them. Soon after this another idea occurred to me.

I made a mill arrangement with four sails, and on each of these arms I fixed an extending arm. These arms were hinged at about the middle of the sail and fitted with weights on their outer ends. The idea was that when they were on the downward stroke they would swing out from the spindle, exert a pull and then draw towards the spindle on the upward stroke. To make the weights I needed more bullets but that was easy, so I off to the rifle range and soon found what I wanted.

It was now a matter of casting these bullets into weights of the size that I needed and this time did not intend to blow my head off or my brains out. I made a hole the right shape in a piece of wood and made that for a mould, and as I now had a long-handled ladle did not need to pinch my Mother's saucepans.

I was now ready to start casting but dare not use my Mother's fire this time, thinking anyhow I should drive her out of the kitchen as the mould was sure to make clouds of smoke when I poured in the hot lead.

So I made a fire in the shed outside and got on well this time, casting my four weights successfully. By the burning away of the wood they were not all of the same size but I soon got over that trouble by shaving them away with my pocket knife, and adjusted them to the right weight. The next thing was to fix them onto the arms. At last it was done and all was ready to try. I do not think that all my life I shall forget that evening.

It was growing dark before I had finished and I had only two tallow dips stuck on nails on a board glimmering in the shed, leaving everything around me in gloom. Boy like I was so sure it would work, this thing that had been so long stirring in my brain, turning about like a live creature that is yet prisoned, as them cabbage caterpillars are when they hang themselves up in cocoons under the eves in the shape of what is to come, twisting and writhing when you touches them with your finger. Times were when I saw it all so clear and simple—when I was half dreaming half waking, and times when I would be thinking of other things and suddenly it would seem I had it—like a rat by the tail—then in a flash it was gone again, and try as I would I could not fetch it back.

Now here it was, the first model that I had put all I owned into, and me standing there all weak at the knees, and feeling sick in my stomach, and the sweat running down my face wondering if it would go. One dip burnt down and spluttered out, and all in a hurry lest

The last of the Seven Famous Snobs.

I should be left in the dark I put out my finger and started it off. It whirled round—made a few turns—and then stopped.

I took that hard as one does when young. I had failed and I had been so sure, but when I came to be able to think it out it did not take me long to see that it was friction and the reaction of the weights which caused the trouble. I made up mind I would not be daunted, other ideas flooded across my mind but at this time I had entered into my apprenticeship with a master builder in the village for whom I worked for many years, so had not so much time. Also, he was the Father of the girl whom long after I married, and perhaps I had other things to think about.

When I tried once more I was better equipped. I had made myself a small portable forge worked by a fan of my own make, a drilling machine, and a lathe with a slide rest for the cutting tools, and having collected a quantity of scrap iron and other metals was able to experiment with all metals.

My new model was on entirely different lines to any of the previous ones. I did not adopt the cam shaft but used a straight shaft with a fly-wheel on each end. The two fly-wheels I built up with brass hobs, stiff wire spokes and cast lead rims, and finished off by turning them up in my lathe. I considered they made well, looking a neat pair of fly-wheels when fixed on the shaft and running on roller bearings. I then made the operating ratchets—the last adjustment was done, I oiled it well and started it spinning round. It spun until—like the other, once the energy I had put into it was expended, it stopped.

This time I was older. Perhaps I had lost a little of the faith one has when very young, that all things are possible to man in the pride of his youth. Perhaps I was wiser and realised how great was the problem I sought to solve, but I did not take my failure so greatly to heart. I found that what I had gained in power I had lost in speed, and must try once more on different lines.

That model still stands on the ground floor of my workshop with several more that I have made at different times—sometimes working far into the night. The embers of my ambition are still burning though I have passed by some years three score and ten, but they do not glow so brightly as they did in my teens.

I have made in my day thirteen different models. Some may say this is unlucky, not staying to think that all through nature there is always the thirteenth. After the birth of each one of us we reach our thirteenth hour, day and year on this old globe of ours on which we live, which is still making its countless numbers of evolutions like a huge fly-wheel, every turn bringing us day followed by night. He who believes in this needs to think a second time, and not be guided by so called Fate and Predestination, as a horse is led with bit and bridle.

I still will not say it is impossible for man to construct a machine with its driving power contained within itself. It does not suggest itself as does the steam engine, the oil engine, electric dynamo, water wheel, wind wheel, watch and clock. All these are set in motion by an outward and onward power or force that does its work and passes on, not being retained within the machine.

He who would build, or endeavour to build a machine that will maintain its motion for ever, without an outward force or power, must first of all seek for a power that is retained within itself. The man or woman who discovers the secret will change the world. I have sought high and low all through my life to find it—and I have failed.

MAN

Not for false and fleeting joys,
Pleasure, that while tasted, cloys,
Not for self-inflicted pain
Born to purchase heavenly gain,
    Did God make man;

But for wisdom, happiness,
Blessed life and life to bless,
Love the soul of Deity,
And progress through eternity,
    Did God make man.

For cultured earth and conquered wave,
Fancy bright, and science grave,
Mind and heart with blending powers,
Building more than Eden's bowers,
    Did God make man.

And for mutual love and aid,
Never weary nor dismayed,
Strength renewing as we rise
Upward to unchanging skies,
    Did God make man.

William Johnson Fox, "The Norwich Weaver Boy," 1786-1864.

CHAPTER XVI

Old Adam when first was created
The Lord of the universe crowned,
His happiness was not completed
Until that a helpmeet he found.
She was not taken out of his Head
To rule and triumph over Man,
Nor was she taken out of his feet
By Man to be trampled upon.
But she was taken out of his side,
His equal and partner to be,
And as they are united in one,
The man is the top of the Tree.

Traditional.

READING OVER what I have written about what happen to me when I was but a boy, it seem but yesterday. A lot of water has run under Bungay Bridge since I was seventeen, and I have seen the world which seemed so fair to me as a boy, pass under the dominion of machinery and grow year by year more troubled. Those inventions by which man could turn it into Paradise have been used for other ends, so that it seems the children of men's brains may finally destroy the civilization they have themselves built up. Most of us when we are young think that we know all there is to be known. As we grow older and begin to understand the world and its ways we find out we are travelling a long road with many turns and windings, never knowing what may be round the next corner. One thing I know. That it is best to be fair and upright with one another, young or old, rich or poor. To give what one can when it is asked. Not to be too hasty in judgement, even of those who will do an ill turn if they can, and to remember when a lame dog asks for a lift over a stile, that one may oneself have a lame leg some day. The rest I must leave just telling what happened in my later life.

My father who came into this old house, where I still live, at Michaelmas 1869 lived here all the remainder of his days, and died on his birthday 1922 at the age of eighty. After that happen with my mother ill in bed, cows to look after, and a hundred and one jobs to do as well, I found I had my hands full, and enough work for another pair into the bargain. Thought to myself even though it is getting a bit late in the day, the best thing I can do is to get married. So I ups and asks the Girl of my Heart if she is willing (my old sweetheart when I was a little lad at school) if she would not come and throw in her lot with me.

She did not want asking twice, and the difficulties that had all along been in the way were gone, so we agreed to start off in double harness, and got married on the first of October 1922.

If I had my time over again I would do that same thing the early side of twenty. As it was if I had waited any longer I should have missed what she had to give me—the sunshine and comfort of my life. I have found again and again it is a true saying—that delays are dangerous.

My dear old mother, whom I was very fond of, survived my father very nearly two years, and died of infantile decay in the eighty third year of her age.

It was now a question as to whether I and my wife should leave the old haunts or not. Half a century is a long time. A man put down roots like a tree into the place which he has known all his life, and I felt more or less like a wild rabbit which lurks round the burrow of its birth. I had the chance to stay on in the old house and did not hesitate for long.

Since that time with the willing help of my best half, we have built bridges over the river, constructed new row boats, rigged up bathing huts, made chairs out of old bedsteads, and tables from rick stands—my grandfather having made thousands of them in his day. So we go along and have been very happy, and very contented we still are, though we know that having married late in life there is a great deal we have missed. Time and time again when we are sitting one each side of the hearth, before we goes up and shifts ourselves for bed, there seems something wanting, and we know what it is—there are none to come after us when our work is done and we are called. Seems somehow, when a man and woman get on in years, one misses 'em more, no chick nor child to have our little bits the missus set such store by. It is not as if they would not have been welcome if things had turned out different, but no man can go back on the same road. Some of them that have children think the world of them—others the sooner they are quit of them the better they are pleased. One thing is certain as the nose on my face, if you cannot laugh with the children as never come to you, neither can you cry for them and the troubles they may bring. It is as true a word as ever the bible tells that there is many a child that brings down them that fathered them with sorrow to the grave.

I write these last words of the story of my boyhood as I wrote the first, to the sound of Bungay bells chiming over the Common. Through childhood, youth, and manhood, and all the troublous ways of a man's life the Lord has kept me, and in his peace, mercy and kindness I abide in my old age.

Come-to-thy-God-in-time
Thus saith thy pealing chime,
Youth, manhood, old age past,
Come-to-thy-God-at-last.

TAILPIECE

Learn to live by faith as I did live before,
Learn you to give in faith, as I did at my door,
Learn you to keep by faith, as God be still thy store,
Learn you to lend by faith, as I did to the poor;
Learn you to live, to give, to keep, to lend, to spend,
That God in Christ at day of death, may prove thy friend.

Verse on the tomb of John Porter, Yeoman at Messing Norfolk (1600).